DAUGHTER OF CHAOS

JEN McCONNEL

Month9Books

Edited by Georgia McBride
Published by Month9Books
Cover designed by Victoria Faye

To W.M. and all the IMPS.

DAUGHTER OF CHAOS

JEN McCONNEL

1

I had been looking forward to tonight all week. It wasn't often that I got the house to myself; my parents aren't really the "date-night" type. That's why I was thrilled when they announced they were going to some cheesy classic rock concert in Raleigh tonight. Mom had tried to persuade me to come along.

"It'll be fun, sweetie. You love concerts!" she'd pleaded. I do love concerts, but she and I have very different ideas about what constitutes music. So I stayed home, planning to relax and shake off the week.

School had sucked more than usual the past five days. Things were getting weirder with Justin, if that was possible. I thought we'd hit an all-time low with our breakup, but I'd been wrong. As if that wasn't enough, it seemed like the teachers were trying to torture us; in one week, I'd had two essays due and three major tests. Somehow, I had managed to pull off a B- on the alchemy test. Science has always been my worst subject, even if alchemy is a magical science.

Since I got that grade without cheating, I thought I deserved a bit of pampering. I popped myself a big bowl of popcorn, grabbed an orange soda, and parked myself on the couch. I had been recording my favorite show for weeks, hoarding the episodes like Halloween candy until the perfect opportunity presented itself. I don't know why, but I love watching the cake show on the home and garden channel. It wouldn't surprise me if they had a Witch or two in that kitchen; they do way more with frosting than Nons should be able to!

Thinking I had hours of sugary entertainment in store, I settled in with the remote. I only made it about ten minutes into the first episode before the power surged and the DVR reset itself. Annoyed, I scrolled through the menu to get back to my show just as a crash of thunder rocked the house. I jumped, spilling popcorn all over the couch. The lights flickered and the power went out.

I leaned forward, groping around the coffee table for matches. The house was full of candles, and my mother left the big boxes of kitchen matches scattered around for easy access. My fingers closed around the thick rectangle and my skin prickled.

Someone was in the living room with me. There was a hunched figure standing in front of the window. Sucking in my breath, I opened the box and struck a match along the side. The smell of sulfur filled the room, and my eyes widened as I stared at the figure before me.

She was a funny-looking old woman, and if I didn't know exactly who she was, I might have laughed at her. As it was, the sight of Hecate standing in my living room made me incredibly uncomfortable. Although I knew that the gods played a role in magic, this was the first time I had ever met one of them face-to-face. I'd never expected in a million years that I would meet a god as powerful and frightening as Hecate.

The Queen of Witches was not given to traipsing through time and space on a whim; in fact, we'd learned in school that historically, Hecate only appeared for one of two reasons: to punish someone who broke the laws of Witchcraft, or to reward an unusually talented Witch. The last time the latter had happened was about five hundred years ago, and I don't think I have much in common with Will Shakespeare, so I figured her presence must be due to my mounting transgressions.

For the first time, I wished I were with my parents. A few hours ago, I couldn't imagine anything worse than being stuck in a stadium with a bunch of old hippies trying to recreate Woodstock. Now I could.

Bowing my head before the goddess, I tensed, wondering if I could talk my way out of the punishment that was inevitably coming. Surely a few little hexes weren't enough to have me chastised for breaking the Rede?

The Rede is the cardinal rule of magic, and it had been drummed into my head by my parents and teachers for years. According to the Rede, Witches are free to act as we choose as long as our actions don't bring harm. I tried hard to follow it, but sometimes I couldn't resist using my magic for a little well-deserved payback. From what I knew of Hecate, she herself was no stranger to small acts of revenge. Maybe, I thought hopefully, maybe she would go easy on me.

"Girl." Her voice was raspy, like a rusty door hinge, and I jerked despite myself. She chuckled without humor. "Girl, look at me."

Slowly, I raised my eyes, sweeping my gaze up her inky black robes that shimmered like water, past the blood-red stone dangling from her throat, and up to her golden eyes. They weren't human, but from what I remembered of the myths we studied at school, Hecate had never valued humanity. Her eyes were the eyes of a night predator—an owl or fox—and they held me spellbound.

"Darlena. Darlena, I have been aware of you for some time now." Her words came slowly, creaking into existence and lingering. I was frozen with fear. "Child, you stand at the brink. A choice must be made."

Confused, I started to shake my head, but her ragged claw shot out and held my chin steady.

"You, child, will be powerful. But you stand at a crossing. Choose."

Silently, I shut my eyes, willing the apparition before me to vanish. She just laughed.

"Darlena, little one, choose your path. Will you walk the White, the Black, or the Green?"

At these words, her visit suddenly made sense. We had spent a good deal of time studying the three paths in school, even taking monthly aptitude tests to determine which path we would follow in our own lives. Most of my classmates already knew which of the three branches they were called to, but I kept getting confused. I never seemed to test high in any of the three areas, and for a Blood Witch to be sixteen and still without a path was shameful. No one had said anything, of course, not outright, but I felt my parents' growing frustration that I hadn't declared yet. At the same time, no one had said what would happen if I didn't choose a path, so I had delayed, waiting for something to take the decision out of my hands.

And now the Queen of Witches stood before me, demanding that I make a choice I wasn't prepared to make.

I shook my head, and her claw tightened on my chin. Her fingernails, sharp and ragged, bit into my flesh with subtle pressure.

"You must choose, child. Choose now, and choose once, for once taken, the path becomes your fate."

I looked into those strange golden eyes, searching for a way out. "Majesty, what would you have me choose?"

She chortled. "It is not what I want, girl. It is what you are called to. I would have you choose now, and choose wisely. You will not have a second choice."

Even though the goddess was staring at me intently, I couldn't keep my mind focused on her words. My thoughts went back to a few weeks ago, when Rochelle and I were hiding in the art room at school. She sketched with charcoal while I worked a spell. I had just bound a hex with red thread when Justin walked in. His brown eyes widened when he saw what I was doing, and he threw an accusing glance toward Rochelle, but he shut the door and sat down across from me without saying anything. Rochelle ignored him, but the sound of her charcoal against the page got louder. I finished up the spell and then looked up to meet his troubled gaze. I could feel the energy radiating off of him, and I resisted the urge to reach for his hand. Instead, I raised an eyebrow, hoping I looked bored.

He cleared his throat. "Who are you hexing?"

I shrugged and looked back at the hex. "Principal Snout didn't even bother listening to my side of things this time."

"Lena, is this really a good idea?"

I glared at him, so he switched tactics.

"I found my path today. I've decided to declare to White magic."

I nodded, and Rochelle stiffened slightly. He didn't seem to notice and I wondered if all White Witches were as oblivious to the undercurrents surrounding them. His declaration was hardly news to anyone but Justin; he'd always been so noble and good that I don't think anyone at school doubted he was destined to follow the White path, the same way everyone seemed to know Rochelle was leaning toward the Black. He smiled unsteadily, still getting used to his new identity. I swallowed, trying to slow my heart rate. His tentative smile was still enough to get under my skin.

"I just thought—I know you haven't chosen yet, but I wanted to ask you something." His eyes were serious, and I couldn't look away from his warm gaze.

It had been bad enough breaking up with him once; why did he have to keep making me fall for him all over again? I tried to reel in my emotions, but I felt my neck starting to flush. Sitting beside me, Rochelle stopped drawing in anticipation of something. I wasn't sure what she was waiting for, so I focused on Justin.

"If you ever wanted to, well, I mean, if you ever thought about—" He floundered, but I couldn't bear to help him. If I spoke, I was afraid I might say something I'd regret.

He took a deep breath and went on. "You know that Whites and Greens can intermarry." He paused as he glanced for the first time at Rochelle. "But a Black is forbidden from marrying at all. I just wanted you to think about that before you make your own choice." His final words came out in a rush, and I exhaled quickly. My heart spun through my body like a yo-yo, and I struggled to keep my face blank.

I nodded once, curtly, and then turned my attention back to my recently finished hex, studiously avoiding meeting Rochelle's eye. Justin sat there, uncomfortable for a moment, before reaching over to squeeze my upper arm in parting. My skin tingled at his touch. I listened to the door click shut behind him, and my calm demeanor cracked.

"Prick." Rochelle spat the word as if she had just tasted poison.

I shrugged and forced a smile. "He's just excited about his declaration."

She laughed sharply. "And he's clearly still in love with you." Rochelle looked at me, her dark eyes piercing my soul. "Why in the world did you break up with him?" Her mocking tone annoyed me, and I shrugged again, even though my heart started to pound. No one knew how I still felt about Justin, and Rochelle would be the last person I'd confide in. She hated him too much to ever understand, and she thought that I did, too.

"It doesn't matter. What's done is done."

***

"Red." I don't know if I spoke the word or only thought it, but it was obvious from her stunned reaction that Hecate had heard me.

"Red." I croaked a little more firmly, even though I had no idea what I was saying. "I choose to follow Red magic." Oh, boy, how would the goddess in front of me react to that? I'd said the first thing that popped into my mouth, but I knew there was no such thing as Red magic. Nervously, I clenched my fists, digging my nails into my palms and waiting for her to chastise me for my insolence.

The punishment I was expecting never came. Instead, there was a crash of thunder outside, and the power flickered on for one blinding moment before the lights went out again. A threatening chuckle filled the air.

"Girl, you have bound yourself with your words, but I wonder if you know exactly what you are now tied to?"

Mutely, I shook my head, and she cackled. Her hand shot toward my face, and I flinched. The goddess ran her fingers through my hair, tangling it more than it already was. I tried not to jerk away from her, but my scalp crawled.

"A Red with red hair. It is fitting."

I stared at her, too surprised to speak. What did my hair have to do with anything? And did that mean there really was a thing called Red magic?

There was another crash of thunder and the goddess stepped away from me. "You will learn all things soon. But you are bound by your choice. Remember that later."

The lights flickered on spasmodically, and the goddess vanished.

2

Part of me wanted to believe that I'd just had a dream, not an actual visitation from the most powerful goddess on earth. I was shaking and cold all over as I made my way up the stairs to my room. Not caring about the mess, I crawled into my closet and sat on the floor, hiding under my clothes. Trying to still my heart, I took three deep breaths, holding the air in my lungs a beat before exhaling.

Red magic. What in the world was that? I'd never heard of anything but Green, White, and Black. They were the balanced triad of crafts taught at my school, Trinity. Did Red magic even exist? Hecate's laughter filled my ears, and I began to feel hot and panicky. I crawled out of my closet and reached for my cell phone, but I didn't call anyone. I thought about it; I was freaked out by her visit and by my impulsive declaration, but when I picked up the phone, the first person I thought of was Justin. I so wasn't ready to go down that road.

Justin and I had dated a few months ago, and it was intense. I've never dated a Non, and he was my first boyfriend, period, so I don't have anything to compare it to, but dating a powerful Witch was a mind-bending experience. Kissing him literally created sparks. It was like holding a hot wire while eating candy: dangerous, sweet, and strange. He still seemed to have feelings for me, but I had a hard time believing it after what had happened in the woods the last night we were together.

***

I'd planned everything. We'd left the prom early to drive around, and I wasn't ready to go home yet.

"Why don't we sit down by the river?"

He glanced at my black dress. "Are you sure that's okay?"

"Of course! It'll be a romantic way to end the night." I slid as close to him as the bucket seats in his mother's van would allow and put my hand on his arm. He shivered, and my heart sped up with anticipation.

We didn't say anything when we got to the park, and when I pulled a cheap bottle of champagne out of nowhere, I saw his eyes go wide. Magic can't make something out of nothing, and I wasn't about to tell Justin that I'd stolen the bottle from the convenience store the day before prom and stuck it in his mom's car. It was better if he thought I was powerful and mysterious.

We sat on the muddy bank of the river and took our shoes off. I leaned against his shoulder, feeling the warmth of his skin through the thin fabric of his dress shirt. He'd left his jacket in the car. The bubbles from the champagne were flat, but they still made me tingle. Or maybe that was simply my reaction to Justin.

When I leaned over to kiss him, I tasted wine on his lips. He laced his fingers through my hair, and I pressed my body against his, gradually pushing him back until he was almost lying down. Water gurgled beneath us, and when I looked down into his face, I couldn't read the emotions flitting across his eyes.

I closed my eyes and leaned forward for another kiss, but Justin turned his head to the side.

"What's wrong?" I tried to make my voice sound husky, like an old movie star, but I suck at glamouring. A skilled Witch should be able to change her voice or appearance at will, but this was one spell I'd never been able to master.

Justin looked up at me and frowned. "Did you just try to use magic on me?"

I shook my head. "What makes you think that?"

Gently, he lifted me off of him and set me to one side on the bank. "Don't lie to me, Lena."

"It was just a little glamour. I wanted to make you want me as much as I want you."

He reached his hand out and cupped the side of my face. "You don't need magic for that."

Eagerly, I leaned forward again, but he pulled back.

"I think we should slow down."

I stared at him for a minute. My cheeks were hot, and I was glad that he couldn't see how embarrassed I was in the darkness. "Why?" My voice sounded whiny, and I winced.

"We're young. There's no reason to rush into this."

I forced a laugh. "You sound like a stupid Non."

"Lena, you know I love you." He leaned toward me, but I pulled away and stood up.

"No, I don't. If you loved me … " I trailed off, trying to get my emotions under control.

"There's more to love than sex, Lena."

"But I want you." I hated myself as soon as the words were said, and I turned away from the river and began walking fast. I couldn't bear for him to know that he was the one thing that made me vulnerable; Justin had often teased me about being unstoppable.

"Lena, wait!" I heard him scramble to his feet behind me, but I didn't look back. I sped up and whispered a spell to keep him from catching up to me. I walked all the way home, ignoring the stars overhead as I listened for his footsteps. But at some point he must have stopped following me, because when I turned onto my street, I was alone in the night.

I didn't cry that night, but the next morning when Justin didn't call, I dissolved into embarrassed tears. We broke up after that, sort of. I never actually told him I didn't want to see him anymore, but I started ignoring him at school. He took the hint and stopped pestering me, but over the summer, he had started hanging around again. Not like a boyfriend, though; I assumed he wanted to try just being friends. I didn't have the energy left to tell him that every time I saw him smile, I felt a knife go through my gut.

So we tried to be friends. After the strange thing with Hecate, I really wanted to call him. I started to dial his number, but then I felt a bubbling of blame. If that night in the woods had ended differently, I'd still be with Justin and none of this would have happened. When Hecate had appeared, I probably would have declared Green, to please him and my parents. My face felt hot, and I thought about how he'd let me down. I scowled at my phone and dropped it to the floor. I put my arms around my knees and dropped my head down, curling into a tight ball. The events of the evening replayed again and again in my mind, and I shuddered.

A thought flicked through my mind that filled me with anxiety. What would my parents say when they got home? Would they even believe me?

***

At dawn, I woke in a sticky sweat, visions of a blood-washed field still fresh in my memory. I thought there had been a castle in the distance, and the sound of strange chanting, but all I remembered for sure was the blood. I took a long, hot shower, trying to cleanse myself of the awful night. Mom and Dad were both already at work when I left the house, and I was grateful that I didn't have to talk to them about Hecate just yet. I'd almost managed to convince myself that the whole thing was a twisted nightmare. Why would the Queen of Witches bother asking me to pick a path? And even if she did, why would she allow me to choose something that didn't exist? I was almost cheerful with my delusion as I walked to school.

Passing beneath the ancient arch, I laughed to myself. Our school gave every appearance of being an old, private Catholic academy: ivy-covered walls, Gothic arches everywhere, and even that name, Trinity School.

It certainly was a private school, but we weren't Catholics. Trinity ran all year, offered a full curriculum, and consistently sent students on to some of the best universities in the country, but in addition to standard courses, Trinity offered training in Witchcraft. Most of the students were legacies, Blood Witches like me whose parents had attended in their own time. Every now and again a Dreamer would make it in. Dreamers were those with magical talent but no magical heritage. Trinity quietly recruited Dreamers from central North Carolina, the area immediately surrounding the school, and due to the large number of people who had moved here in recent years, my graduating class boasted a record number of five Dreamers. Rochelle was one of them. Costs to attend Trinity were high, but the alumni were fairly active and money never really stood in the way of a student who sought admission there.

I hated everything about it.

My parents were both Green Witches, and they had met at Trinity when they were teenagers. Dad managed a research company in Raleigh and Mom was in charge of various community projects. Her latest crusade was creating a community garden in our city, Durham, and she and Dad both traveled easily among

Witches and Nons. They assumed I would have the same easy time of it, but schooling at Trinity had only made me feel more isolated. I hardly trusted Blood Witches or Dreamers, so what made them think years of private school would enhance my trust for Nons? I couldn't wait to graduate and leave home. I didn't have any kind of future planned, but I knew I couldn't be the kind of Witch my parents expected. I guess the previous night proved that.

I hurried toward my first class, suppressing a yawn. The night before had been pretty awful, and the nightmares I'd had after seeing Hecate kept me from getting much sleep. I'd have to try extra hard to stay awake for classes, but the topic written on the board when I walked into my history class made me want to drop into a coma right then and there. Magical Ethics. Could Ms. Minch pick any topic that was more boring?

Rochelle rolled her eyes at me as I slipped into my desk beside hers in the back corner of the room. "Can you believe it's another ethics lecture?"

Trinity was always trying to remind us to be good little Witches, and frequent ethics lectures popped up in every class. The ethics of alchemy, the ethics of magical literature, even the ethics of gym class. I shook my head at Rochelle. "If we haven't figured out how they want us to act before now, I doubt this lecture will be much help."

She nodded, examining her fingernail. "I'm getting really sick of these stuffed shirts telling me how to handle my magic."

Before I could respond, Ms. Minch rapped on her desk with a ruler. I dragged my eyes to the front of the room, and I heard

Rochelle sigh loudly beside me.

"Magical Ethics." Ms. Minch looked sharply around the room, making eye contact with a number of students before she continued. "Why do we follow the rules that we follow?"

There was an uncomfortable pause. Finally, Justin raised his hand. "Ethical behavior is just common sense. There's no reason to do anything harmful just because we can do magic. Besides, the payback isn't pleasant."

Ms. Minch nodded once, but her lips were pursed and she looked disappointed in his answer. "The Rede is important, I'll grant you that, and the threefold law guarantees that your magic will rebound on you with a magnified effect, regardless of the intention of the spell. But that isn't what I want this discussion to be about."

In every ethics discussion at Trinity, they harped on the importance of following the Rede, and I was sick of it. What's the point of magical power with boundaries? At least Ms. Minch didn't seem to want to talk about *that* today, but I still didn't want to be there.

"Miss Agara." Ms. Minch's voice pulled me out of my reverie, and I jerked my head up to meet her gaze. "Would you tell us another component of the ethics of magic?"

Everyone turned to look at me, and I heard Rochelle snicker under her breath. Out of the corner of my eye, I could see Justin smiling from the front of the room, but I didn't want to think about him.

"Miss Agara, anytime, please."

I glared at Ms. Minch. "I guess there's the fact that we don't show off in front of Nons."

"Can you elaborate on that, please?"

I shot her a dark look, but her stare was unwavering. "Nons can't know about us, so it's better if we use our magic only when we're around other Witches."

"And can anyone tell us why Nons are forbidden from magical knowledge?" Ms. Minch shifted her eyes from me, and I relaxed slightly. I hated being called on in class, but the teachers seemed to love singling me out.

One of the Dreamers, Liza, raised her hand. "Doesn't it have to do with Salem?"

Rochelle snorted. "Not just Salem. All the Witch trials." She didn't bother raising her hand, but she seemed unconcerned when Ms. Minch shot her a withering look.

"That's right, Liza," Ms. Minch simpered, ignoring Rochelle. "There was a time when Witches didn't bother to hide from Nons. Magic and everyday life existed side by side for centuries. But with the spread of the Church, people grew more suspicious of things that couldn't be explained."

Justin raised his hand eagerly. "But weren't the victims of the trials not actually Witches?"

"Some Witches were accused, but you're right, many more innocent Nons were swept into the mania." Ms. Minch turned to write on the board.

"Not so innocent if they caused the trials in the first place," Rochelle muttered, but Ms. Minch acted like she hadn't heard her.

"It took many years, but by the nineteenth century, the magical community had finally agreed that it would be better for everyone if Witches and Nons didn't mix. Since that time, secrecy has been carefully preserved."

Liza spoke up again. "It seems really stupid. I mean, I can't even tell my parents about magic. They're not likely to burn me at the stake or anything."

Ms. Minch nodded at Liza once. "We are safe from Nons. The secrecy has more to do with keeping them safe from us. If we advertised our abilities, there's no telling what would happen. Nons are happier believing that magic is nothing more than superstition." She pointed to the timeline she'd drawn on the board. "Now, can anyone tell me which Witches have nearly destroyed the balance by advertising their power?"

The timeline had fifteen dates on it, all from the last two centuries. I raised my hand and pointed to 1939. "Hitler."

Ms. Minch nodded, writing his name on the board. "Hitler was a Black Witch, but he shouldn't be seen as representative of the dark path. It's likely that he was insane, and his actions were only magnified, not dictated, by his magical abilities."

Rochelle sat up sharply. "But couldn't it be argued that he shaped the modern world? If it weren't for World War II, things would look a lot different now. Shouldn't we revere him for pushing us forward in history?"

The room was silent for a minute, and even I felt shocked. Rochelle was defending Hitler? Before I could ask her what she meant, Ms. Minch regained control of the discussion.

"Whether he propelled us into the modern era or not, Hitler broke the ethical rules of Witchcraft by using his power in such a visible fashion. Witches must not reveal themselves to Nons."

The speaker over the door crackled to life, and Ms. Minch looked at it, annoyed.

"Yes?"

"Ms. Minch, Miss Agara to the front office. Immediately."

Everyone turned to look at me, and Rochelle chuckled. "What did you do now?"

I shrugged and grabbed my bag. I really wasn't sure why I was being called to the office, but I had a bad feeling in the pit of my stomach that it had something to do with my bizarre dream about Hecate.

The look on Principal Snout's face when he spotted me crossing the courtyard told me that whatever was going on was worse than I thought.

"Miss Agara," he whispered hoarsely, "you should not be here!"

"Where should I be?" I snapped.

He didn't answer. Glancing warily around, he grabbed my arm and dragged me into his small office, shutting the door behind me. I sighed, wondering what I'd done now and taking my customary seat in the chair facing his desk and staring at a spot on the wall above his bald head. The office was decorated with magical objects: a row of cauldrons hung on the wall above the window, and small figures of different gods lined the windowsill. It was sort of creepy, as if Snout was trying to make his office look like a shrine; it had been like that for as long as I'd been at Trinity. Most Witches didn't put their tools on display, but Snout wasn't most Witches. I waited for him to begin shouting.

The shouting never came. Instead, when I glanced up, Snout suddenly looked away from me and began fiddling with a glass paperweight on his desk. A bead of sweat stood out on his forehead, and it occurred to me that he was nervous. What could possibly make the principal nervous to be around me?

He dithered around a bit longer before he finally spoke. "I have been, erm, informed, that you have made your declaration." He still didn't look at me, and his nervous twitching began to irritate me.

I stared. So it hadn't been a dream after all. But who had told him about last night? "Yes," I began slowly, "I have decided to follow—"

He made a jerky motion and the words died on my lips. He sealed his silence spell, and I closed my lips, annoyed.

"I am aware. You will complete your training elsewhere. Starting now. Trinity no longer has the resources that you will need. There are … certain individuals who have expressed interest in you." His eyes flickered to the door, and I turned my head to see what he was looking at. A black plaque hung there above the doorway, showing a goddess with three heads. I shuddered, recognizing Hecate's face on each of the heads.

Snout nodded at me once, and I realized that Hecate must have told him everything. Why in the world was she taking an interest in me? I tried to speak, but I was still bound by his spell.

"Your records will not indicate expulsion, but you will not be admitted onto these premises again. Not now, and especially not after your training is done. You will receive your diploma in the mail. Is that quite clear?"

His voice shook as he spoke, but I was too angry to feel sorry for him. My eyes burned, but I nodded. He sank back in relief and waved his hand, freeing my jaw. Still, I couldn't speak.

"Darlena, if I may offer you a word of advice: don't overreach yourself. You have chosen your fate, heaven help you, but don't try to become the best. To be the best on your path is to be the next to fall. Remember that."

"So it really exists."

He stared at me like I was an idiot. "What did you think, that you'd declared to follow an imaginary path?"

I shrugged, feeling foolish. I hadn't really thought at all. When Hecate appeared, I had been too confused to think. I had said the first thing that popped into my mind, but evidently, there really was a Red path. "What kind of magic is it?"

He mopped his forehead with a handkerchief. "A very dangerous kind. You will leave the school grounds immediately, and not return."

With a wave, he dismissed me, and I thought I saw regret in his eyes as I turned and stomped out of his office.

A dark shape came slipping out from behind one of the columns in the entry hall, and Rochelle fell into step beside me.

"What happened?"

I shook my head, not trusting my voice just yet.

22

She glanced over her shoulder at the principal's door. "Well, whatever it is, coffee can't hurt." Rochelle grabbed my arm and steered me off campus in the direction of our favorite spot.

***

"So then what did you say?" Rochelle's heavily lined eyes were wide and the coffee in front of her sat untouched.

"I told her I wanted to be a Red Witch."

Rochelle crinkled up her nose. "But what does that even mean?"

I shrugged, my heart sinking. Rochelle was the first person I had told, and some desperate hope had made me think that she might know more about Red magic than I did. She was always studying strange things that none of our classes covered. "I don't know, but I guess I better find out fast." I took a swallow of my latte, and Rochelle sipped her black coffee thoughtfully.

"I wish Hecate would show up in my living room." Her voice was wistful, and I shuddered at the memory of the goddess's claw-like hand gripping my chin.

"Trust me, Rochelle, it wasn't fun. And what would your parents say? They'd freak out!" Rochelle's parents thought Trinity was the expensive prep school that it looked like; they had no idea that their daughter was training as a Witch. How she kept it a secret, I didn't know, but Rochelle managed somehow.

We'd been best friends almost since the minute she enrolled. I met her in the janitor's closet. I used to sneak in there during

Algebra to practice spells that our teachers thought were too dark or advanced for freshmen to learn, and Rochelle had had the same idea. I walked in on her binding a hex, but I never told on her. I was too fascinated by the powerful magic Rochelle had taught herself before enrolling. In exchange for silence, I begged her to teach me, and by the end of the week we were inseparable. Hexes aren't exactly part of the standard curriculum at Trinity, since they flagrantly violate the Rede. Rochelle wasn't intimidated by breaking the rules, and I loved her for her bravery.

I took another sip of my latte, relishing the flavor, and looked at my best friend. Her hair was cropped short, and this week she had died the tips teal. Everything else about her, though, from her eyeliner to her shoes, was black. My parents didn't like Rochelle; they had a real prejudice toward Black Witches, although I didn't see what the problem was. Black was just another path, and clearly it wasn't as dangerous as whatever I'd pledged myself to. Rochelle hadn't been expelled; I had.

Rochelle chugged the rest of her still-steaming coffee. "Well, when you see Hecate again, be sure you tell her 'Hi' for me."

I laughed nervously. "I doubt I'll be seeing her again. I mean, how often does she ever show up? Her visit was a once-in-a-lifetime thing, and I'm glad. She won't have any reason to check up on me." I hoped.

My best friend shot me a look that I couldn't read. "Don't count on it, Darlena."

***

24

Rochelle cut classes for the rest of the day, insisting that I shouldn't be left alone in my current mood. We took her sporty little Honda and headed to downtown Raleigh. I felt a little foolish, but I convinced her to spend the day wandering in and out of the free museums near the State Capitol building. It was the only thing I could think of that would make the day feel normal.

My parents used to drive into Raleigh every month, taking me to one museum after another. While a lot of people who live in this area tend to stick to their city, my parents were never shy about exploring Raleigh and Chapel Hill. Rochelle didn't object when I asked to go to the State History Museum, but she sighed loudly and rolled her eyes the entire time we were there. I ignored her, lost in the past. Indulging in childhood memories seemed a lot safer just now than dealing with my new reality.

We spent the entire day in Raleigh, but eventually Rochelle said she should get home for dinner. I felt a guilty tug in my gut; I had barely thought of my parents the whole day. What would they think when I told them what had happened? Rochelle dropped me at the end of the street and I walked home, stewing. I'd wanted to believe Hecate's visit was just another dream, but now I knew better. Snout had made it clear that Red magic was real, and what's worse, it seemed to scare him. What had I gotten myself into?

By the time I reached my house, both my parents were there waiting to pounce on me. When I saw their cars, I almost turned and walked back down the driveway, but I squared my shoulders and decided to face the music sooner rather than later. I wasn't sure how I'd tell them about Hecate, but I thought that maybe, since Snout had known already, I wouldn't have to say anything. I wasn't sure if that would be better or worse than telling them myself.

Mom was sitting on the tattered floral sofa, something she had dragged around since her college days. Her face was blotchy and puffy, and I realized with a shock that my stoic mother had been crying. I froze on the threshold, digesting the unsettling sight. Dad was leaning against the wall, his back to the door, but he and Mom both looked up at my entrance. Dad stiffened and looked away, but the tears that welled up in my mother's eyes as she gazed long and hard at me hurt more than his snub.

Still unsure, I crossed the room and took a seat beside Mom. The smells of coffee and cigarettes wafted up to greet me; that couch had had quite a life before I was born, and the lingering scents of its past were often present. The old smells should have been comforting, but I was too confused to really notice.

Hesitantly, Mom took my hand in hers and clutched it. She and Dad were both holding their breath, and they exhaled loudly after Mom held my hand for a few seconds. She didn't let go, but tightened her grip.

Dad cleared his throat and I looked up into his face.

"We have been informed that you will be continuing your education here at home." I didn't bother to nod, and Dad didn't wait for my response. "Your mother and I will help you in any way that we can, but the training you will receive is different from anything we've ever experienced. Darlena—" He paused, looking at my mother first and then at me. "Darlena, this is still your home.

That may change in the future, but for now, this is still a safe place for you."

At those bizarre words, Mom started to sob loudly. Her grip on my hand was crushing, but I was squeezing back just as hard. Dad looked away uncomfortably, and an eerie silence descended.

"We love you, Darlena. Remember that, whatever else happens." Mom's usually strong voice was reduced to a breathy whisper, and the sound of it brought tears to my eyes. I stood up quickly, trying to mask my hurt from my parents.

"Why is everyone freaking out?"

They looked at me, confused. Finally, Dad spoke. "You mean it's not true?"

"What, the fact that Hecate showed up last night? Yeah, that's true."

Mom shuddered, and Dad turned pale.

"I don't know why you are being so calm about this."

I glared at him in shock. "Calm? I'm not being calm! First that goddess, then I get kicked out of school, and now you guys are treating me like a leper. Trust me, I'm anything but calm."

Mom reached for my hand, but dropped her arm before she touched me. "Darlena, honey, sit down. We have a lot to talk about."

I shook my head. "Not right now. I don't want to deal with any of this tonight."

"You'll have to face your choice sooner or later." My dad clenched his jaw as he spoke, and the muscle above his eye twitched. It hurt to look at.

"Not tonight. I'm going to bed." I knew I sounded like a sulky brat, but I didn't care. I wasn't ready to deal with any of this, and in the back of my mind, I still wanted it all to be an awful dream.

Mom and Dad let me go without complaint, even when I slammed my bedroom door so hard it shook. I stood, helplessly flexing my fingers, staring around my room in confusion.

What exactly had I done when I pledged myself to the Red path? I sank to my floor and, for the first time all day, I didn't try to stop the frightened tears that poured down my face.

3

My phone buzzed as soon as I started to cry. I was tempted to ignore the call, but then I saw Justin's number on the screen.

My heart soared into my throat, and my hands were shaking when I answered the phone. I didn't say anything, because I didn't want him to hear me cry, but he started talking before I needed to worry about it. I struggled to get a grip on myself.

"What happened to you today?" Justin's voice was concerned, and I smiled despite the tears drying on my face.

"I got expelled."

"I know that! It was all over school. Gods, Lena, what did you do?"

My happiness at hearing his voice was quickly turning to irritation at his tone. "What do you mean, what did I do?"

He pressed on. "Rochelle left school with you. Is she kicked out, too? Were you dabbling with something dangerous?"

"Why would you assume that Rochelle had anything to do with what happened?"

Justin paused. "She's not as … focused as you are. And she's dangerous."

I laughed humorlessly, fighting back tears. "Not as dangerous as I am now. She had nothing to do with me getting kicked out. She just cut class to try to make me feel better. Unlike some people," I spoke quickly, not giving him the opportunity to interrupt, "who seem to think now is the perfect time to make me feel like shit."

I hung up the phone and threw it across my room. It didn't ring again, and I didn't care.

***

It sounds cliché, but when I woke up, I felt better about everything. I hadn't had any nightmares, and as the sunlight streamed into my room, I felt a new sense of purpose. I needed to figure out what Red magic was, and fast, if I wanted to know what I'd become.

When I emerged from my bedroom, the only member of my family who was there to greet me was Xerxes. He rubbed his whiskers against my legs as I stood in the kitchen, searching the cupboards for food. Desperate, I grabbed a banana and some toast and headed back to my room with the cat trailing after me.

I shut my bedroom door and cast a quick circle to seal my room from intrusion. Mom and Dad were at work, but I wasn't taking any chances. I added a protective ward for good measure. Xerxes looked at me, bored, and rolled around in a sunbeam on the floor.

"Why don't you help me for once, cat?" I was annoyed that he insisted on hanging out with me, but it was hard to stay mad at Xerxes for long. He'd been in the household before I was born, and even though he was close to nineteen years old, he acted like he had as much energy as a kitten. I loved Xerxes, and I had considered him my cat, not my parents', since I was in first grade.

Ignoring the blissful purrs coming from the side of the room, I grabbed my *Encyclopedia of Witchcraft* off the shelf above my desk. If there was any common knowledge about Red magic, I would be able to find it there.

***

Xerxes pressed his head against my side and mewed pitifully. Dazed, I looked up from the book and glanced out my window. It was dusk outside. I had been in my room reading for most of the day. Stretching my arms, I cracked my knuckles and dropped my head in a slow circle, focusing on my breathing. I glanced back at the open page in my lap. This book was full of knowledge, but it didn't mention Red magic anywhere. Rubbing my temples, I leaned back and closed my eyes.

I needed to think about this logically. First, I thought, running through what I'd just read and what I'd already known, I should start with the other magics. White is pure goodness, and White Witches are usually a bit above the nitty gritty details of the real world. Those on the White path are more concerned with grace and old wisdom than with daily living, they are sworn enemies of Black magic, and, I ticked off on my fingers, White magic governs all intellectual and spiritual endeavors. I smiled grudgingly. Justin had certainly chosen his path well! He was always lost in thought, and even his behavior on prom night indicated that he was above the actions of the real world.

I moved on to the Black path. Black Witches value power, influence, and vice, I recited to myself, and they also work with spirit. They are the opposite of Whites, focusing on the darker aspects of spirituality. They aren't evil, but they're usually misunderstood. My parents have a deep prejudice against Black Witches, and they hated that Rochelle and I were friends.

Green Witches, like my parents, govern the realm of earth and are much more grounded in day-to-day reality than Whites and Blacks. Greens have the easiest time living among Nons, and Greens are also very globally minded. My parents are two perfect examples of Green Witches using their power for the good of all. They don't worry as much about spirit as Whites or Blacks; they are more concerned with the here and now.

Somehow the three paths balance each other, but, I wondered, where did Red fit in?

Unfolding myself from the floor, I crossed the room to my dresser and pulled out a slim red candle and a matchbook. Mom relied on her herbs, and Rochelle had her old deck of Tarot cards, but I had always preferred to use candles for divination. I guess fire suits me.

Sinking down onto the floor, I crossed my legs into full lotus and closed my eyes. After whispering a quick prayer for clarity of sight, I lit the candle and placed it on the floor in front of me. I stared at the flame, shutting my mind down to all other sensations. As my vision focused and my breathing slowed, I began to feel words in my mind. I let them come, knowing I could analyze what I learned later. I breathed in and out and watched the red candle until it was nothing but a puddle of wax on my bedroom floor. Just as I started to shake myself out of my trance, my cell phone buzzed beside me, and I grabbed it, hoping that Justin was calling to apologize.

My heart fell when I saw the message. It was a text from Rochelle, wanting me to meet her for a movie. I was tempted to say no, remembering our conversation yesterday, but I needed to think about something other than magic. I was getting burnt out. There would be time later to think about what I'd seen in the candle flame. Just in case I forgot, I jotted down some notes to look over when I got home.

I texted her to say I'd meet her at the end of my street in fifteen minutes. Straightening my stiff legs, I got off the floor and started getting ready. I probably could have told my parents, but I was still mad at Dad over his reaction the night before. Besides, they hadn't come up to my room to bother me when they got home from work, so maybe they didn't want to deal with me right then, either.

Instead of going downstairs, I opened my window and climbed down the massive ash tree right outside my window. I had done it many times. There was something thrilling about sneaking out, even though my parents were usually easygoing. I never had to sneak out, but I liked the rush.

I reached the last branch and dropped silently to the ground. My heart was pounding, and I felt dizzy with adrenaline. For the first time since I'd met Hecate, I felt like myself again. I ran to the corner of the street, fighting back the urge to laugh, and hopped into Rochelle's waiting car.

***

The movie was some stupid zombie flick, but that didn't surprise me. Rochelle always picked the worst movies! Still, it was good to hang out with her like nothing had changed. I was on edge, but she didn't bring up Red magic or Hecate, and I was grateful. After the movie, Rochelle wanted to stop at an all-night diner, but I just wanted to go home and sleep; I kept clinging to the idea that everything with Hecate might still be an awful dream. Rochelle seemed annoyed, but she took me home anyway.

The house was dark when she dropped me off, and although I was relieved, I felt a twinge of loneliness. I hadn't seen either of my parents since the blowup last night. Were they avoiding me because they were afraid of what I had become? Or did they think I was angry and they were trying to give me my space? Either way, it was weird not to have spoken to them at all in over twenty-four hours. I used the front door, noisily letting myself in with my key. I sort of hoped I'd wake them up and they would come ask where I had been, but the house remained silent. As I climbed the stairs to my room, I promised myself that I would at least come downstairs for dinner the next night.

Even though it was past midnight, I wasn't all that sleepy. I looked at the notes I had scribbled after my meditation one more time, searching for something comforting. Goddesses were listed on the left side of the page, and words on the right. I scanned the list of goddesses, and my stomach sank as I recognized the names: Aphrodite, Pele, Kali, and Freya. On the other side of the page, I skimmed the words I recalled from my meditation: fire, lust, destruction, chaos, blood. My mouth felt dry as I stared at the list.

Each branch of magic taught at Trinity had a patron or patroness among the Pagan gods. Most of the instructors said it was old-fashioned to work with a patron, and that modern Witches could do magic with the aid of all the gods without swearing allegiance to any one god in particular, but Trinity still focused on the connection between the gods and the different kinds of magic. We had mostly studied the Greek gods, with Demeter and Dionysus in charge of Green magic, for example. I knew that other deities were associated with the three colors in some way, and I also knew that none of the goddesses on my list were linked with the three colors I was familiar with.

Aphrodite was the goddess of love in the Greek tradition, and she was famed for her short-tempered acts of vengeance when she was displeased. I swallowed, my eyes skimming the list again Despite Trinity's focus on the Greek gods, we had covered other mythologies briefly, and I wracked my brain, trying to remember what I knew about the other names on my list.. Pele was a

Polynesian goddess, but I didn't remember much about her. Kali terrified me; the Hindu goddess symbolized blood lust and chaos. I didn't know anything about the last name on my list, but Freya sounded like something Celtic. I would have to do more research on the four goddesses, and maybe then I'd understand a bit more about Red magic.

A soft knock at my bedroom door jolted me out of my reverie. I shoved my notebook under my bed before standing up to call, "Come in."

My dad entered the room, carrying a stack of newspapers. I tensed and crossed my arms over my chest, waiting for him to berate me for coming in so late. Instead, he wore a strange expression that I couldn't decipher.

"These were delivered. For your first lesson." He extended the stack of papers to me as if they might burn him, and he wiped his hands on his jeans once the newspapers were handed off. Dad looked like he wanted to say more, but instead he walked back into the hall, shutting the door quietly behind him.

I looked down at the stack of newspapers in my arms. There was a yellow sticky note on top of the pile: "read these—look for chaos—lesson one." The handwriting was spidery, and with a chill I felt certain that Hecate had been the one who delivered my homework. No wonder Dad had looked disturbed! Gingerly, I moved the stack of newspapers to one side. I didn't want to deal with them tonight: between the meditation and the note from Hecate, I was starting to get a picture of Red magic, and it wasn't one I liked. Exhausted, I fell into a deep sleep.

4

Dinner the next night was a strained affair. I guess I could have stayed in my room. I always kept a stash of granola bars and dried fruit that I saved for whenever I can't bear to be around my parents (plus, eating after doing magic is one of the quickest ways to bring you back to reality), but I felt like I owed it to them to at least pretend to be their normal daughter for a bit longer. Besides, I hadn't really seen them since the day after Hecate's visit, and sooner or later, Mom was bound to come looking for me.

Mom's a vegetarian and she does the cooking, so I've grown up on tofu and lots of spices. Vegetarian food is great, but for some reason, I was craving a juicy, red steak. I'd never had a steak before, juicy or otherwise, so I thought this was pretty weird and didn't say anything. I just tucked into the chana masala Mom served, keeping my mouth as full as I could to avoid talking.

I was sopping up the last of the spicy orange sauce with a piece of freshly baked flatbread when Dad cleared his throat. He set down his glass of wine and looked at me. Mom paused, her fingers twitching with anticipation, and I looked at them both, too nervous to swallow the food that sat on my tongue.

Instead of the lecture I was expecting, Dad reached his arms across the table, clasping my hand and Mom's in his. Now was not when I would have expected Dad to start saying grace at the table. Besides, we were done with the meal. I looked at him curiously. Mom squeezed my other hand in hers, but didn't speak.

"Darlena," Dad began, "I know I may have sounded harsh yesterday. This—" He cleared his throat. "Your path has come as quite a shock to both your mother and me. However,"—he looked at Mom for a minute, and she nodded back at him gently—"we are your family. It is up to us to raise you, to shelter you, and to aid you, even in the face of something like this." He was staring at me intently, and I forced a small smile. I still didn't understand what Red magic entailed, but his words were the first real comfort I'd had since Hecate had appeared in the living room.

Mom began to speak. "There will be many things you can't tell us, and many things we might not want to know. But you need to know that we will support you, and if our actions can ease this burden you now bear, we will do what we can. We love you, Darlena." I looked at my beautiful mother, realizing that she suddenly looked years older than she should have. I suppressed the feeling of guilt that surged into my mind.

They both looked at me expectantly, and finally I asked the

question that I had been struggling with. "Just what exactly have I chosen?"

They looked startled, so I hurried to explain. "I know I said I would practice Red magic." At the word 'Red', my mother blanched and my father looked angry, but I pushed on firmly, "But I didn't know what I was saying. I thought it didn't exist, but everyone seems to believe otherwise."

Dad raised his eyebrow. "You swore to follow a path as a joke?"

I shook my head. "That's not what I meant."

"You just said you didn't think it really existed. That sounds like some kind of ridiculous joke to me." He crossed his arms and gave me *the look*. My dad had always been the disciplinarian, and his look could usually make me apologize for whatever he thought I'd done, but I resisted the urge.

"She was pressuring me! I didn't know what I wanted; I still don't." I looked down, fiddling with the tablecloth. "I guess I thought that if I pledged to an imaginary path, everyone would back off for a while."

Mom looked stunned. "What do you mean, everyone?"

I didn't look up. "Ever since my birthday, it seems like everyone has been on my case about my stupid path."

"It's important, Lena. Your path is your future." Mom touched my cheek, and I looked up into her concerned eyes.

"But I don't even get why we have to pick our paths, anyway. Can't I just practice magic and not worry about the color?"

Dad exhaled through his teeth. "That's a childish thing to say."

Mom shot him an inscrutable look. "Either way, her choice has been made."

I swallowed my irritation at Dad. They seemed to know more about what was going on than I did, and right now, I needed all the help I could get. "I don't know anything about any magic but the Trinity paths. I'm scared. Should I be?"

Dad nodded, and my heart sank. "The path you have pledged is challenging."

"And dangerous," Mom whispered.

"It is dangerous," Dad echoed, "to others and to yourself."

Confused, I looked at both of them, searching for answers. It was Mom who began to speak.

"The magic you will practice is ancient. And powerful. There is so much about it that is unknown, and so much more that seems like half-remembered myth. I don't know enough to teach you anything." Her face looked defeated, and I felt small and alone. My mother was brilliant and a skilled Witch; there had never been anything magical that she couldn't explain to my satisfaction.

Dad opened his mouth and the lights in the dining room surged brightly and then went out. I let out a startled shriek. Mom stood up, and I heard her rummaging around in the dark. I guessed that she was searching the junk drawer for matches to light the candles that sat unused on the table. The sulfuric smell of the match brought eerie illumination, and my mother's head looked like it was floating in the darkness. Then the candles were lit, and everything felt normal, if somewhat quaint. We didn't usually eat in candlelight, since candles served more of a purpose for my family than providing romantic lighting. Witches rely on candles to focus their magic for all kinds of spells, but the two that stood ready on the table for power outages were plain white tapers that had never been used for magic.

Across the table, Dad shifted uncomfortably and gestured to the candles. "I don't think we're supposed to tell you anything else right now. Otherwise, the power would still be on."

His words made my skin crawl. "What do you mean?"

"Someone is watching you, Lena," Mom said, "and she's not a goddess I want to cross."

That pushed me over the edge. I stood up so fast my chair toppled over behind me, and Mom jumped at the crash. "I need to know! This is going to be my life, and I can't be ignorant!" I ranted, stomping around the table with pent-up anger. "I've been kicked out of school and now you two just told me that whatever it is I am is dangerous, but you won't tell me how, or why, or anything. It's not fair! None of this is fair!"

A shadow moved in the corner of my eye, and Mom gasped. I turned and found myself facing a shimmering specter, a woman robed in blue. Her hair was black as ice and her eyes were cold. Her mouth was stained unnaturally red, and at first I thought she was some kind of vampire until I saw the halved fruit in her hand. Pomegranate seeds tinkled to the floor as she moved forward, and my mother bent her head in reverence. That's when I figured out who this goddess was: she could only be the daughter of my mom's patron. Dad hadn't moved since the apparition had appeared; it was as if he was frozen.

"Of course it's not fair," Persephone whispered. "If it were fair, would I have been forced to choose between my love and the light of the sun?" She clenched the fruit in her right hand. Juice squirted onto her blue gown, but she didn't seem to notice. "You are a Red, girl, like it or not, and like myself, you are bound by forces beyond human conception."

I darted a panicked look at my parents. Mom still had her head bowed, her eyes turned to the floor. Frightened, I looked back at the goddess, not sure what she expected me to say or do.

"I'm sorry," I said lamely. Persephone didn't answer.

She considered me for a moment, and then her expression altered. She didn't seem angry anymore, but I couldn't tell what emotion now possessed her. She stretched her hand out to me.

"Take a seed. Take three. Keep them. If you ever feel that you've made a devil's bargain, you may eat them." A smile played across her lips, but I didn't think she was really happy. What did the seeds have to do with anything? Suspicious, I shook my head, and her eyes turned to steel.

"Take them. What you do with them is up to you, but do not refuse a gift from the gods."

Hesitantly, I held out my palm and three jewel-like seeds dropped into it. I closed my fingers cautiously, almost as afraid of crushing the gift as I was of accepting it. Persephone seemed satisfied.

"The Red is the blood. My blood was virginal when I was taken from the springtime, but now I am neither of this world or that. The blood changes, but the blood compels. Remember this lesson, and obey your own blood."

With these strange words, red light filled the room and I blinked. In that instant, the lights came on and the goddess who had stood in our dining room was gone. I looked at Mom, then down at the pomegranate seeds clutched in my hand. Mom looked at Dad, who was blinking in the suddenly bright light, and I realized he had no idea what had just happened. Mom shot me a warning look and I nodded. We wouldn't say anything about this to Dad for now.

I tucked the seeds carefully into my pocket, my mind racing. What had Persephone meant about blood? I was sure that her presence had something to do with Red magic, but I wasn't sure what to make of her words. She hadn't given me advice, exactly, but she had given me the seeds. I just didn't know what she wanted. Dad was watching me warily, and I tried to remember what had happened before the power went out. Oh yeah, my outburst. I righted my chair and forced an apologetic smile.

"I'm sorry I got upset."

Dad smiled faintly. "This has upset all of us, I think. Maybe we should call it an early night."

Mom nodded, but when Dad looked away, she pointed upstairs once. I understood. We would talk about everything later, away from Dad. I nodded, wondering what she would be able to tell me alone that she hadn't said at the table.

5

When I headed to bed after loading the dishwasher, Mom followed me into my room and closed the door.

"Lena." She choked on my nickname, tears threatening to well up in her eyes. I looked at the floor and waited, and in a minute she continued. "Persephone is, well, she is the daughter of my patron, Demeter." She paused, sorting things out in her mind before speaking. "Maybe," she paused, "her presence might mean that Red magic isn't as different as I thought. Maybe the things I've heard—" She broke off with a nervous glance at me.

"Demeter is the goddess of the harvest, right?" I interjected. Mom nodded, relieved to have the conversation back in familiar territory. "And she lost her daughter to the lord of the Underworld, right?"

"Hades. He broke through the earth and took the girl, kept her in his kingdom against her will and broke her spirit." Mom recited the words like a well-learned lesson, but her eyes looked uncertain. The goddess herself had seemed to allude to a different version of the tale.

"And then she ate the pomegranate seeds and was forced to return to the Underworld."

Thoughtfully, Mom nodded. "But from what she said, it sounds more like the seeds caused some kind of balance, not entrapment."

Our eyes turned to the three pomegranate seeds I had set on my dresser.

"Not yet," I whispered. "She said to eat them if I ever felt like I'd made a bad choice, but right now I still don't understand the choice I've made. I need to know more."

Mom looked into my eyes and I felt her strength filling me. "I thought blood magic was just about death and chaos. But now I think there is more to it, and I know that if Demeter's daughter is involved, I must be involved, too. I will try—" Her voice cracked. "I will try not to be afraid anymore of what I think you have become."

Her words startled me. I had realized my parents were upset, but I hadn't thought they were afraid. What force could make a mother fear her own daughter? And twice now I'd heard that word: *blood*. Persephone and Mom had both called Red magic *blood magic*. What had I gotten myself into? I sank down onto my bed and looked at Mom in confusion.

People had always said I looked like my mom, but I didn't see it. She was beautiful, with her long hair flowing down to her shoulders. She'd never colored her hair, yet women were constantly asking her what product she used; no one believed that rich reddish-brown color could be natural. But if Mom's patron was indirectly involved in Red magic, maybe I was more like her than I thought.

As if echoing my thoughts, she said, "Persephone would make a nice patron. Maybe you should consider—"

"I don't want to take a patron yet. I don't even understand Red magic; how am I supposed to know who the Red gods are?"

Mom pursed her lips. "Lena, it would be good to have help, and a patron can provide you with more help than your father or I can."

I turned over, pressing my face to my pillow. "I don't even know if I want a patron."

"You're young. You don't understand how wonderful it is to work directly with a god."

I looked up at her curiously. Mom had never talked about her relationship with Demeter that much, and I had never asked. "When did you swear to Demeter?"

Her eyes got misty as she remembered. "When I was fifteen." She noticed my startled expression and laughed self-consciously. "We did things differently back then; the patron and the path sort of came together."

I counted on my fingers. "So you've been a Green Witch for—"

"A long time." She laughed. "And since day one, Demeter has been there to guide me."

"Does she appear all the time? How do you work with her?"

Mom hesitated. "She appeared to me during my Dedicancy ceremony, but other than that, it's mostly been a long-distance relationship."

My mouth dropped open. "And that's what you want me to get myself into? How can she help you if she isn't here?"

"It's hard to explain. But my powers have sharpened because of her presence in my life."

"Your green thumb." Mom could grow anything in the thick clay that pretended to be our yard, and the neighbors were always amazed by her garden.

She shrugged modestly. "That, and other things. Trust me, Lena, a patron is a huge blessing."

"Who's Dad's patron?"

I couldn't read her expression, but her tone was tense. "That's a question you'll have to ask him."

"You know he and I can't really talk anymore." It was true. Once, I'd adored my dad, but then he'd grown overbearing and distant. He'd always been the one to dole out punishment, but it was as if he stopped going easy on me all of a sudden when I hit high school. There were days that I hated him, although I'd never say something like that out loud.

Mom sighed. "Your dad loves you. It's just hard for him to understand you. Remember, he was never a teenage girl."

I snorted. "You can say that again."

"Think about what I've said, Lena. If you worked with Persephone, maybe I would be able to help you."

"You can help me even if I don't have a patron, right?" I tried to keep the panic out of my voice, but she heard it.

"I will always do everything in my power for you."

It wasn't really an answer, but it would have to do. I forced a smile. She touched my cheek softly before she left my room, but her eyes looked troubled.

I lay back on my bed, staring up at my ceiling. Instead of thinking about what Mom had said, I found myself wandering through childhood memories.

My parents used to take turns reading to me every night before bed when I was younger. I don't know how old I was, but I must have been old enough to go to school. I hadn't always attended Trinity. My parents had started me out at a public elementary school. Most Witches didn't mix with Nons, but because Mom and Dad were Greens, or maybe just because of their personalities, they weren't inclined to segregate themselves. I don't know when they would have sent me to Trinity if I hadn't run into a narrow-minded teacher at the public school. Maybe they'd planned to keep me with Nons as long as possible, or maybe they would have sent me to Trinity that year anyway. I'd never thought to ask.

The night everything changed, Dad and I were reading together before bed. I remember we were reading the story of Rapunzel for about the millionth time. Right after the witch cut Rapunzel's hair, I turned to my father.

"Witches are nasty, right, Daddy?"

He looked down at me for a second, stunned. "What makes you say that?"

I pointed at the book. "It's true! Ms. Brenamen said so today in class."

My father frowned. "Witches are not nasty, sweetie."

I was confused. "But look at what the witch did to Rapunzel! That's mean."

Dad sighed. "Magic is powerful, so you have to be careful to do the right thing."

I giggled. "You're silly, Daddy. Magic isn't real."

He closed the book and looked at me with a serious expression. "Darlena, you are a Witch. So am I, so is your mother. This doesn't mean we are evil. It just means"—he snapped his fingers and the candle beside my bed dimmed and then flared up—"that we have to be careful with our magic."

He kissed my cheek and tucked me in, but I still didn't believe in magic. It wasn't until later that week, when my parents pulled me out of the public school and enrolled me in Trinity, that I began to understand what he'd been talking about. At first, it was really cool, like falling into a fairy tale. But Trinity didn't believe in using magic unnecessarily, and soon I felt more stifled than before. I'd always hated the fact that I could do magic, but I wasn't supposed to use it all the time. What was the sense in that?

***

When I finally fell asleep, I plunged immediately into a dream. I was walking along a dark, stone corridor, feeling my way with hesitant steps. In the distance, I could see a dim glow. As I walked, the glow brightened and I realized the light was tinted red. I hesitated, but a gust of wind swept down the tunnel and forced me forward. I stumbled and reached out to catch myself, but my hand grabbed something fleshy and soft. I shuddered. When I looked, I was relieved to see that I was gripping a rotten pomegranate, not something human. My hand was stained red from the juice, and I was suddenly overwhelmed with an urge to lick my fingers. Before I could, I heard a crash in the corridor ahead of me and dropped the fruit, distracted.

I took a few more hesitant steps down the corridor, rounding a bend. The red glow grew blinding. As I struggled to see, a shape began to form in the red light. A figure stood before me, robed in black and engulfed in flames. I felt my skin prickle, and all of a sudden I realized that I was looking in a mirror. I was the one burning.

***

I woke with a thump. Startled and disoriented from my dream, I couldn't quite figure out why I was staring at a pair of glowing green eyes. As my awareness returned, I realized that I was on the hardwood floor of my bedroom. I must have fallen out of bed as I struggled to escape my nightmare, and Xerxes was eyeing me with something approaching interest. The old gray cat had never seemed to care about anything that wasn't tuna, but clearly my new sleeping habits were intriguing. He stretched languorously and touched his cold nose to mine. The cat and I both flinched at the static charge that zapped us. He looked at me, offended, before turning tail and stalking into my closet.

I stretched my tired muscles and touched my face. No burn scars. I exhaled in relief. My dream had seemed so real.

As I sat up, I noticed the stack of newspapers sitting by the foot of my bed. The yellow sticky note winked up at me, and, curious, I reached for the first paper. I skimmed the headlines, wondering what kind of chaos I was supposed to be looking for: robberies, terrorism, natural disasters; what did Hecate want me to see? The headlines on the first page were gruesome: a bomb in the Middle East, flooding in the Caribbean, and a high schooler in the Midwest who brought a gun to school. Those all sounded pretty chaotic to me, but I kept turning the pages. I made it more than halfway through the paper before I found any stories that weren't about chaos. By that point, I was too depressed to keep reading.

Tossing the paper aside, I picked up the next in the stack and began skimming. Once again, it seemed like the only news stories were about horrors around the world. Announcements of births and weddings and interviews with interesting people were buried in the back. Why did the press insist on sharing only the bad things that were going on? Surely these articles couldn't represent the ratio of misery to joy in the world, could they?

"Now you see why your choice is so valuable." The voice made me jump. A woman had materialized out of thin air and was leaning against my dresser. Her hair was like a black waterfall across her shoulders, and she wore a red floral dress that set off her caramel-colored skin. Her eyes were glistening amber, like the burning embers of a fire. I stared at her, stunned.

"The world feeds on the chaos generated by Red magic. Without it, what would people read in their paper each morning?" Her voice dripped with power, and I wanted to shrink back against the bed to avoid her reach. She went on, oblivious to my revulsion.

"You have chosen to be a keeper of chaos. You will remember to honor me as you keep the balance." She smiled like a cat, and my hair stood on end.

"Um, I don't want to be rude ... " I paused, searching my mind frantically for some clue about this goddess. I was terrified of being incinerated, but my mind was completely blank. "But I don't know who you are." I cringed, waiting for her reaction.

The goddess growled. It sounded like a rumble, as if the entire house were on the verge of collapse.

"I am Pele. You will not forget me, girl. It is my fire that creates your realm."

"I don't understand." I scrambled to my feet, spreading my hands in an apologetic gesture. At least she hadn't killed me yet.

"You are one of the keepers of Red magic, and the boundaries of your territory are set by my fire mountains."

"You're a goddess of volcanoes?"

She rumbled again. "I am the great keeper of the fire mountains. They worshipped me in the South Pacific, but my realm includes all mountains of rock and flame."

"But how should I honor you? I don't even understand what my job is yet." My throat tightened around the words. I was starting to understand Red magic, but I still had no idea what it meant to be a Red Witch.

Pele stared at me, her eyes sparking. After a moment, her gaze cooled and I could breathe again. "I see that is true. You do not know yet, but you are starting to understand. And when you take your power, you will honor me with sacrifices. My mountains do not like to be silent."

The room suddenly filled with the smell of burning flesh. My eyes watered and I rubbed my hand across my face. When I looked up, Pele was gone, but my room still smelled like rancid barbeque. I shuddered. What did she mean about sacrifices? I shook my head and attempted to return to my newspaper reading but was distracted. The scorched smell lingered in my nostrils, and my stomach rocked sickeningly. I set down the paper and stood up. I had learned long ago that the best way to re-ground my body after an intense magical experience was to eat, and I hadn't had breakfast yet. Glancing over my shoulder just in case Pele had reappeared, I shut my door firmly and headed downstairs. Maybe if I got food, I could forget about the goddess who had appeared in my bedroom. My thoughts raced. Where were all these goddesses coming from, anyway?

6

The kitchen seemed oddly empty, and after rummaging around in the fridge for a few minutes, I decided to hit the bakery around the corner from Trinity. For some reason I felt a little uneasy leaving the house, but I scribbled a note to my parents and grabbed my scarf from beside the door. The weather in North Carolina is bright and sunny most of the year, but this was one of those strange days that cropped up in late summer. It had been a steamy eighty degrees the day before, but the air had turned crisp, and I was grateful to have the warmth of the ratty wool scarf my dad had brought home from a trip to Scotland. Soon the days would all be like this: chilly and beautiful. Drinking in the blue sky overhead, I tipped my head back with a smile.

Fall is my favorite season not only for the perfect weather, but because my two favorite festivals are in autumn. My parents always made a big deal about celebrating Mabon, the fall equinox, since it's directly connected to Mom's patron. I'd grown up weaving grass crowns for each of us, and the annual ritual was always punctuated with rich apple cider and donuts. I loved it, but not as much as Samhain, which most Nons, and even many Witches, now know as Halloween. To most Witches, it is the crux of the year, and my parents always did a great job of blending magical traditions with the things Nons expected to see. We decorated the house like crazy every year, and I was hoping to help my dad this year by hiding under the candy table and making ghostly noises. Later, after the trick-or-treaters went home, the three of us would light a fire in the fire pit and talk quietly. Mom always told a different story of the Underworld: some years, it was the tale of Orpheus, while other years, she spoke of Inanna. I loved everything about Halloween, and I couldn't wait for the weather to change into true fall.

I was jolted out of my reverie by the sound of squealing brakes. I looked over my shoulder as a green car flew around the corner. The driver had clearly lost control and was headed straight for the sidewalk—and me. Frozen to the spot, I put my hands up in an instinctive gesture. I squeezed my eyes shut, ready to be crushed by the hunk of metal barreling toward me. Instead, I heard glass shattering and metal grinding.

Confused, I cracked one eyelid, and then blinked stupidly. The car that had been about to hit me was flipped over in the middle of the road like a turtle on its back. I was fine; in fact, I felt buzzed.

Probably a reaction to a near-death experience, I thought foggily. Realizing that the shapes inside the crumpled vehicle were stationary, I pulled out my cell phone and dialed 9-1-1. That's when I noticed the red sparks on my arms. They faded as I looked at them, but for a minute, my hands had looked like sparklers on the Fourth of July. Puzzled, I turned my hands over, but the sparks were gone. Maybe I had imagined it.

A crowd of gaping onlookers had started to gather, and I saw a few more people pull out their phones. I swayed dizzily and remembered that the whole reason I had been on the street this morning was because I hadn't eaten yet. I shifted from foot to foot for a moment, wondering if I should stay at the scene as a witness. But since I hadn't really seen anything, and there were so many other people around, I decided I should get some food before I fell down. Besides, the accident looked bad, and I was feeling squeamish. I didn't want to hang around in case the people in the car were badly hurt. I could handle the sight of my own blood, but I'd never been around a car accident before. Making a decision, I disconnected my phone while it was still ringing. My stomach lurched, and I took one last look at the still figures in the car. Fighting nausea, I turned into the bakery where Rochelle and I usually hung out.

The bell above the door jingled, and the smell of warm bread enveloped me. I breathed in for a minute, letting the familiar scent steady my stomach. As I approached the counter, Cindy, the pink-haired Non who always waited on me, looked up. Her expression was blurry, like she was trying to remember something and failing miserably, but that wasn't too out of the ordinary. Cindy was a college student at NC Central, and she was usually stressed out from studying. I smiled at her warmly, waiting for her to rattle off my regular order: everything bagel with cream cheese and honey and a vanilla latte, but she just stared at me, unspeaking. I cleared my throat, and she shook her head.

"What can I get you?"

Startled, I stared at her. In the past year, Cindy had only ever asked me that question once: the first time we met. She looked at me with bored expectation, and I found myself glancing at the menu.

"I'll try ... the vegetarian breakfast wrap. I guess. And a cup of iced pomegranate tea, to go." She rang up my order and I paid, wondering why I had deviated from my normal morning routine. I never ordered iced tea, even though southern sweet tea is the best invention known to man. Maybe the car accident had shaken me more than I realized. Shrugging, I put my change in the tip jar and slid down the counter to wait. Instead of starting my sandwich, Cindy slipped into the kitchen, leaving the counter unmanned. As I waited, bored, I strained to listen to the conversations around me. I like to eavesdrop; it passes the time, and I usually learn something bizarre about the strangers around me. It's amazing what people will say in a public place. As I listened to the couple behind me discussing their sex life (not what I want to hear about before breakfast, thank you very much), I suddenly tuned in to Cindy's voice.

"That freak out there, the girl at the counter. I saw her curse those people."

"What are you talking about? Cindy, there's a customer, get out there."

"She flipped that car. You saw the accident."

Cindy's companion murmured something I couldn't hear, but my palms had started to sweat. Cindy's retort made me turn cold.

"She held up her hand and it was like a tsunami hit that car. There were sparks and everything! That weirdo is deadly. Would you just finish her order? I don't want her to curse me, too."

The other girl must have agreed, because a few minutes later I received my breakfast from a girl with braces whose name tag said "Hi! I'm Ginger." She stared at me as I left the shop, and I felt Cindy's eyes on the back of my neck, too. I raced home, wishing I could fly.

I had to cut around the long way to avoid the accident, but after what Cindy claimed she had seen, I didn't want to be anywhere near the wreck. What if I had caused it in some way? I remembered the faint red sparks on my hands; were they left over from some kind of crazy magic? And what had happened to the driver? Nobody was moving inside the car when I left, and I felt a sick sensation in my stomach that had nothing to do with hunger. With a flash of intuition, I realized that the people in the car hadn't survived. Did that mean I had committed murder? I shuddered at the thought. My magic had never been strong enough to manipulate large objects, but it was definitely odd that the car hadn't hit me. It should have, based on everything I saw before I threw up my hands in that foolish defense. I unlocked the back door and slipped into the kitchen.

Hecate was waiting for me.

7

The goddess looked totally at ease, and I glared at her. The first thing that came to mind was the accident I had just witnessed. "Well?"

She stared at me impassively. "Well, what, little Witch?"

I threw my breakfast on the counter and rounded on her. "Well, did I just kill someone?"

"Life always gives way to death. It is the way of things."

Her answer infuriated me. "Look, lady," I said, dangerously rude but beyond caring, "you still haven't told me anything, and now I think I just killed those people in that car!"

She looked at me, her face calm but her eyes smoldering from my insulting tone. "Someone was supposed to die today."

I sank down in a chair and buried my head in my hands, but she continued talking. "Two people were meant to die; two people died. But those two were not the two that were meant to die."

I looked up at her, startled.

"A pedestrian like yourself was meant to perish. As was the passenger. But," she added tonelessly, "you called upon the power of chaos and altered the course of events."

Horrified, I pressed her. "So I killed the two people in the car? It's my fault?" I waited for her to tell me no, but I knew the truth in my gut. I was a freak, a murderer, like Cindy said.

The goddess shook her head slightly. "It is more complicated than that. You have done something I do not usually see Reds do. You turned the chaos of the situation inside out."

Seeing my dumb expression, she explained herself. "The driver of that car would have been injured, but lived. He would have lived with the crushing guilt that he had killed two innocent women, and in three years' time, the pressure would have been too much for his mind. He would have purchased a rifle, walked into the street, and opened fire on a large crowd at a summer picnic. He would have killed a child and wounded three others before turning the gun on himself."

Her words washed over me like a death sentence, and I shivered at her emotionless tone. "How can you know what he would have done?"

"You forget your training. I am the goddess of the crossroads, and I see three ways."

I remembered the strange triple-headed wall plaque in Principal Snout's office and shuddered. "The past, the present, and the future?"

She inclined her head without speaking, and I tried to process everything she was telling me. It was impossible. My brain kept getting stuck on the fact that two people had died today because of me.

The goddess answered my thoughts. "What you did today—" She paused, her yellow eyes fixed on me. "You confounded chaos. Two people died today, but the thread that bound those future deaths to today has been snapped."

Her words sank in, and I started to cry. No matter what she said might have happened in the future, I had used Red magic to kill. I'd broken the Rede and every other rule that had ever been instilled in me about magic, and I hadn't even meant to. No wonder Dad said I was dangerous! Hecate watched me for a moment, her features like stone. I gulped for air and wiped my cheeks, trying to straighten my shoulders under the goddess's harsh gaze. If she could see the future, maybe she could help me sort things out. Finally, I got a grip on myself and looked her in the eye.

"I need to know. I need you to tell me, right now, without any more games, what Red magic is. I need to know what I am doing before this happens again."

Hecate looked past me and spoke. "You would have done well to have raised this child with manners. Her arrogance displeases me."

I followed her gaze over my shoulder and nearly fell out of my chair. Mom was kneeling on the floor behind me, her forehead pressed to the cold linoleum. How long had she been there? Had she heard that I was a murderer? I twisted in my chair, petrified at the thought that Mom might have heard I'd become an uncontrollable monster.

When she spoke, her words weren't directed at me. "Your Highness, I am sorry. She is headstrong. I taught her as best I could, but I never thought she would meet you. I never thought I would have that honor. Perhaps I have been lax in her upbringing."

The supplicating tone of my mother's voice made me even angrier. "Now, look here, both of you," I cut in, and Mom gasped. "She is a great mom. If you think I've got an attitude problem, lady, that's all because of you. My parents aren't to blame for anything I do. I'm sixteen, for gods' sake; I can do what I want. So if you're pissed, blame me, not her." I glared defiantly at Hecate for a moment, even though my heart was racing.

Hecate smiled slowly, and that was scarier than anything else I had lived through that morning. She looked like a spider gazing at its next meal, and I had to tighten my muscles to keep myself from recoiling in reflex. I had already cried in front of her once; I wouldn't show her that I was afraid. I clenched my fists and lifted my chin, not breaking eye contact with her even though her yellow eyes were the creepiest things I'd ever seen.

Her smile widened. "Little Red one, you are well suited for your task. Today was a fluke, I see that now. Clearly, I do not need to worry about the chaos you will bring."

With a thunderclap, she was gone. I sank back into a chair. "I am getting so tired of these melodramatic exits!" I muttered. "Don't goddesses ever use the door?"

On the floor behind me, Mom let out a strangled chuckle. In a second, she was laughing hysterically. Quickly, I knelt beside her. It sounded like she might start crying at any time, and I didn't think I could handle that on top of everything else.

"Mom, she's gone. Get up. It's okay." Talking to her like I would a two-year-old, I slowly coaxed Mom from her crouch on the floor and seated her at the table. Gradually, her laughter died down, and I could feel her eyes on me. I couldn't look at her; what would she think of me now? Desperate for something to do, I put the kettle on the stove and started to make tea. Mom kept her loose herbs in neatly labeled jars on the top of the cabinets, and I climbed up on the counter to reach for the peppermint. It would soothe us both. Pausing for a moment, I grabbed the jar of dried roses, too. A little bit of joy wouldn't hurt, especially if Mom had heard as much as I was afraid she had. Like so many things, tea can have two purposes for Witches: we drink it because we like the taste, just like Nons, but we are more intentional about the ingredients. A well-prepared cup of tea can be a spell, affecting the person who drinks it in different ways depending on the properties of the herbs used.

Mom didn't speak, even when the kettle began to whistle and I poured the water into the mugs. When the infusion had steeped long enough, I took the mugs to the table. Mom clutched her cup reflexively and closed her eyes as the steam washed over her face.

I sat across from her and eyed her nervously. She was sipping at the tea slowly, but she wouldn't look up or meet my eye. We couldn't ignore what had happened forever, and after a few sips of the still-hot tea, I took a deep breath.

"Mom. We need to talk about this."

My words sounded surprisingly adult, and she glanced up at me. I faltered for a minute, but I kept talking.

"I don't care what Hecate says; none of this is your fault."

Tears welled up in her eyes and she blinked rapidly. I kept talking, trying to distract her.

"I chose this, Mom. I still don't really know what I've picked—" I forced a laugh to lighten the mood, but she didn't even crack a smile, so I went on, "I don't know what it is that I am now, but I picked it. Nobody forced me to do this, and you certainly didn't raise me wrong. You and Dad are amazing. It's just that Hecate only likes to talk to weak Witches; strong ones irritate her." Even as I said it, I realized it was true, but I stopped talking for a moment in confusion. Had I just called my mother a weak Witch? Worse, had I implied that I was strong enough to make Hecate uncomfortable? I took a sip of tea and tried to collect my scattered thoughts. Before I could speak again, however, Mom began talking.

"Darlena, if she's mad, that means that something about you isn't what she thought. That might be a good thing or a bad thing, but it's definitely dangerous for you to make the Queen of Witches angry. We have to try to figure out what upset her. Why did she come here today?" Mom looked at me, searchingly, and I drew a shuddering breath. So she hadn't heard about the car accident. I wished I could pretend it had never happened, but I realized that I was in way over my head. Maybe confiding in Mom would make things easier.

Quickly, I told her about the morning. She stared at me intently, and raised an eyebrow when I repeated what Hecate had said about me altering the fate of the man in the car. When I finished, she was still. What if she ordered me out of her sight? I don't know why I thought that—confrontation isn't Mom's style—but telling her about the horrors of the morning had been hard. Hearing the words coming out of my mouth made me feel even more like a monster, and I wouldn't have been able to stand it if Mom had thought the same about me.

Mom tapped the side of her mug rhythmically and looked up at me. She didn't look angry, just thoughtful, and I exhaled in relief. "Darlena, I think I understand a little bit of this. Red magic has something to do with death and disaster, right?" I nodded, thinking of the stack of newspapers under my bed and the visit from Pele. Mom kept talking, not noticing how pale I suddenly was. "And the car accident today was supposed to happen. Two people were supposed to die, but the accident would have also served as a catalyst to more deaths down the road, right?" I nodded again. Mom drew a deep breath before continuing. "So. So you are a Red Witch, and you changed death today." I started to interrupt, but Mom plowed over me. "Two people still died today, but the man who would have killed others later on was one of the two. You balanced chaos."

I stared at her, not sure I understood. Mom reached across the table and took my hands in hers.

"Darlena, this is a good thing. You saved lives today!" Her voice rang with pride.

I pulled my hands away. "But two people are still dead because of me! Nothing can change that."

Mom looked at me sternly. "Hecate said even more were meant to die. You changed that, Darlena. It's a tragedy, don't get me wrong. But you made the tragedy smaller."

We stared at each other for a minute, letting it sink in. I tried to wrap my mind around the idea that I'd done something good through doing harm, but it went against everything I'd ever been taught. Good was good, bad was bad, and harm was always bad, right?

An idea occurred to me. "Do you think that's what a Red Witch does? Controls chaos?"

Mom nodded thoughtfully. "But clearly Hecate doesn't want you to limit chaos. When you flew off the handle at her, she said that she wasn't worried anymore, right?"

I nodded, ashamed that I had let my temper get the better of me. "So I have to control my temper, because somehow Red magic is affected by my moods. Great. I'm sixteen, and the fate of the world rests on me keeping a cool head." I sat back in the chair, sulking. Mom squeezed my hand.

"Not the whole world. There must be other Reds."

8

I stayed in the kitchen with Mom that afternoon. She was preparing some food to take to a potluck that night, and she said she needed my magical touch. I knew that was a lie; I'm not much of a Kitchen Witch, and Mom has certainly had years of experience making amazing food, but I let her lie to me. I wanted to be close to her, too, after the shock of the morning.

Mom had the kitchen window flung open and the crisp air was wafting over us. I laughed when she said she wanted to make apple pie.

"How TV family is that?"

She chuckled. "There's nothing wrong with wanting things to be perfect for an afternoon, is there?"

I took down the flour tin and tossed some on the counter. "I guess not," I said, patting the flour down and tracing shapes in it, like I did when I was little. Mom came up beside me and laughed when she saw what I was doing.

"I think you learned your first spell in this kitchen with me, playing with flour. Do you remember?"

Instead of answering, I smoothed the flour and began deliberately drawing symbols. Mom squeezed my shoulder.

"That's the one. The spell to make sure the food you cook won't burn. You did that so naturally the first time, I only had to show you once! And you were such a little thing. I was sure—"

She broke off as a shadow crossed her face.

"What?" I asked, even though her expression begged me to stay quiet. She turned to the sink and began washing the apples.

"Oh, it's nothing." She wouldn't look at me.

Now I really wanted to know. "Mom. Please tell me what you thought when I did that spell."

Her shoulders slumped, and she kept her back to me when she whispered, "I was sure that you were going to be a Green Witch like me."

Silence filled the kitchen, and I stared at her back for a moment. Dad had always talked about how great it would be if the whole family was Green, but Mom had never pushed. I should have realized that she'd want me to follow in her footsteps, but it had never occurred to me. And the fact that I'd declared to a weird and dangerous form of magic that was about as far away from Green as I could get probably wasn't helping the situation. I struggled for a minute, trying to think of something I could say, but I gave up and turned my attention back to the dough.

69

We continued our work in tense silence.

She was peeling apples over the sink while I rolled out the piecrust when I heard her gasp.

"Oh, sugar and salt!" Her tone was sharp, despite her quaint words, and I turned around quickly, hiding a smile.

"Can't you just say *shit*, Mom? What's wrong?"

The blood on her hand answered my question.

"It's just a little nick. I was clumsy, that's all." She wrapped her finger in a paper towel and sat down at the table. I couldn't look away from her blood, and instead of feeling unsettled, I realized I was—hungry. I felt my head begin to spin, and even though she kept talking, her words sounded as if she were underwater.

"Darlena! What is it, sweetie?" Mom leaped up in concern, her own injury forgotten at the sight of my pale, confused expression.

"I don't know. The blood—"

Mom glanced down at the crimson-stained paper towel and shrugged. "But it's not a deep cut, sweetie. Don't worry about me; I'll be okay." She put her uninjured hand against my forehead. "You're cold as ice! Go lie down in the living room. I'll finish up in here."

I wanted to stay in the kitchen with her. The blood wasn't making me woozy; it was making me excited. With a shudder of disgust, I wrenched my eyes away and headed into the living room, trying to ignore the strange thoughts that were flitting through my mind. Xerxes curled up immediately on my stomach, and his rhythmic purr eased my nerves. Gradually, the scent of blood faded from my nostrils, and I stroked the cat. What in the world was wrong with me? Blood shouldn't excite me; that was a freakish reaction. It was becoming impossible to deny that Red magic had changed me in ways I wasn't prepared to deal with.

***

When I felt well enough to climb the stairs, I retreated to my room. I began restlessly scanning my bookshelves for something that would distract me. I paused, and stared intently at my shelf. I'm a little OCD, and I keep my books in alphabetical order, filed under the author's last name, just like in a library. Rochelle teases me about it, but I like to be able to grab any book I want without having to waste time looking for it. I wouldn't have noticed the error if it weren't such a gigantic book, but my *Complete Works of Shakespeare* wasn't where it belonged. I skimmed the shelf again: it wasn't there.

I started rooting around my room, wondering where it could have gotten to. I didn't particularly feel the need to read any of the plays right now, but I was curious. I dug through the stack of boxes under my bed without success. My hand brushed the pile of newspapers and I felt a chill down my spine. Would I be the cause of a headline tomorrow?

I kept looking for that book. I even went so far as to poke my nose into my closet, even though there was no way the book could have wandered in there on its own, and I'm the only one who can enter the closet. When I was young, I used one of the first powerful spells I ever mastered to ward my closet. No one could enter without my consent, including Mom. The closet had been the messiest part of my room for years because Mom got zapped the first time she tried to clean it after my spell. She'd avoided it ever since, and I liked the mess: it made a good place to hide things. The clothes didn't look like they'd been disturbed, but something thumped behind me and I spun around.

The huge book was sitting on top of the log cabin quilt my grandmother had made for me when I was born. It hadn't been there a second ago; I was sure of that. I would never have missed such an obvious, visible location.

I picked it up, ready to return the text to its place on the shelf above my desk, but something about the book seemed odd. It felt lighter than a two-thousand-page book should, and I cracked the cover open, wondering what was different about it.

There was strange, spidery handwriting all over the page.

At first, I was pissed. I know it sounds dorky, but I love Shakespeare. It helps knowing he was the greatest Green Witch in recent history, but the man had a serious way with words. I love reading *Lear* if I want to get depressed or *Midsummer* if I want to laugh my ass off. And someone had messed with my book. I don't even dog-ear the pages of my books, let alone scribble notes in the margins, and I had no idea who would sneak into my room to deface one of my treasures. My blood started to boil at the thought, but then I looked at the page more closely.

The handwriting was spidery and golden, and the letters seemed almost fluid, like the ink wasn't dry yet. The words didn't stay on the page, but the text scrolled like a teleprompter. I flipped to another page: same situation. Glancing around my bedroom, I checked to make sure I was alone. As far as I could tell, I was, but given the past few days, I didn't trust my appraisal of the situation. I considered for a moment and grabbed the flashlight off my dresser. Taking the book, I crept into my closet and shut the door.

I sat on a pair of crumpled shorts, the smell of sand and surf filling the small space. I flicked the flashlight on and opened the book. Right away the golden words began scrolling again, but this time I concentrated on the text and I was able to read the loopy writing.

"Darlena," it began, "pay attention. Everything you read will be erased as soon as you read it."

I paused and looked back up the page. The words were gone. I'd seen weird magical objects before, but this book took the cake. Who would use magic to write in one of my books? Mom and Dad wouldn't bother; they'd just tell me whatever they wanted to say. Clearly, somebody didn't want to say something out loud, and I was intrigued. I closed my eyes for a minute and willed my short-term memory to kick in.

I opened my eyes and looked at the book. The gold script appeared and started moving again, but more slowly than before. It was almost as if it knew I needed to take my time with this information. I leaned forward eagerly, trying to decipher the next line.

"I am not supposed to tell you any of this. Make sure you do not tell the Queen, or else things will be much worse than you can imagine."

The ominous words vanished, and despite the threat, I relaxed. Whoever had written in my book wasn't Hecate, which made me inclined to trust them. Right now, I'd even take Pele over Hecate. I continued reading, ignoring the tingling sensation in my arms.

"There is so much you need to know. I try not to get involved with the Reds anymore. But Helen was dedicated to me, and her failure haunts me. I'll try to remedy that now."

I looked up into the darkness of my clothes overhead. Helen? Who was that? And why should she matter to me? But whoever she was, she had something to do with Red magic. I gripped the book tightly; this might be my only chance to figure out how to control chaos.

I kept reading. My eyes grew wider and wider in the dim light of the flashlight, and my pulse started to race. I didn't notice when the golden words started to blur: I had to keep reading. I had to know what I had become when I pledged to follow the Red path. And the mysterious author certainly seemed to know about that.

Two hours later, I crawled out of the closet carrying the book. There was no writing anywhere inside it. I returned the book to my shelf, glancing around to see if I was being observed. The skin on the back of my neck prickled, but I didn't see anybody. If anyone like Hecate was watching, maybe she'd think I'd spent the afternoon doing homework. Trying to move calmly, I picked up my purse and shuffled through it. When I found my cell phone, I sent a quick text. I grabbed a pair of sunglasses to hide my haunted eyes and sauntered for the door, working hard to look casual. The book had taught me that I could never be too careful now that I was a Red.

9

Justin opened the back door as soon as I jumped the privacy fence surrounding his yard. His eyes blazed with curiosity, and I could feel protective energy radiating off his skin. I tried to smile at him as I slipped inside, hoping I had made the right choice. I needed to talk to somebody, and no matter what hadn't happened between us at the prom, Justin was still the person I trusted more than anybody else. If I was being honest, maybe I'd admit that I texted him because a part of me wanted him to leap to my defense and prove that he still cared about me, which was sort of silly, really, but I couldn't help it if I had a romantic streak. I could, however, keep those thoughts to myself.

He closed the sliding door behind me and sealed it by drawing a pentacle in the air. I almost saw the line of energy; he was getting stronger since his declaration of White magic. My skin tingled, and

I felt myself being pulled toward him like a magnet. I took a careful step back, trying to get a grip on my emotions. I hoped Justin wasn't feeling as awkward as I was, but he acted calm and collected. Had he forgotten that he had sort of proposed to me before I went Red?

He put a finger over his lips, and I nodded. We slipped upstairs silently and shut the door to his bedroom. Justin again sealed the door, this time with a gesture I had never seen before. I studied the white light as it faded, but I couldn't quite make out the shape. I made a mental note to ask him later if that was a White magic thing. When he turned to face me, his eyes were shining with excitement, and I felt my own heart speed up in response.

"So tell me what's going on."

I smiled, despite the empty pit in my stomach. Justin's straightforwardness had been one of the things that attracted me to him the year before, combined with his casual sense of comfort. When Justin moved, there was a sensual grace in his step, but whenever I watched him, it was clear that he was oblivious. There weren't many Witches who weren't at least a little bit arrogant, but Justin was humble even before declaring White. It was one of the things I loved about him, although I'd never admit that out loud. Instead, I focused on the matter at hand.

"I'm a Red."

He nodded, unsurprised, and I realized that word of my unconventional choice had probably circulated around the school on the heels of my expulsion. That annoyed me, but I didn't think now was the time to get defensive about my privacy.

I took a deep breath. "I think I've found out what that means."

He leaned forward. "What?"

"Reds control chaos. There are never more than three Red Witches at any given time, because they are so powerful." I felt my cheeks flushing; Justin was a powerful Witch, and I was making it sound like I was better than him. I'd always accepted that the boy I'd fallen in love with was more powerful than I was, but everything had been flipped on its head. He didn't look offended, though, so I pushed on. "Reds have been responsible for some of the worst events in history. Helen of Troy was a Red, and we all know how much better she made her world."

Justin snorted with suppressed laughter, and I smiled.

"The three Witches in *Macbeth* really existed, and they were all Reds. Reds aren't allowed to know each other anymore, because every time the Reds have gathered in history, chaos has gone spinning out of control."

"You can't control chaos." Justin was quiet, but his words were powerful. I paused for a second, considering.

"I don't really understand it all yet, but I think you—I mean I— can. I think Red magic exists to shape the chaos that happens. There will be chaos in the world no matter what; it's a primal force, and we can't ignore it."

Justin nodded thoughtfully, but I could tell he wasn't sold. I sighed. I hadn't wanted to tell him what had happened that morning, but he needed some kind of proof that what I said was true.

"Red Witches might not control it, not fully, but they can

manipulate it." I told him about the car and everything Hecate, Pele, and Persephone had said to me. Then I told him about the writing in my book. His eyebrows drew together and he looked worried.

There was a long silence as he digested what I had said. I fiddled with my sleeves, worried that I'd said too much. Mom hadn't been freaked out, but what if Justin hated who I'd become? I watched him nervously.

When he finally spoke, his words surprised me. "Why are you here, Darlena? Don't you tell Rochelle everything? She's the one who taught you to hex, so why isn't she helping you deal with this?"

I shook my head. "I trust Rochelle, but ... " I struggled to put my fears into words. "She's a Black. I don't know if she's declared or not yet, but there's no other path for her. I want to learn to control my magic, to filter out harm, and I don't think Rochelle would ... "

" ... be cool with that," Justin finished for me as I trailed off, and I nodded, relieved that the words came from him. I hated thinking ill of my best friend, but something in my gut told me that she wouldn't be too concerned with controlling chaos. Even so, that wasn't the real reason I'd come to Justin. I kept hoping he'd open his arms and embrace me, but he was staying a careful distance away. Still, any help would be better than none, so I waited for him to think about everything I'd said.

He stared at me for a long minute. "If this is all true"—I heard the slight emphasis he put on the word "if" and had to fight down my anger—"you are really dangerous."

I jerked my head, but his eyes were smiling. Maybe he was just trying to tease me, but his words were true. I was dangerous, and I hated it.

"I don't want to be a pawn. These goddesses have already started messing with me, and I don't want to give Pele victims or stir things up for Hecate. Red magic may be primal and under their control, but I'm not, right?" My voice cracked with emotion, but I didn't care. I wanted Justin to tell me that I wasn't trapped. If he said I could handle this mess, I'd believe him.

Justin stared at me for a long moment before he answered. "Energy is never good or evil; it just is."

I nodded eagerly. I had been thinking the same thing, and I hoped it applied to Red magic as well as the other three.

He continued, "If you use the power in a negative way, you will create negative things. But—" He paused, raising his eyebrow. "—I can't think of a way that chaos could be good."

I chose my words carefully. "Maybe I should try to make it as harmless as possible. After the thing with the car this morning, I've been thinking about it a lot. What if I could limit chaos? People would still get hurt, but what if I could pick who would be hurt, and choose as few people as possible?"

Justin shook his head, looking worried. "It's not up to us to decide. Remember the Rede, Darlena: 'An' it harm none, do what you will.' If you start believing you can choose who lives and dies in this world, you're going to go crazy."

I voiced my worst fear. "But then what is the point of having

Red magic? Why am I a Red if there's really nothing I can do besides blow things up?"

Justin was silent. I flopped down on his desk chair and gritted my teeth, determined not to cry. If I cried, he might feel sorry for me, and I couldn't bear that thought. He hadn't seen me cry the night we split up, and I wouldn't let him see that now if I could help it. My emotions swirled around in my chest, but gradually I felt the tears subside and sink down my throat without falling. I swallowed, tasting salt water and snot, and tried not to make a face.

After what seemed like an eternity, Justin spoke. "Darlena, I'm sworn to the White path. It is my duty to uphold life and goodness. If you do have power over chaos, I should encourage you to stop all chaotic events entirely, for the good of mankind."

He turned and began pacing, not noticing my gaping jaw. Before I could figure out a counter argument, he sighed heavily.

"However," he said, sounding defeated, "chaos formed the universe and exists outside the laws of good and evil. It would be evil for you to use your power for personal gain. But—" He looked at me expressionlessly. "I think it would be evil for me to refuse to help you. You came to me for comfort, and I owe you that. Not," he added quickly, "because of anything we had in the past, but because as a White I am sworn to help all who are just. And Darlena, you might be crazy, but you're never unfair." He smiled broadly, and I felt an answering grin spread across my face. Justin could make any situation seem better.

I jumped up and hugged him without thinking. He still smelled the same, like pine trees and campfire smoke, and I melted into his warm embrace. He held me for a moment before I reminded myself that he'd made it clear he didn't want to be with me last spring. I broke away, tugging on the hem of my shirt for a second so I had an excuse not to meet his eyes. "So what do we do?"

Justin studied me, and I could tell he was sifting through everything I'd told him. "First," he said, "we need to figure out what your territory is. When Pele showed up, she mentioned boundaries, didn't she?"

I looked at him, startled. "Yes. But why would territory matter?"

"If there are three Red Witches, you can't all control the same chaos, right? You'd have to work together for that, and you said you are forbidden from meeting the others. So you must each be in charge of a territory."

That made sense, and I was annoyed that I hadn't thought of it myself. "Should I meditate on a world map and see what I come up with?" My question was meant to be sarcastic, but Justin didn't notice my flippant tone.

He shook his head earnestly and turned on the small TV sitting on his dresser. "I have an idea. Watch the news. Concentrate on changing whatever they're talking about."

The reporter on the tiny screen looked morose as she talked about an uprising going on in the Middle East. I stared at her and the video clips, concentrating on redirecting chaos. The reporter switched to a story about a hurricane in the Caribbean. I looked at Justin. He shrugged, but pointed to the screen. I watched the images, concentrating on changing the force of the disaster. I tried to think about calm weather, happy people, and peace treaties. Nothing happened.

Frustrated, I flopped down on the bed. "It didn't work." I sulked, punching a pillow once without much effort. Justin sat next to me and put his hand on my knee.

"But it might work. Those news stories had already happened. Maybe you need to focus on things right before they happen." I tried to listen to his words, but I was distracted by the tingling warmth where his hand was touching my leg. Just when I thought I had myself under control around him, he did something small like that and I started to fall for him all over again.

I looked up into his brown eyes. "How? I'm not clairvoyant!"

"No, but, Darlena, sometimes people can predict chaos. Think about it: hurricanes don't happen out of the blue, and wars are always somewhat expected. So maybe we need to start paying attention to the things that are almost chaos, and see what kind of change you can bring." He finally took his hand off my knee, and I tried to ignore the surge of disappointment that swept through me.

"So we just watch the news and wait? This doesn't seem like it will help very much."

Justin sighed. "I know. But do you have a better idea?"

I didn't. I was out of ideas, but doing something had to be better than nothing.

10

I sifted through my thoughts on the walk home. If there were three Reds, as I had been told by the strange golden writing, then it would be ridiculous for the Reds to have control over the same things. It made sense that the division of power would be geographic, but the world did not easily divide into thirds. As I puzzled it out, a fear crept into my mind: what if the Red Witches were divided by power, not location? I had already begun to understand that there are many types of chaos; what if we each only had power over one of those types? If my power wasn't localized, Justin and I wouldn't get anywhere with our plan.

I tried to recall some of the other things that had been written in gold ink in my book. Usually, I have a great memory, but everything I had read that afternoon seemed fuzzy, as if I had been sick when I first learned it. The indigo twilight was darkening to black when I let myself into the kitchen, and Dad pounced on me as soon as I was inside.

"Where have you been, young lady? Your mother and I have been worried sick!" Mom was sitting at the table, in the same seat she had crumpled into that morning. She didn't meet my eyes, even when I crossed the room and stood right in front of her. She just kept staring at the object in her hands, and I stared at it too. It was her athame, her ritual knife, the blade still sharp after a lifetime of use. I'd only ever seen the knife once, when she threw a ritual for me when I turned thirteen.

I had just gotten my first period, which, in addition to being a real pain in the ass, is the event that marks a turning point in a female Witch's power. Mom tried to downplay the cramps and invited over a bunch of her friends to celebrate my first "moon blood." Mom had used her athame that night to stir the honey into the water in the ceremonial chalice. She had handed the cup to me, still holding her knife, kissed me on both cheeks, and said, "May you never hunger or thirst."

The ceremony had been really special, but I hadn't seen the athame since. I knew enough about magic to know that no Witch brought out her most precious magical tool just because she was worried about her daughter. Something big had happened, and part of me didn't want to know what it was.

I looked between my parents, unsure who to ask. "What is it?"

Mom sighed. "Hecate dropped by. Again." I glanced at her sharply, but given Dad's lack of reaction, he had clearly already found out about the whole thing with the car. I drew a deep breath, trying to steady myself. Hecate had been around a lot lately, but while that was strange, it shouldn't have been enough to throw my parents into the state they were in.

"And?"

"She warned us not to let you go out on your own. She implied that the car might not have been the only close brush you'd have with chaos." Mom's voice was calm, detached, but my dad was turning purple and I could practically see the steam coming out of his ears.

"I was afraid of this, but your mother tried to tell me she could watch you. What happened tonight?"

I wanted to tell them everything: about the book, about the plan Justin and I were hatching, about what I'd learned about being a Red. But fear and anger bubbled up together in my throat, and I flung my head back in defiance.

"I'm just trying to understand what I am. Don't you get it? Everything has changed and I don't know where I fit anymore." I kept my hands clenched tight to my sides, afraid that if I opened my palms, I would conjure up the Red magic that I had used that morning. No matter what I was, I wouldn't hurt my family, not even accidentally. That was one thing I could control.

Mom and Dad stared at me in shock. I didn't usually fight with them; I used silence as my weapon until they forgot we weren't getting along. I turned on my heel, ran up the stairs, and crawled into the sanctuary of my closet.

I had just shut the closet door when the tears I had been struggling to hold back all day finally burst out of me. I sobbed into the skirt of the dress I had worn to prom with Justin the year before, not caring that the black tulle was coarse and itchy. There was a gentle tap on my bedroom door, and I held my breath.

"Darlena? May I come in?" Mom's voice was muffled by the clothes surrounding me, but I let my breath out in relief. I couldn't talk to Dad when I was upset like this, but I thought I might be able to handle Mom.

"Just a sec." Snuffling, I scooted out of the closet and sat down next to my bed. I hastily rubbed at my face, trying to wipe away the evidence of my meltdown. Mom was already worried enough about me; she didn't need to know I'd been crying on top of it all. "Come in."

The door opened, and Mom flicked on my light as she shut the door behind her. She paused for a moment when she saw me but didn't say anything. Sinking to her knees beside me, she sat quietly. Her shoulder bumped mine, and I impulsively reached over and took her hand. She squeezed my fingers and turned my hand palm-up. I watched with interest as she began tracing the lines on my palm with her fingertip, muttering to herself. Her beautiful auburn hair fell in front of her face, masking her from my view. Then she cocked her head to one side the way Xerxes does when he's thinking about jumping up on a window ledge, and I had to fight back the urge to giggle.

Her eyes met mine, and I sobered. "Things won't be easy," she said solemnly. I nodded. I had already realized that. She placed something in my still-upturned palm, and I was startled by the feel of it. A glance confirmed my suspicion.

"You can't give me this!" I held her athame gingerly, feeling the magical energy stored in the blade. "It's your most powerful tool!" It felt like her, warm and strong, but I knew the blade was sharp. Mom was like her knife, I realized with a flash of intuition: simple but deceptively powerful.

"But you need it more." The weight of her words settled over the room like a curse, and I shuddered. She kept speaking in a quiet, sad voice. "I am sworn to Demeter, Darlena. Above all else, she is a mother. She was willing to sacrifice the world in her grief at losing her daughter. I don't," she choked, "want to lose you, so shouldn't I be willing to sacrifice a knife if it will keep you safe?" She stroked my cheek with her finger. "You are my beautiful child, and I am afraid I won't be able to protect you anymore."

I hugged her close, the athame still clutched in my hand. Neither of us rushed to break the embrace, but finally Mom pulled me back and looked at me hard.

"Remember," she said, "declaring a path is not the same thing as swearing to a goddess. You do not belong to Hecate. When you finally choose a patron—" Her eyes glistened with tears when she said this, "choose someone who can shape your life. Hecate would not be the best choice for you." I nodded silently. I had been worried since meeting the goddess that she already took my allegiance for granted, when I wanted nothing more to do with her. Like I'd said to Mom the other day, I wasn't sure I wanted to deal with a patron at all.

"You don't walk my path, but you are still my daughter. I will stand by you, and if you keep my blade, I think I will be able to help you." She kissed my forehead and got to her feet. I rose to stand with her and realized that my eyes were level with hers. When had I gotten so tall?

"Thank you. For everything, but thank you especially for this." She nodded and stepped out into the hall, gently closing the door behind her. I still felt fragile, like a soap bubble, but Mom's words had reminded me that I wasn't alone. I had her, and I had Justin. Maybe Dad would even come around eventually, but if nothing else, I was sure he wouldn't stand in my way. I fell asleep with the knife beneath my pillow, and for the first time since I met Hecate, I didn't have any nightmares.

11

My dad had already left for work when I got up the next morning. I know, because I lay awake waiting to hear the car engine turn over and pull away before I ventured downstairs. Avoidance seemed like the best policy right about then. I had hoped to have the house to myself, but I wasn't that surprised to see Mom in the kitchen.

"Oh, good, you're up. I made muffins." Mom handed me the steaming basket of cherry and chocolate chip muffins, and my mouth watered.

"Thanks. And thank you again for—" She waved her hand in a dismissive gesture and blushed, so I trailed off. Hopefully, she knew how much her gift meant to me. She smiled at me, and I sat down at the table.

"Did you want any coffee? There's still some left from Dad's breakfast."

I shook my head. She seemed surprised. I usually wouldn't turn down coffee, but for some reason, that morning, I didn't want to be jittery. I had a feeling that I couldn't afford a caffeine crash, although I wasn't sure why.

"What about some tea? I was just about to boil water."

"No, but you go ahead." I bit into a muffin and burned the roof of my mouth. Mom looked at me for a long second before turning to put the kettle on the stove. She rustled around in the cupboard for a minute, then took down a box of loose-leaf green tea.

Mom sighed softly as she sat down, and I looked at her. "Lena, you know Dad loves you, right?"

This was not at all what I had been expecting to hear, and I stared at her for a minute without reacting. She took my silence as denial, and pressed on.

"He's just shocked, that's all. Even though your father seems happy as a Green, I've always thought he walked awfully close to the White path."

"What does White or Green have to do with any of it?"

"Surely you've noticed that White and Black Witches don't tend to be aware of"—she smirked slightly—"gray area, if you'll pardon the pun."

I nodded slowly. Taking Justin and Rochelle into consideration, I saw exactly what she meant: neither one of them seemed capable of finding any middle ground. I'd always thought that was just part of their personalities, but maybe it ran deeper than that.

Mom continued, pouring water over the herbs in her mug. "Greens have an easier time seeing balance, since that's one of our

91

purposes, to balance White and Black magic. But for some reason, your father isn't able to see anything in this situation but the danger." She stirred her tea and I took another muffin.

"Why won't he listen?"

"He's scared, sweetie. I'm scared, too, but remember, I saw Persephone that first night. I know there's more going on here than all the legends and rumors. But Dad doesn't know that."

"Why don't you tell him?"

Mom sighed and looked at me sadly. "You know better than that, Lena. Can you ever get Justin or even Rochelle to believe anything once they've set their minds on something else?"

Mutely, I shook my head. She had a point.

"Your father makes up his mind very quickly, and sometimes he never unmakes it. But we have to be patient."

I coughed on a chunk of cherry. "Mom, I can't be patient. Whether or not Red magic is as bad as he thinks, I better learn how to control it, and fast. I don't want to be responsible for any more deaths!"

"I know. But whatever you plan to do, be careful. Hecate is not someone you want to directly oppose."

"Mom," I said thoughtfully, "Justin and I came up with a plan—"

"I don't want to hear about it." Her words were final and I closed my mouth, feeling shut out.

"But you said you wanted to help me!"

"I do. But I don't think you should tell me anything."

I stared at her. "Why not?"

She sighed again, sadly. "Because, to be honest, I'm frightened of Hecate. I don't want to know anything that could hurt you if she found out, and I don't know if I could keep a secret from her." Her eyes welled up with tears and I reached across the table for her hand. Sniffing to regain control, she continued. "I am sworn to obey Demeter. You know that. But you do remember the only god who helped Demeter when she was searching for her daughter, right?"

A chill passed over me as I remembered the myth. Demeter had appealed to all the gods, but they refused to help her find Persephone. All except one, who defied Zeus and accompanied the distraught goddess into the Underworld to collect her daughter.

"Hecate. I had forgotten that."

Mom nodded miserably. "That's why I don't want to know. Demeter has strong feelings for the Queen of Witches, and if she could compel me to speak against you—"

I squeezed her hand. "I understand. I won't tell you anything." I felt a heaviness in my stomach when I spoke, as if I had swallowed a stone, but I tried to ignore the strange sensation. Mom was being honest with me, and I had no right to make her choose between her patron and me.

The next week was quiet. I didn't come downstairs much because I was avoiding my dad, and he knew better than to come to my room. Justin texted with a few suggestions, but nothing seemed to happen. If it hadn't been for the athame sitting on my desk next to three ruby pomegranate seeds, I would have had an easy time believing that I had imagined everything. I almost wished

I could pretend that things were normal, but I had a feeling they would never be normal again.

The following Saturday, I finally agreed to Mom's request that I come down for a family meal. She had made blueberry pancakes for brunch, and she knew I couldn't say no to that. I slid into my chair, trying not to meet Dad's eye. He smiled at me over the newspaper, and I started to relax. Maybe he'd forgotten that he thought I was dangerous. I poured syrup over the stack of pancakes on my plate, then chewed in silence.

"Linzi, we better check the crawl space today. They're calling for that tropical storm to be a full-blown hurricane by tonight, and it looks like it will come up the coast. There's a flood watch in place for the next three days." He folded his paper and set it down beside him to take a bite of pancake. Mom brought the last plate for herself and sat down.

"I hope it passes us by. We've been lucky; there hasn't been a really bad hurricane to hit North Carolina since Fran. Do you remember that at all, Darlena?"

I shook my head. Dad chimed in. "You were so young, I'm not surprised you don't remember. You had just turned one when it hit."

Mom laughed. "We ate birthday cake for a week when the power went out! I was so thankful that you'd made that cake, Richard."

"What happened?" I asked.

"The hurricane hit Cape Fear, and the whole state was pretty much under water and without power." Dad looked thoughtful.

"We got really lucky. We had rented a beach house that summer, but your mom insisted that we come home early. She said she didn't want your first birthday memory to be away from home."

I looked at Mom, then at Dad. A hope was forming in my mind, but I didn't want to say anything in case Hecate or another one of the gods was watching me. As casually as I could, I asked, "What about this storm? How bad will it be?"

Dad answered. "There's really no way to know for sure until it becomes a full hurricane. It's still a tropical storm, but they're anticipating that it will hit the Caribbean by tomorrow morning at the earliest. We'll just have to wait and see what it does. But," he added, "I'm going out to the grocery store today to pick up some bottled water and bread, just in case. Can't be too careful." He finished his last bite of pancake, hesitated for a moment, and then planted a syrupy kiss on my forehead. I looked up in surprise and met his eyes. "I'll check the generator when I get back. You girls better enjoy the sunshine while you can!" He picked up his keys and headed out the door.

The kitchen was silent for a moment, and I forced myself to swallow another mouthful. Finally, Mom spoke without looking at me. "Don't tell me. Don't say anything. Just be careful."

I took the stairs two at a time. Acting on impulse, I grabbed the athame, a box of matches, and the stub of a red candle in one quick sweep, and then I picked up the tattered old atlas my grandfather had given me. I was in my closet with the door shut in an instant, but my breathing was ragged. If I hadn't moved fast enough, it didn't matter how warded my closet was; if Hecate was watching, she would stop me. I had no illusions that the Queen of Witches wanted me to use my new powers to avert chaos, and I only hoped I had moved fast enough not to catch her attention.

Closing my eyes, I drew in a long breath through my nose. I held it for a moment, then slowly exhaled, feeling the fear slip to the back of my mind as I grounded and centered.

Kneeling on the floor, I picked up the athame in my right hand. Slowly, whispering a prayer to the elements of air, fire, water, and earth, I traced a wide circle in the air with the knife. I opened the atlas to the map of North America and set it down before me. Gently, I laid the blade on top of it. Then I struck a match. The smell of sulfur flared up for a moment and was replaced by the comforting smell of burning wood. I lit the red candle as I slipped closer toward my trance state. Even if Red magic was new to me, spells and rituals were as ingrained in me as breathing.

Without questioning myself, I called upon the goddess who I suspected was willing to help me, based on the clues she'd left in my book. "Aphrodite, protect me. I do what I do out of love." If I was wrong, I hoped it wouldn't matter, but I was more and more certain that she was the goddess who had reached out to me. I placed the glowing candle at the top of the map and leaned forward and studied the page. Placing my open palms against the map with my right hand covering the Caribbean and my left hand covering the Atlantic coast, I began to hum. Tunelessly, I buzzed like a bee, pausing only to draw breath. I filled my mind with images of clear skies, and I imagined the warm caress of a gentle breeze against my face. As I hummed, I felt my hands pulsing with energy, and I concentrated hard to direct it out and into the map. Red sparks raced up my arms, but I didn't stop. When I felt like I was about to burst with energy, I stopped humming and lifted my hands.

I whispered a prayer of thanks and snuffed out the candle. Then I sat in the darkness of my closet for a moment, concentrating on my breathing. When I was steady, I stood up. I couldn't hide in my closet all day: I needed to be where I could listen to the weather. I hoped I wouldn't have to wait too long to know if I had accomplished anything.

12

I convinced my mom to let me go see Justin that afternoon, but I felt a little guilty. I made her think that I was pining for him, which was sort of true, although I wouldn't readily admit that under normal circumstances. I knew Mom had always been fond of Justin, but I hadn't realized how much she liked us as a couple until I asked to go over there. Despite Dad's warnings, she let me leave the house with a smile and a wink.

I took the back way to his house and texted him while I walked. He was waiting for me at the gate in his backyard, and for once I didn't hop his fence. I was surprised when he leaned forward and brushed his lips against mine, and I froze, my skin tingling from his kiss.

"In case anyone is watching," he murmured in my ear, and I nodded. Of course he was right. The lie I had told my mother just might convince Hecate, as well. Swallowing, I leaned forward and kissed him gently, trying to ignore the way my heart was throbbing between my ears. A slow heat began to climb through my feet and into my legs, and I broke away before I could make a total fool of myself. Justin draped his arm casually across my shoulders and nuzzled my ear as if he didn't notice.

"Wait 'til we're inside." His voice was so low I had to strain to hear it, but I faked a laugh and reached up to hold his hand. As I glanced over my shoulder, I made eye contact with a sleepy-looking owl sitting on a branch in the next yard. It blinked its golden eyes at me twice, and I shivered. Justin had been right to be careful; we were being watched. There was only one other creature with eyes like that, and I didn't doubt that the owl would report directly to Hecate if Justin or I said or did anything out of the ordinary. Hopefully, I thought, the goddess hadn't been watching me for long, or she'd realize that kissing Justin was way out of the ordinary for me lately. I tried not to worry as we headed inside.

Once we were safe in Justin's bedroom, I stepped away from him quickly. It wouldn't do either of us any good if I let him see the way he still stirred me up. I had to get my feelings under control. Justin didn't mention the kiss. Instead, he sat down on the edge of his desk and looked at me.

"So what did you do?" His question was laced with excitement; despite the danger, Justin was enjoying himself.

His energy was infectious, and I smiled as I told him about the hurricane. "I don't know if it worked, but I threw everything I had at it."

Justin immediately crossed to his computer and pulled up a news site. He clicked around for a minute, but then shook his head. "Nothing on here so far. But we should know soon if it was supposed to make landfall in the islands today or tomorrow." He glanced up at me, and he suddenly seemed nervous. "Did you want to stay here while we wait? We could play a game or something." With his brown eyes and unruly hair, he was a strange combination of sexy and sweet, and my heart lurched. I didn't want to be alone, and if there was any way I could pretend to be a normal teenager one last time, I wanted it. Besides, I'd give anything to spend a few hours alone with Justin.

"Do you still have that old Nintendo in the basement?" He nodded, and I grinned.

"Bet I can still kick your ass!" I waited for him to open the door, and he smiled at me. I almost melted.

"We'll just see, won't we?"

***

After spending four blissful hours beating Justin at the old video games of our childhood, I was almost able to forget the spell I had attempted that morning. Almost.

I remembered everything when we took a break from the games to scavenge for some food in the kitchen. The small black and white TV on the counter was turned on and playing quietly to the empty kitchen when we emerged from the basement, and I immediately heard the words *freak weather pattern*. I rushed across

100

the room and fixed my eyes on the screen, with Justin following close behind me. He reached over my shoulder to turn up the volume.

The reporter looked confused as he said, "For those of you just joining us, I'm pleased to announce that a freak weather pattern has caused Tropical Storm Helene to dissipate just hours before it was predicted to make landfall in the Bahamas." A satellite image flashed on the screen, first showing the swirling mass of the storm before switching to a blank map.

Justin squeezed my hand, but I kept my eyes on the reporter. "Meteorologists are stumped by this turn of events and warn citizens of the islands and the eastern United States to take precautions as if the storm were still coming. In case the storm re-forms, people are advised to seek shelter in high, inland areas."

My mouth hung open as Justin hugged me.

"You did it!"

I hugged him back for an instant, overwhelmed by the heady sensation of power coursing through me. I'd never tried to do anything so important with magic before.

After a moment, I pushed him away as shock replaced my initial euphoria.

He looked at me, confused, and I forced myself to take a step back.

"Right. I did it. I defied Hecate." As my words sank in, his jubilant smile faded, and I saw a flicker of fear in his eyes. Just then, a rumble of thunder shook the house. I glanced outside at the cloudless blue sky and looked back at Justin. "Get it? I'm in trouble." I turned away from him, my mind whirring frantically. I couldn't let Hecate come after me here; something might happen to Justin, and then I'd never forgive myself.

"Where are you going?" Justin rushed to block the door, and I groaned in exasperation.

"Don't you see? Okay, great, we figured out what I can do. But Hecate told me not to try anything like this. I have to get home."

His eyes were filled with concern. "It's not safe for you to leave. This house is warded."

"It's not safe if I stay! Justin, I can't let Hecate hurt you because I'm with you, but it's even more important that I get home. If I'm there, maybe she won't hurt my parents. I don't think anyone else has pissed off this goddess and lived."

Justin frowned, thinking about what I had said. Lightning flashed outside, and I jumped.

"I'm going with you." His voice shook, but his jaw was set. He grabbed his keys and propelled me out the door before I could argue or think.

13

The house was dark and the shutters were drawn, even though the sun had barely set by the time we arrived.

"Shit," I hissed under my breath. Justin looked at me, startled. "Hecate was here recently."

"How can you tell?"

I paused, wondering at my certainty. "I'm not sure. But I guess she's been around so much lately that I can sense her," I finished lamely. Why on earth would an untrained Witch like me be able to tune in to the presence of the Queen of Witches? Unless, of course, she wanted me to know she was there. That thought made my heart race, but I tried to smile reassuringly at Justin. "I can handle this, if you want to go home."

He shook his head wordlessly, and I sighed. I was glad that he wanted to help, but I didn't want to have to protect him if things went badly with Hecate. Still, it was nice to have him there.

I put my key in the lock and looked over my shoulder at Justin. "Fine, but don't say I didn't try to warn you."

"I can handle whatever is coming."

I doubted that. I wasn't even sure I was ready to face Hecate's wrath, but I had no choice. I needed to make sure she hadn't done anything to my parents.

I pushed the door open and stepped across the threshold, Justin close behind me. The air smelled crisp, like burnt plants. Everything was still except for my wildly pounding heart.

"Hello?" I called, feeling foolish. "Mom? Dad? I, uh, brought Justin over for dinner."

My dad emerged from the hallway, looking dazed. "Justin." He flicked his eyes toward me. "Tonight's not really a good night for company." He paused. "We have a family matter to discuss."

Justin was too well-mannered to argue with my dad, and even though I had just been pleading with him to stay out of this, I felt desperately empty when he squeezed my hand and said, "Okay, Mr. Agara. I just wanted to walk Lena home." As he turned to leave, he whispered to me, "Text me later, so I know, okay?" I nodded, and he closed the door behind him.

Dad waited a beat before he lit into me. "Darlena, how could you defy a goddess? What is wrong with you? I told your mother you were out of control with this Red stuff, but she wouldn't listen to me."

His words struck me a mile a minute, and I couldn't even form a response before he was onto the next painful statement.

"You can't stay here anymore."

My heart turned to ice. "What do you mean?"

Dad rubbed his eyes tiredly, and all at once his shoulders slumped. "She was here. Again. I can't handle any more visits from her."

"So, what, you're just sending me away? How is that fair?"

He shook his head. "We aren't sending you away. Hecate is taking you."

"Excuse me?" My mouth hung open.

"She wants to supervise your training personally. There's not much your mother and I can do for you, really." He shrugged. "Maybe it will be better for everybody."

I couldn't believe what he was saying. "Dad, do you honestly think that I'll be safe with Hecate? She wants me to cause chaos, and when she finds out that I don't want to—"

"Lena, you can't ignore what you are. You're a Red, and your mother and I can't help you. Hecate might be your only choice."

I didn't answer, but I knew my expression told him I thought it was all ridiculous.

He sighed. "She said she'd be back to collect you in an hour." Was it my imagination, or did Dad glance meaningfully at the front door? "I suggest that you be ready to leave in case she gets here early." He emphasized the words leave and early, and I narrowed my eyes at him, trying to understand.

"Do you mean—"

"Make sure you say goodbye to your mother." He turned on his heel, but not before nodding at the door again. Unless I was going crazy, Dad was telling me to run.

I didn't need to be told twice.

I was out of the house in fifteen minutes. I climbed down the tree outside my bedroom window; I figured that I shouldn't use the door, in case Hecate blamed my parents for helping me. I didn't want them to have to lie to her, so I didn't leave a note, but I did loosen the ward on my closet to allow Mom to enter. I had to hope she'd think to look there, and that she would understand why I'd left my copy of the Greek myths open to the story of Atlanta's footrace. That was the only clue I could leave, but Mom was smart. She'd be able to figure out where I was headed, and she might even realize which goddess I hoped to meet along the way.

I carried my worn nylon backpack. The only food I'd packed was the pomegranate seeds from Persephone, and I didn't plan on having to eat those. If my years at Trinity had taught me anything, it was never to eat or drink something that came from an immortal source unless there was no other choice. I wasn't that desperate, yet. The seeds bounced along beside Mom's athame, wrapped up in my favorite sweater.

Other than that, I had a small wad of cash and my emergency credit card. Our house was just a few blocks away from the highway, and it wasn't long before I was standing under a bright streetlight with my thumb out.

I got picked up by the third car that passed me on the on ramp.

14

"Where are you headed?" The tired-looking woman in pink scrubs glanced at me.

I shrugged, wary of drawing a Non too deeply into my issues. "Just needed to get out of town." That seemed like the safest response, and I hoped she wouldn't ask me any more questions.

She nodded thoughtfully. I saw her eyes flick toward me again, sizing me up, and her shoulders relaxed slightly. Evidently, she had decided I wasn't a threat. I didn't know about that, but I was grateful to be moving west.

"Thanks for stopping. I know nobody hitches anymore." I tried to sound bright and nonthreatening, but a tremor of worry crept into my voice. The nurse looked at me again.

"You didn't do anything illegal, did you?" I shook my head quickly. "That's okay then. And you're not fourteen or anything?"

"I'm almost seventeen." Even though I had just passed my birthday, I didn't feel guilty about the lie. Seventeen sounded a lot better than sixteen.

She nodded. "I thought you looked old enough. I don't want any trouble, but I couldn't leave you standing there when it's getting dark. You might have gotten hit. Drivers are crazy at night."

"Thank you."

She paused, squinting at the road ahead. "I live in Greensboro, so that's as far as I can take you."

My heart sank. I shouldn't have expected to get very far in one night, but I had hoped I'd at least make it across the state line. I didn't know how quickly Hecate would pursue me, and I wanted to put as much distance between us as possible. "That'll be fine. I'll try to get a ride from there."

We drove on in silence. The sixty-mile drive went much too fast, and before I knew it the nurse was dropping me off at a rusty gas station on the highway. "This is a safe stop; I always get my coffee here, and nobody ever bothers me."

I nodded, shouldering my bag. "Thanks again. Can I give you anything for gas?"

"I should be the one trying to give you some cash." She drummed her fingers on the steering wheel. "You sure you don't want to crash on my couch and get started tomorrow morning?"

The offer was tempting, but I shook my head. I couldn't do that to her; what would happen when Hecate caught up with me?

I waved as she drove off, but as her brake lights receded, I felt a wave of panic. What if I was stranded at the gas station for the night? Glancing around at the dark parking lot, I pulled my bag higher on my shoulder and headed inside to get a snack and to see if I could find another ride.

The bell over the door jangled, and I looked around to see if anyone had noticed me. The bored clerk was snapping his gum and reading a magazine, and there was only one other person in the store, a man in a baseball cap back at the coffee machine. Neither of them looked up as I came inside.

I paid for my candy bar with cash; I decided that I would try not to use my credit card unless it truly was an absolute emergency. Maybe the longer I stayed off the Nons' radar, the longer I could stay off Hecate's, as well.

As I pocketed my change, the guy in the hat stepped up and paid for his coffee. "Got a long ways 'til Atlanta!" he chortled as the clerk raised an eyebrow at the size of his steaming coffee. My ears perked up. This was almost too good to be true!

"Are you headed to Atlanta tonight?" I asked, trying to seem nonchalant. The man looked at me curiously and nodded. I exhaled and forced a smile. He wouldn't have been my first pick of traveling companion, but beggars can't be choosers, and I really didn't want to be stuck at that gas station all night. "I'm trying to get there. Could you give me a ride?"

"You hitchin'?"

I nodded, trying to look confident. The guy stared at me for a long time before he finally nodded. I suppressed a shiver; something about his eyes unnerved me. I didn't let myself dwell on it, because anything was better than dealing with Hecate. So what if his eyes were creepy? He was probably just tired. I followed the guy out to a big red semi and hauled myself up into the cab. The road looked strange; I'd never been up that high in a car before, and the windshield distorted my depth perception. Still, the truck was headed west, and it would take me where I needed to be.

Ever since the golden writing had appeared in my book, I'd had a suspicion that Aphrodite was the one who was helping me. Because of that, I was headed toward Atlanta. Besides being a huge city where I could hopefully hide from Hecate, Atlanta was named after a myth. There was a girl named Atlanta who swore she'd never marry. Aphrodite got involved, being the goddess of love and all that, and the girl agreed to marry anyone who could beat her at a race. The goddess picked a suitor that she liked and gave him three golden apples. For some reason, the Atlanta chick was distracted by the gold, and the suitor flung the apples off the path whenever he needed a chance to pull into the lead. He won the race and the girl, and supposedly they lived happily ever after.

Even though my experience with the goddesses I'd met indicated that they could pop up anywhere at any time, I thought I stood a better chance of winning Aphrodite's favor if I could get to a city named after one of the mortals she had liked. Besides, getting as far away from my family as I could seemed like a good idea; even if Hecate came after me in Georgia, they wouldn't be around to be harmed.

The trucker and I passed the first hour in relative silence, each lost in our own thoughts as the countryside passed by the windows.

When we drove through Charlotte, the trucker leaned forward

and turned the knob on the old radio wedged in the dash. He glanced over at me.

"Mind if we have some music?"

I shook my head. A twangy country song filled the cab, and I suppressed a smile. How stereotypical, I thought.

"Damn, I hate that whiny country shit." I was startled to hear his response, and I laughed despite myself. He changed the station to classic rock and sat back, satisfied. "I bet you thought I was one of those rednecks who chews tobacco and listens to Patsy Cline, right, girly?"

I blushed, embarrassed that he'd read my disparaging thoughts. He chuckled when he saw my uncomfortable reaction. "I'm a good southern boy, but nothing beats the Stones."

We settled back into silence, but when I looked across the cab, I thought I saw a smile playing around his lips.

"I don't even know your name!" I blurted out. It had just occurred to me how odd that was. "And you don't know my name," I added lamely.

"Well, girly, I'll tell you mine if you tell me yours."

I hesitated for a minute, but I decided to tell him the truth. "Darlena."

"Darlena." For some reason, I didn't like the way my name sounded in his mouth, and I tensed. But all he said was, "That's real pretty. Mine is Hank."

"Thanks for taking me to Atlanta, Hank."

He grunted noncommittally, and again I felt a shiver of apprehension. I leaned back in my seat and recited a spell for protection in my head while I looked out the window. I hadn't really paid attention to protective magic in school, and I kept forgetting the words to the spell, but I hoped it would be enough to keep me safe. I started to doze midway through the spell, and we had almost made it to Atlanta when all hell broke loose.

I was dreaming in red again. I stood in a rich red room that smelled like roses and something rancid. The room was vast and empty, but I had the sensation of eyes watching my every movement. Suddenly, I felt a hand grab me from behind.

I woke from the dream to realize the sensation of being grabbed was very real. The truck was stopped on the shoulder of the road, and there weren't any cars passing us. It must have been really early in the morning, if the highway was empty. Still disoriented from my dream, I twisted in my seat only to realize that Hank was pressed up against me, his meaty hands gripping my biceps. If I'd had any doubt what was happening, his next words confirmed it.

"Glad you're awake, girly. It'll be more lively."

The truck smelled like sweat and cigarettes, and I fought back the urge to gag. I twisted my arms, but Hank only held on tighter. His breath was warm on the back of my neck, and he pulled me across the bench until he was pressed against my back. Suddenly, I wasn't just frightened. I was furious. How dare he? Just because I was traveling alone, what made him think he had the right to do whatever he wanted to me?

With strength I didn't know I had, I wrenched out of his grip and thrust my hands against his chest. He made a grab for my hands, and just as his fingers closed on mine, I pushed again, barely noticing the red sparks that covered my arms.

Hank and the truck flipped to the left, the sound of metal on gravel like an explosion. I clutched the door handle so I wouldn't fall into him. He growled, confused, and I pushed the air in front of me again with my free hand. The trucker slammed against the driver's-side door, which was now parallel to the ground. His eyes were bleary with shock. He wasn't unconscious, though, just stunned, and I knew I had to move fast.

Adrenaline coursing through me, I pushed against the passenger door. It wouldn't budge, but the window was down, so I tried to lift myself out of the cab. A hand grabbed my foot and I kicked out wildly. Grabbing my backpack, I shimmied out the window. Without any thought other than escape, I flung myself to the ground feet first.

The drop from the truck winded me, but I didn't let the pain in my ankles slow my pace. I ran away from the deserted road into the brushy area along the shoulder. I didn't hear anything behind me, but I wasn't taking any chances. I didn't slow down, dodging around trees and garbage, propelling myself farther away from the road. I ran until I felt like I was going to burst, and then I sank to my knees beneath a shrub. There wasn't time to get to Atlanta, and I hoped the goddess I was seeking would understand my urgency.

"Aphrodite, I need you here now!" I called out as I struggled to pull the athame from my backpack. Impulsively, I put the knife against my skin. If she was a keeper of Red magic like I thought, she would have some kind of affinity for blood. That was one thing all the Red goddesses I'd met had in common. I pushed the blade of the knife into my left palm, grunting with effort, until I drew blood, and then I switched the knife to my wounded hand and sliced my other palm. It's really hard to cut skin, and harder to cut yourself, but I finally did it. Ignoring the raw pain, I pressed my palms to the earth, panting, "Goddess, please, help me now!"

I knelt there for a moment, frozen in fear, listening to the sounds of the night for any sign of Hank. For a moment, everything was still, and I worried that I'd made a terrible mistake.

"Well, you don't have to be so melodramatic about it." The annoyed voice came from behind me, and I turned to face the first goddess I had ever summoned intentionally.

15

She eyed me with a cynical twist to her mouth, but she didn't speak. The goddess was beautiful; even in the middle of the night, her blond hair hung in perfect ringlets, and her red dress looked like she'd just come from a fancy party. What must I look like to her? I was drenched in sweat, my hands were bleeding, and dirt from the road clung to my skin. I pushed my hair out of my face and stood up.

"It was you who helped me, right?"

She sighed. "I left the instructions in your book, yes." She sounded like she regretted it, and I scanned the path behind her, worried that the trucker would find me here and she would do nothing to save me.

Aphrodite waved a hand. "He's already forgotten everything."

I looked at her skeptically. "What about his truck being turned over?"

She shrugged elegantly. "He thinks he fell asleep at the wheel. He's going to take a vacation after he finishes this run." She rubbed her hands together as if they were dirty. She sighed again, deeply, and squinted at me in disapproval.

"Why did you come when I called if you don't want to help me?" I hadn't been racking up many politeness points with goddesses lately, but my ordeal in the truck had left me in no mood to mince words.

"Who says I don't want to help you, you silly thing?" Her laughter chimed through the dark night, both soothing and irritating at once.

"Then help me. Please," I added belatedly as her eyes narrowed slightly.

"If you can learn manners, Darlena, I might do just that." She put her hands on her hips and glared at me.

I bowed my head, waiting for her to take the lead.

"Do you understand Red magic yet, child?" Her voice held a trick, so I thought a moment before I spoke.

"I think so. Red magic causes chaos. Death, destruction, and disasters all seem to be a part of it."

The goddess sighed, and I shot her a quick look. "There is so much more subtlety to it, child. Red is the magic of chaos, yes, but chaos is the greatest force in the world. Chaos is neither good nor bad; it simply is." She paused to let me absorb this. "Do you realize the world was created in chaos?" I nodded, dim memories from mythology class tugging at my mind.

"Chaos is higher than all else, and chaos magic is the magic of the cosmos. Red magic does not cause chaos, child, it governs it."

Her words sank into my mind, and suddenly I felt like I could see clearly.

"So I don't have to kill people to be a Red?"

Aphrodite's laugh tinkled like sleigh bells. "You don't have to do anything to be a Red. You use chaos magic, for good or for ill. It's not the power that causes death and destruction, but the Witch who wields that power."

I thought about that for a moment. "But what else can I do with it? Hecate seems to think I will kill more people, Pele asked for a good disaster, and Persephone said I'm not strong enough to handle it. What else is there to chaos?"

"Love." That one word echoed around me as if Aphrodite spoke with a thousand voices, and tingles raced up my spine. "Love is the greatest chaos of all."

She had a point. I'd never felt so out of control, so consumed by chaos, as when Justin and I had been dating. Still, I hesitated. "But what do I do?"

"Choose me."

I stared at her in shock. Even though Mom seemed happy with her patron, I'd never considered making the same kind of vow. Working without a patron didn't mean you couldn't ask the gods for help from time to time, and that had always seemed preferable to the binding of choosing just one god to serve forever. I drew a shaky breath.

"Why?"

"Without a patron, you are at the mercy of the many forces of chaos. You have only met a few. There are others who make those goddess look like kind old aunts and grandmothers." I swallowed in fear and she went on. "If you are mine, they cannot touch you. They cannot manipulate you."

She had a point, but I wasn't sure I was ready to trade freedom for security. "But you would have control over me. I'd give up the fear of these unknown gods to become your slave. Tell me if I've got it wrong."

She glared at me. "There is always free will, Darlena. Unless you swear to be a slave, you will never be one. But yes, if you were mine you would obey me. It is a small price to pay for the protection I can offer you. And," she pressed on, a glint in her eyes, "there is beauty in the service of love. More beauty than in the service of fire or madness."

I considered her words. Even though this might be the only way to gain protection from Hecate, I wasn't sure it would work. Besides, something had been bothering me ever since I'd first read the golden words in my book. "Helen of Troy was sworn to you, wasn't she?"

"Yes." Her smile slipped. "I was Helen's patron."

"And she was a Red Witch, wasn't she?"

Aphrodite nodded, looking uncomfortable.

I glared at her, amazed that she would try to convince me that serving her was safe. "What protection did you offer her? She started a war!"

"Because she was beautiful and beloved. I made her famous. She is, after all, the face that launched a thousand ships."

I felt anger boiling up inside me. "Ships that came home empty! How many men died at Troy? How many people were murdered when the city was sacked? And," I continued, ranting, "I don't seem to remember Helen making it out of that situation the way she wanted! She ended up right back where she started. What a great deal." I had been an idiot to think Aphrodite could help me. She was as dangerous as the other Red goddesses I'd met.

"Helen lived. My protection spared her." The goddess spat her words. "I led Aeneas onward to safety. He founded the greatest empire the world had ever seen, with my protection. Troy may have been a battle, but those who swore allegiance to me lived to see another day. You would do well to follow their example."

I looked at her flushed face and shaking hands, and I tried to reel my emotions back in. The last thing I wanted to do was make a goddess angry enough to attack me. I wouldn't stand a chance, even with Red magic at my disposal. Besides, Aphrodite was the only help I'd received, and unless another god swooped out of the sky and offered to protect me, I had to make the best of what I could get. I drew a deep breath.

"How do I know I'll fare any better than Helen?"

"You don't. But I offer you the protection of my name and my power. Has anyone else offered even half as much? Be grateful, Darlena, that I did not just turn you over to Hecate immediately."

I licked my lips, deciding to do it. I couldn't possibly be in any worse trouble than I was now, and maybe Aphrodite's protection would allow me to go home. If Hecate was no longer hunting me, things could return to normal. "Are you still offering to be my patron?" She nodded. "Then tell me how to make my vow."

"First you must kneel. Now, here, before me." Her hands spread wide in a gesture at the ground in front of her. I knelt gingerly, hoping I wouldn't cut myself on any broken beer bottles or other roadside garbage.

"Good. Now, you must speak these words: Aphrodite, Queen of Love, Daughter of the Sea, I promise you my loyalty and give to you freely this pledge. For all of this life, I will honor you above all others, and I will act in a manner which pleases you. May all the waters turn against me, may all the creatures of the air become my hunters, and may I never rest if I break this trust with word or intent."

I repeated the speech haltingly, and I felt my pulse speed up when I spoke the words that would condemn me if I broke my vows. The goddess wasn't playing around; I had to obey her now or suffer the consequences. Aphrodite placed her slender hands on the crown of my head and I looked down. My own arms and torso had begun to glow with a rosy light, and I sat, spellbound, after finishing the vow.

My reverie was broken by the sound of slow, mocking applause. Hecate emerged from the shadows, clapping her hands loudly. I jumped to my feet, but the air around me solidified, holding me in place. The Queen of Witches moved forward until she was standing barely five inches from me, her owl eyes piercing my soul.

"That was a lovely ceremony, my daughters. So touching! I

haven't witnessed such an impassioned Dedicancy for many years."
Her tone belied the kindness of her words, and I shivered despite
myself. The pink glow that had surrounded me had faded, and the
clearing was instead lit in the eerie gray glow radiating off of
Hecate. "You are safe, Darlena. For now." She leaned forward and
whispered in her rasping voice, "But how many of those ships
never left Troy?" With a cackle, she vanished.

16

Aphrodite sent me home using magic, and the journey that had taken me over six hours took under a minute. It was like I blacked out: one minute I was standing with the goddess by the side of the road, and the next minute, I was there in the street in front of my house. I took a step and crumpled to the ground. I struggled to crawl up the walk, then pulled myself upright and drew a few deep breaths. Everything had happened so fast: the trucker, my Dedicancy to Aphrodite, and then Hecate's threat. I wanted to crawl up to my bed and sleep for a month.

The old door creaked painfully and I paused, clutching my keys in one hand to muffle any telltale clinks. I counted slowly to one hundred, my heart thundering in my ears. Nothing. No parents, no angry goddesses, nothing made any sound. Maybe the door had only sounded loud to me. I breathed a quick sigh of relief and stepped into the house.

Suddenly, I froze in my tracks. There was a faint rustling noise coming from the kitchen. I paused, praying that it was only my overwrought imagination. As I stood there, my eyes adjusted to the dark and I began to count slowly, the way I used to during thunderstorms. One, two, thr—

I heard it again. There was definitely somebody in the kitchen. Creeping around the corner, I tried to still my frantic heart. The blue streetlights outside cast strange shadows, and everything in the familiar old kitchen suddenly looked alien and threatening. Unless my eyes were playing tricks on me, there was a vaguely human shape seated at the table. Had Hecate changed her mind and decided to go after me despite my patron? I drew a deep breath and flicked the light switch, flinging my hands up in preparation for a protection spell.

Rochelle laughed softly. "Turn the lights off, you idiot. Do you want your parents to know you're back?"

My mouth hung open. "What are you doing here?" I flicked the switch after she lit the stub of the white emergency candle that still sat on the table. It took a moment for my eyes to adjust to the sharp glow.

She shrugged. "Waiting for you. Your mom called my house when you took off, guess she thought you might have been with me."

"What did you tell her?" I grabbed a chair and sank into it.

"That we were having a slumber party, that you were pissed and you'd call them in the morning."

"Thanks."

She cocked her head to one side. "Where were you, really?"

I hesitated. I'd gotten so used to keeping secrets since I became a Red Witch, I'd almost forgotten how good it felt to confide in my best friend.

"Atlanta." Rochelle arched an eyebrow, so I continued, "I went looking for Aphrodite. I thought she could help me."

"Why Atlanta? I mean, can't the gods come and go wherever they want?"

I struggled to put my confused thoughts into words while Rochelle stared at me, unblinking. "I thought that if I could find Aphrodite anywhere, it would be in the city named after one of her devotees."

"But why not just summon her here?"

"Because I hoped she could protect me from Hecate if we were on her own turf."

My best friend whistled. "Dang, girl, I've never talked to any goddesses, and here in one week you've chatted it up with two!"

"Four, actually," I interjected without thinking. "Persephone and Pele have both been here, too." I shuddered as I remembered Pele's request for sacrifices.

Rochelle looked stunned. "What do they all want with you?"

I sighed. "Red magic. It turns out that being a Red Witch means I have power over the forces of chaos. Pele wants me to kill people for her, and Persephone ... well, I'm not sure what she wanted." For some reason, I didn't want to tell Rochelle about the pomegranate seeds. "And Aphrodite offered to help me find a middle ground that won't require death and destruction."

Rochelle scrunched up her nose. "But why would a love goddess care what you do with chaos magic?"

I shrugged. "I don't totally get it, but I guess Helen of Troy was a Red, and I think Aphrodite feels bad that she didn't help her more." I held up my hands at the skeptical look on my best friend's face. "That's what she said! I just knew I didn't want to face Hecate again without some kind of protection."

"So, what, you have a patron now?"

I nodded, hoping that Rochelle wouldn't tell me I was an idiot.

She shrugged thoughtfully. "I haven't found the right god yet, but I think it's a good thing for you."

"Really?" I was surprised. Rochelle always complained about old-fashioned Witches, and I had just assumed she considered patrons old-fashioned.

She nodded. "I mean, you won't be any worse off than you are now, right?"

I exhaled quickly. "Right." I covered a yawn, but Rochelle kept talking.

"Red magic must be pretty powerful, huh, if so many goddesses have been paying attention to you?"

"I don't know," I lied, suddenly self-conscious about my magic. "But there are only three Red Witches in the world. It's not that the magic is powerful," I hurried, "but I think it's just too much to unleash in large quantities."

She leaned forward. "How did you even know about it?"

"I didn't."

Rochelle eyed me skeptically. "Seriously?"

"Seriously. When Hecate showed up, I panicked. I didn't want to pick a path, so I said the first thing that popped into my mind."

"That was dangerous: what if you'd said something that didn't exist?"

I shrugged. "I just hoped it would throw her off and she'd leave me alone. Instead, I made a vow I still don't understand."

"What else do you think they're keeping from us at Trinity?"

I looked at her in surprise. "Do you really think they'd do that?"

"They clearly knew enough about Red magic to kick you out after you declared." She closed her eyes, thinking. "I bet they only teach us the watered-down stuff. Red magic seems way more powerful than even Black."

"But why wouldn't the teachers at Trinity want us to be powerful? Wouldn't they want us to know as much magic as we can?"

Rochelle sighed. "Grow up, Lena. Why would they want us to be powerful? We're easier to control if they spoon-feed us baby magic." She sighed, tipping her chair back. "You'll teach me some of the stuff you learn, right?"

I only hesitated for a moment, but I saw a flicker of anger pass across her eyes when I paused. "Of course. You're my best friend."

She smiled. "Forever."

17

Rochelle left around dawn, and I made myself a cup of tea to take up to my bedroom. I cradled the steaming mug carefully as I padded up the stairs, but when I opened the door to my room, a gray ball of fur ran into me and I slopped scalding water all over myself.

"Damn it, Xerxes, what were you doing in there?" I set the cup down carefully and wiped off my hand. Turning on the light, I sucked in my breath to choke back a scream.

"That's no way to greet your patron, Darlena."

Aphrodite was lounging on my bed, eating one of my emergency chocolate bars. I narrowed my eyes at her, wondering why she was there.

"Why are you in my bed?"

"I'd expected to find you asleep and dreaming. I sent you home hours ago. Did you get lost?"

I shook my head. "My friend was here. She knew I was missing, and she wanted to find out where I was."

Aphrodite looked at me hard. "What did you tell her?"

I closed the door, willing my voice back down to a whisper. "I told her what happened. You didn't say I couldn't tell anyone, and now that Hecate knows, I figured, what the heck?"

The goddess was silent, so I tried another tack. "Did you already think of something you would like me to do?"

Her face lit up as she smiled at me. "Yes." She patted the bed and rose. "You should sit down. You've had a long night."

I perched on the edge of my bed, clutching my half-empty cup. "Well?"

She clasped her hands and closed her eyes. "I want to help you, Darlena. I told you that already. And I decided that the best way to help you is to teach you. If you learn to control your magic, you'll feel much better about being a Red."

I nodded, relieved. I had been afraid she was here to demand that I start making people fall in love.

She smirked. "That will come later. For now, I just need to show you some individual spells."

I gaped at her. My patron had just read my mind; clearly I was in far deeper than I had imagined. I'd have to watch what I thought around her.

"Can you cast a glamour?"

I blushed at her question. "No. I tried, once. It didn't exactly turn out the way I thought." The goddess looked hard at me for a moment, and I busied myself watching the steam waft out of my mug. I tried to focus on the shapes in the steam, willing my mind to stay blank. She squinted once, but didn't seem inclined to pursue my train of thought. I was relieved; I didn't want to talk about that disastrous night with Justin.

"It's an easy enough spell, once you know what you're doing." Aphrodite casually tossed the candy wrapper onto my floor and rose. Her red robes shimmered and looked almost translucent, and I blushed again, trying not to look too closely at her curvy frame. Even if she was wearing a glamour, my patron was by far the most beautiful woman on the planet!

She faced me, her head cocked to one side. I felt as if I were being examined under a microscope. I glanced down at the rumpled shirt I hadn't had a chance to change. Surreptitiously, I brushed at a stain on my jeans. I kept my eyes down, ashamed for the first time to have sworn my craft to the patron of love. There was no way she had ever been a patron to anyone as ordinary looking as me.

"Actually, Helen was quite plain before I taught her the art of glamour." She was reading my thoughts again, and I bit my tongue before I could snap at her. The goddess shot me a long look before she began to show me the spell.

She was right; it was simple. I hadn't done a spell that required so little planning in a long time, and I wondered why I had screwed it up when I tried to glamour my voice with Justin. On my third try, I got it right.

Aphrodite clapped approvingly. "Oh, well done. Take a look!" She handed me a copper hand mirror, delicately carved with vines and buds. The face I saw in the glass was striking. I looked at least three years older, and my skin had flushed to a rich olive complexion. Instead of my usual dull hair color, the shiny hair that framed my face was so bright it looked like it had been expertly dyed. For the first time, I agreed with the people who said I looked like my mother. I stared at myself in wonder.

"How long does it last?" My voice was eager, and Aphrodite smiled indulgently.

"Right now, without practice, it will only last as long as you are absolutely focused on being beautiful." The face in the mirror flickered, and I wavered somewhere between selves.

"Is there any way to make it last longer?"

She nodded. "The more you do it, the easier it gets. There are ways to tie off a spell and make it permanent, but I think we'll wait to go over those until you get the hang of the simpler things."

I felt my heart thrill at the possibility of forever altering my average appearance, but just as suddenly a shard of guilt pricked my fantasy. I set the mirror down quickly, not wanting to watch my features morph back into my normal appearance.

"I don't mean to be rude, but what good does it do?" Aphrodite stared at me blankly. I swallowed and tried to smile. "It's really cool, and I appreciate you teaching this to me, but it's just that I've got all this power now that I'm a Red. Isn't this spell sort of a waste?"

Instantly, I regretted my choice of words. Aphrodite's smiling face had turned stiff, and the temperature in the room dropped considerably. I shivered, facing the goddess.

"You came to me for protection. You swore an oath to serve me. Would you break that oath on your first day in my care?" She spoke softly, but with each word, the goddess seemed to grow in size, filling my room. I shrank back in fear. I wasn't sure if it was an illusion or not, but I really didn't want to piss her off. Aphrodite was famous for her temper, and the last thing I needed was another goddess out to get me.

"That's not what I meant at all! Of course I want to serve you." Her size didn't diminish; she continued to stare threateningly down at me. "It's just that I want to do something with Red magic. I don't want to cause chaos, but ... isn't there a way that I could work to harness chaos, to help people?"

The goddess laughed, and instantly she was the size of any average human. "Silly girl. Chaos cannot be controlled. Forget those thoughts and focus on learning the magic I will teach you."

She kissed my forehead in blessing, and I felt energy gently caress my arms. "Now. You've had quite enough learning for tonight. Sleep, Darlena. I will see you again soon." I started to hand the mirror back, but she shook her head. "Keep it. Mirrors carry the power of water, and they help us to know ourselves. You will need it, I think."

She glided into the hall and I crawled into bed, too tired to even strip off my travel-stained clothes. Carefully, I set the mirror down on my bedside table. I tumbled into bed, my limbs heavy and my mind clouded. Right before I drifted to sleep, I realized what had bothered me about Aphrodite's last statement: I had controlled chaos before. Perhaps my patron didn't know as much as she claimed. With that dangerous thought, I fell into a deep sleep.

18

I woke up with sunlight streaming across the bed, but my mouth tasted like old socks and honey. I stretched groggily, and my hand brushed against the mirror Aphrodite had given me. I picked it up and began to examine it.

It sparkled too much to be copper, and I realized: it was actually finely hammered rose gold. The handle was narrow but fit comfortably in my hand, and the round frame was etched with roses and vines. I turned it over and almost dropped it.

Staring up at me out of the glass was my reflection, still wearing the glamour. Even as I looked, the magic began to fade and my features returned to normal. Had the mirror carried some residual energy from the spell, or had I really managed to hold onto the glamour while I slept? I checked the mirror again, but now my hair was its usual frizzy, dull auburn. My eyes still gleamed, however, and it was hard to look away from myself. That was odd. What had Aphrodite said about the spell? It should have only lasted for as long as I was focused on it, but I was pretty sure I hadn't been thinking about the spell while I slept. I'd have to ask her about that the next time I saw her; maybe I'd done something wrong.

Crossing my room, I set the mirror on top of my bookcase, next to the athame Mom had given me. Seeing it sitting there reminded me that I would have to face the music with my parents sooner or later. I was glad Rochelle had lied about where I was last night, but that wouldn't change the fact that I'd run away. True, Dad had sort of suggested it, but I hadn't stuck around to say goodbye to Mom, and I wasn't sure what kind of reception I'd get now. I ran a comb through my hair and changed my shirt, but I decided I would wait to shower until I'd gotten the confrontation out of the way.

I headed down the stairs and paused before stepping onto the main floor. No one came around the corner screaming at me, so I took a deep breath and called, "Mom, Dad? Good morning?"

"Morning, sweetie! We're out back." Their chorused response sounded far too cheery, and I slunk toward their voices with trepidation. When I reached the sliding glass door that led out to the garden, I paused to take in the scene.

My dad was sitting in the old wicker chair, holding a cup of coffee. Mom was beside him, on her knees in the herb garden. She was trimming back the rosemary with a small pair of shears. Her sun hat shaded her face, but she wasn't wearing any gloves; Mom loves to feel the dirt as she works her plant magic. The image was so normal, so perfectly average, that I started to sweat. Who were they trying to fool? I eased the door open and stepped outside.

"There you are, sleepyhead. Did you have a good time with Rochelle?" Mom smiled up at me. Cautiously, I nodded. Dad set his coffee cup down and looked at me with a slight grimace, and I braced myself.

"You know I really don't like you spending so much time with that girl. Has she made her declaration yet?"

Before I could answer, Mom jumped to my defense. "Oh, let it go, Richard. They're best friends, and there's nothing that says Black and Green Witches shouldn't be friends."

It took a minute for her words to sink in, but when they did, I asked, slowly, "Black and Green, Mom?"

She laughed. "Of course. You think we don't know that Rochelle is going to follow the Black path?" She patted my foot with her dirt-covered hand.

"It's been pretty obvious," Dad hissed under his breath.

"But you said Black and Green. What are you talking about?"

Dad looked up at me in concern. "Are you feeling alright?"

Mom rose, dusting off her legs swiftly. "She's probably just tired. You know girls, Richard, they stay up all night talking, then pretend that they were asleep the whole time." Mom kissed my cheek as she turned to go inside. "But I hope you aren't too tired to remember your Dedicancy ceremony. Dad and I are so proud of you!"

As she went into the house, I looked at my dad. "What ceremony?" They couldn't possibly know the details of last night, could they?

He looked up, surprised. "I think you do need to lie down! It's all you've talked about for a month. You declared to the Green path last month, on the night before your birthday. I don't think I want to know what you girls were doing last night if you can't remember something as important as that!"

***

Shaking, I raced up the stairs to my room. I shut the door and looked around. The athame and the mirror sat side by side, right where I had left them. I dug through my backpack, and I breathed a sigh of relief when I found the three pomegranate seeds in the bottom. Clearly, I wasn't the one who was going crazy. With that thought, my relief left me. What in the world had happened? My parents were acting as if the last month had never happened, and what was worse, they seemed to have a whole different set of memories than I had. It was like I had stumbled into some kind of alternate universe.

I grabbed my phone and texted Justin a quick question. "What path do I follow?"

My phone buzzed almost immediately.

"Justin," I answered quickly, "tell me."

"Calm down, Darlena. What's wrong?"

"Just tell me what kind of magic I practice."

Justin paused. "I don't know if that's something I should say over the phone. What if she's listening?"

"Who, Justin?"

Silence.

"Can I come over?"

"Give me ten minutes, Darlena."

"I'll give you five."

I hung up. I paused for a second, remembering that I still hadn't showered. I didn't want Justin seeing me after the mess in Atlanta. I shuddered when I thought of the truck driver and what had almost happened. Deciding that a few minutes wouldn't make a difference, I sent a quick text and headed for the bathroom.

I turned the water up as hot as I could, letting it scald my skin as I tried to forget everything that had happened last night. Why in the world did my parents think I had declared to their path? It didn't make any sense. Unless, I thought, not noticing the shampoo running into my eyes, someone had made them forget. But who would do that? And, a bigger question: why bother screwing with my parents' memories but leaving mine intact?

19

Dad winked at me when I told him I was going to see Justin, and I tried to smile, but my stomach felt hollow. My mind was racing, but the streets were quiet. I realized that it was Sunday afternoon. Sundays in the South are like a whole summer vacation packed into one day, and I felt my steps slowing despite the frantic pounding of my heart. I closed my eyes and took a deep breath, savoring the chill in the air that reminded me that fall should have already begun.

By the time I got to Justin's house, I was feeling a lot less frantic. I hesitated for a minute, considering jumping the fence again, but I decided it was best if I acted like a normal person. I fought back a laugh at the thought; was anything normal anymore? I walked up the front steps, but Justin answered the door before I even touched the doorbell.

"What's going on?" Worry filled his face as he pulled me inside. I shook my head, aware that we were in the open foyer and could be overheard. Once we were safely inside Justin's room with the door sealed and warded, tears spilled out of my eyes.

"Darlena!" Justin's shock was obvious; in all the time we'd know each other, he had never seen me cry. I sobbed harder, feeling the pent-up energy and fear of the past few weeks bubble to the surface without stopping. "Tell me what's going on. What happened after I left last night? You never texted, and I was so worried that Hecate—" Justin broke off and pushed me into the chair at his desk. He knelt on the floor beside me, keeping hold of my hands.

"First," I managed to say, "I need you to answer my question. What kind of magic do I practice?"

Justin's eyebrows knit together. "Did something happen with Hecate? Is that what this is about?"

Hope rose in my throat, but I shook my head, refusing to speak until he confirmed what I thought I knew.

"You're a Red Witch, Darlena. How could you forget that?"

The relief I felt at those words turned quickly to fear, and I began to cry harder. "My parents don't know."

Justin looked confused. "I thought they found out when you got kicked out of school. How have you managed to keep something like this a secret?"

I shook my head, frustrated. "I didn't. They knew, they've known since the beginning. But this morning, it was like none of this had happened. They acted like I hadn't run away."

"What?" Justin exploded and stood up beside me. "You ran away? When did that happen?"

I waved my hand. "That doesn't matter. My parents are acting like nothing has changed."

Justin sat back down, frowning in thought. "Tell me exactly what happened after I walked you home last night."

Taking a deep breath, I told him everything. He almost broke my hand when I talked about the trucker, and his mouth gaped open when I told him about my vow to Aphrodite, but he didn't interrupt me. I didn't tell him about finding Rochelle in the kitchen when I got home, or about the glamour and the mirror. My first lesson with Aphrodite came a little too close to the night we broke up, and I didn't want to remind him of that. When I was done, I felt like I had run a marathon, and I collapsed against the back of the chair, totally drained.

For a long time, Justin didn't say anything. He sat on the floor, holding my hand tightly and staring into space. I closed my eyes and let him think, relieved that I had told him. At least Justin knew I was a Red Witch; maybe I wasn't going crazy. My brain felt empty, and I sat in silence, just happy to listen to Justin's breathing beside me. Finally, after what seemed like hours, Justin shook himself like a dog after a swim and looked up at me. I opened my eyes and stared back.

"Darlena, the only thing I can think of is that someone altered reality for your parents."

"But you know I'm still a Red, right?"

"I do." He squeezed my hand and I felt a little better.

"So why would anyone wipe Mom and Dad's memories, but leave yours?"

He paused, considering his words carefully. "Maybe they don't want you to have any help."

"But you're helping me!" My voice shook, and I braced myself for his declaration that he didn't want to have anything to do with my problems anymore.

He squeezed my hand again. "And I will keep helping you. But your Mom had offered even more help than me, and both your parents are sheltering you with the safety of your home. Maybe compared to that, my help didn't seem like that much of a concern."

"But who would be concerned that I was getting help?" It didn't make any sense.

Justin looked at me intently. "Who would want you to feel isolated and out of control?"

And suddenly, I knew. I opened my mouth only to find Justin's lips against mine. In my confusion, I kissed him back. He still tasted like vanilla and mint, and I closed my eyes, savoring the feel of his lips. Energy coursed through my veins, and I pulled him close, pressing my body against his solid warmth. I felt sparks dancing on my skin, and I knew that if I opened my eyes, I would be glowing like a coal.

I was starting to really get into the kiss when Justin broke away from me. I blushed, confused.

"Don't say her name. You don't want to attract any more attention from her."

He'd only been kissing me to shut me up? I tried to get my emotions under control, and finally I nodded, not meeting his eyes. It wasn't his fault that he didn't have feelings for me. I was the one who was still hung up on him. He wasn't trying to screw with me; he was just trying to keep me safe. I sighed. "So what do I do now?"

Justin sat back and a shadow crossed his face. "The question is, what don't you do?" I must have looked confused, because he continued. "You don't talk about Red magic anymore with anyone except me. You don't draw attention to yourself. You don't argue with your parents; let them think you're a Green, let them believe you're harmless, and hopefully they'll stay safe."

"That'll be hard. I had really begun to depend on my mom for her support."

Justin nodded. "I think that's what she had in mind when she fixed your parents' memories. She wants you to feel helpless so that you stop trying to control chaos. If you just sit back and let things happen, she'll be happy."

I clenched my fists. "But I won't just sit back and let it happen. I don't want to be the cause of any more tragedy!" The images of the flipped car shot through my mind, and I remembered Pele's fiery eyes. "I don't want to humor any crazy, bloodthirsty gods."

"I know. But maybe you should take a break for the time being."

I stared at him, surprised. "What are you saying?"

He looked at me earnestly. "Learn. You have a patron now. Let her teach you everything she can, and let anyone watching think that you have accepted your fate."

I saw the value in his plan, even if it made my stomach churn. "But if I am in a position to avert disaster again—"

"I know you'll have to act. But until then, don't go looking for disaster. Let the gods think you are compliant; they'll spend less time thinking about you if you don't seem like a threat."

"But even if I learn fast, how can I do this without help?" Tears welled up in my eyes again, and I blinked frantically.

There was a pause, and I felt the electric crackle of magic in the air. He leaned forward and kissed me again, gently. This time, I kept my eyes open, trying to watch him. His face was sweet and intense, and it looked like he was enjoying himself, too. All I knew for sure was he didn't kiss me that time just to shut me up, and the thought made my heart leap.

When he pulled back, he traced my lips with his finger. "No matter what, Lena, I'll always help you."

20

I walked home in a daze, struggling to think coherently while still feeling the pressure of Justin's lips on mine. I shivered in the twilight, giddy with adrenaline.

By the time I turned the corner onto my street, I had nearly convinced myself that my parents' mind wipe was actually a good thing. Maybe this new development would be a blessing in disguise; if no one in my house knew what I really was, there wouldn't be as much tension and fear as there had been.

"I'm home!" I yelled, happy to be able to walk in the front door without worrying what new issue I would find waiting for me.

"How's Justin?" Mom looked up from her book with a smile. I smiled back, feeling really happy for the first time in weeks.

"He's good. We didn't do much, just hung out."

"I know better than that!" My dad's voice drifted around the corner from the kitchen, and Mom laughed.

"Stop teasing her, Richard. Darlena's allowed to have some fun." She looked at me and her expression darkened slightly. "Just not too much fun, right, sweetie?"

I nodded, embarrassed. It was a good thing she didn't know that Justin wasn't the one who wanted more in our relationship; she might have locked me in my room and thrown away the key if she'd had any inkling that I wasn't the good little girl she thought I was. I kept my face blank, glad that Mom couldn't read my mind the way Aphrodite seemed to.

Dad came into the living room with a glass in one hand and a dish towel in the other. "I'm glad you got home when you did. I wouldn't want you to miss curfew on a school night."

"A school night?" Confused, I looked at my parents. They smiled at me, and I felt a shiver run across my neck.

"It's Sunday night, Lena. You can't be so infatuated with Justin that you forgot what day it is, right?" Mom's voice was light and teasing, but her eyes were fixed firmly on mine. I drew a deep breath.

"Right. School. I didn't forget. I just … wish I didn't have to go back tomorrow."

"Now, sweetie, that's no way to talk. I know it's hard now that you've found your path"—Dad patted my shoulder consolingly with the dish towel—"but you still have to get your diploma. You never know when you'll need it; magic isn't enough to make a living!" He chuckled, and Mom smiled up at him.

"Lena's a good student. I know she takes her studies very seriously."

I leaped at the chance to leave the room. "I do. Actually, I just remembered that I have a test tomorrow, so I really should go upstairs and finish studying."

Mom nodded and Dad grinned. "That's our girl. Just don't stay up too late!"

"Don't worry. I'll keep an eye on the clock."

As I went upstairs, I glanced over my shoulder and caught Mom's eye. Did a flicker of sympathy cross her face? Dad had already turned back to the kitchen to finish the dishes, and Mom broke off her gaze almost immediately. I must have been imagining things.

***

Once I was safely inside my room, I sat down at my desk, puzzled. I had thought Mom and Dad's ignorance might be a blessing in disguise, but I had never considered they wouldn't remember that I had been kicked out of Trinity. Obviously, I would have to get ready tomorrow morning and leave the house, but I couldn't go back to school. Principal Snout had made that very clear, and frankly, I wasn't sure I wanted to go back to my old life. I had enjoyed the time I'd had at home, studying and trying to discover the limits of Red magic. How would I continue my training outside the house?

"You could just go to the mall." I jumped out of my chair, startled. Aphrodite was standing beside the window.

"Don't you ever knock?" I asked, irritated. She glared at me, and I reminded myself that this was my patron, my only protection from Hecate. I needed to keep her on my good side, and being grumpy and rude wasn't likely to do that. I took a deep breath and tried to start over. "I'm sorry. I was thinking, and you startled me."

She smiled wryly. "I could tell." Glancing around my room, she wrinkled her nose. "Haven't you tidied up in here since my last visit?"

"You just left this morning! Besides, I like clutter. It helps me think."

"Well, it's not doing a very good job of that, now, is it?" She smirked at me, and I had to fight to control my thoughts.

Her eyes narrowed. "You shouldn't try to keep secrets from me, Darlena. I'm disappointed in you for even thinking such a thing."

"How do you do that, anyway?"

She batted her eyes innocently. "Do what?"

"The mind-reading trick."

"It's not a trick! Don't think to compare me to some fortune-teller at a street fair. It's magic, and it's magic that I could teach you—if you didn't insist on being so rude."

I rolled my eyes. "If you teach me, won't you stop being able to read my thoughts?"

She laughed. "I can teach you the magic of mind reading without teaching you how to guard your own mind, silly child." Aphrodite crossed the room and took my chin in her hand. "Don't presume to outthink a goddess. And don't believe everything you read in those silly novels. Real magic isn't always a two-way street."

Her nails bit into my chin, and her stormy blue eyes were making me feel hot and cold in turns. I nodded my head, but she stared at me a moment longer before releasing me. I rubbed my jaw and felt the indents left by her fingernails.

"I'm sorry. I didn't mean to offend you." I lowered my head in a bow and held my breath. She laughed lightly.

"Submission does not become any Red, but most especially not a Witch who is sworn to me. See that you save your sass for someone other than your patron in the future, and spare me your apologies." She crossed my room and again stood by the window, looking up at the sky. "Come here, Darlena."

I hurried to her side, tripping over my discarded backpack as I did. Maybe she was right; I needed to clean things up a bit. She smiled, but didn't say anything to my unvoiced thought. I was grateful.

"Look at the moon." She pointed to the window, and I drew in my breath in awe. I had been so wrapped up in fear the past few weeks, I had stopped paying attention to the moon. It was almost full, riding low on the horizon: a true harvest moon, tinged orange and floating like a magical orb.

"The moon is just a rock, floating in space. But," Aphrodite continued, "she is also a goddess."

"But one of those things is scientific, and the other isn't."

The goddess laughed in her tinkling voice. "Everything in life is a contradiction. Nothing is ever only one or the other. Remember that."

I looked at the moon, and I thought about what she had said. Perhaps the goddess was trying to help me view Red magic as something more than chaos.

"That will come to you with time and practice." She spoke softly and I met her eyes. "Tonight, I only want to teach you to look at the moon."

21

That night, I dreamed of an earthquake: fire and blood, sirens and screams. But I wasn't afraid, and I didn't try to stop any of the chaos around me. In fact, I danced in the street, and each time my foot hit the ground, another tremor shook the earth. When I looked down at my hands, they were stained red, and even as my mind realized I was covered in blood, I couldn't take control of the dream. I lifted a hand to my brow, then brushed it across my lips and my heart. I licked my lips, tasting the metallic tang of the blood, all the while dancing and causing the earth to shake. In the dream, I began to laugh wildly.

I woke somewhere between a laugh and a scream. I sat bolt upright in bed, drenched in sweat. I rushed from my room into the bathroom and shut the door. I examined my face and hands in the mirror under the blindingly bright vanity lights. I couldn't find a trace of the blood from the dream, but when I rinsed my mouth out with a cup of water, my saliva stained the sink red. I gradually became aware of the sharp taste of blood.

I rinsed my mouth again, this time with peroxide, but the spit in the sink was still crimson. Horrified, I brushed my teeth, but nothing could get rid of the metallic tang that filled my mouth. Had some part of my dream been real? The blood in the sink was real enough, unless I'd started hallucinating. I didn't like either option. I was either going crazy or, worse, I was a maniacal killer.

Frightened, I sank to the bathroom floor and clutched my knees to my chest.

"It is a shame, girl, that you are sworn to another. You have the bloodlust to serve me, that is certain!"

I almost didn't look up. *Please*, I prayed, *let that deep, rasping voice be a hallucination. Please don't let me be locked in the bathroom with another goddess.* I drew a deep breath and counted to three.

When I looked up, I almost screamed. Perched on the edge of the sink was a grotesque woman. Her lips were stained red, and from the trickle that was smeared across her chin, I didn't think it was makeup. Her skin was the color of campfire ash, and her eyes were wild. But what was even more frightening was her jewelry: a necklace of bones and, draped across her hips, a belt of white skulls. I shut my eyes, willing her to disappear.

She just laughed. "You know better than that, girl. You know who I am."

It wasn't a question, and I nodded. There was no mistaking the goddess who crouched before me.

"Tell me."

I shook my head, not looking at her. I felt the bathroom floor sway.

"You are not stupid. You will do as you are told." Her unspoken threat hung in the air, and my stomach churned.

"You are Kali Ma. You are the destroyer."

She threw back her head and laughed gleefully. The bones around her neck danced, and her belt rattled. My throat convulsed but I kept my eyes down, still not looking at her.

"And you are a Red. Why did you waste yourself, girl? Red magic belongs to me. That goddess you serve is nothing but perfumes and passion. You will not go far in her service."

"But I am sworn."

She waved her hand in the air. "A waste! You would be better at my feet. What work can a goddess of love have for a Witch such as you? With me, you would be unstoppable."

She leaned forward, and I caught a whiff of decay. I started breathing shallowly through my mouth and tried not to grimace.

"Let us make a deal, no? You want more than the bargain you have made. There is a way to unmake your choice."

Suddenly, I remembered Persephone and the pomegranate seeds. I stared at Kali, my thoughts flying. If I could somehow trick her into telling me what to do, maybe I could unbind myself from Aphrodite if I ever got tired of her.

"What would happen then?"

She grinned wickedly. "You would be unclaimed. And then you could be mine."

"But—" I didn't want to belong to this goddess. I didn't even want to be stuck in the bathroom with her for another minute, but I had to tread carefully. "But what would you ask of me?"

"Blood. And you would love it; I have seen it in your heart. You crave chaos, and your mistress will not let you have your fill. I would never stint you on your share of blood."

I nodded even as I tried to swallow the bile rising in my throat. "How do I become free?"

Her eyes lit up with joy, but after a moment she bared her teeth at me in a snarl. "You will not hear it from me. You smell like deceit. Unless you will bind yourself to me, why should I help you find your freedom?"

I nodded at her, palms sweating. "Then I'll just figure it out for myself."

Kali laughed. "It will not be as easy as you think. Maybe I shall enjoy watching you ruin what little you have left."

She leaned back against the mirror above the sink. There was no reflection behind her.

***

I didn't even try to go back to sleep that night. I lay awake in my bed, thinking about everything Kali had said. I didn't want to believe that I would be better off serving such a bloodthirsty goddess, but I had this annoying fear that she might be right. Even if I didn't want to accept such a thing, there was my dream to consider. I had been enjoying the destruction I caused, and reveling in the blood of my victims. Dreams had to mean something, didn't they? What if that dream meant Kali was right?

I tossed and turned, my thoughts shifting from the dream to the frightening goddess I had just met. They came to rest on the three pomegranate seeds.

Silently, I got out of bed and crossed the room. My eyes were accustomed to the dark after hours of wakefulness, and I didn't need a light to locate the blood-red seeds. I held them in my hand and stared hard at them, wondering.

"I wouldn't do that if I were you." Aphrodite's voice rang out sharply. I turned to face my patron.

"Why not?"

"Things will not work quite the way you are thinking."

I closed my fingers around the seeds, but made no move to set them down. "How are things working now?"

"No other god or goddess can harm you. You are under my protection. And I am going to help you learn how to manage your power."

"That sounds great. But why haven't you done anything yet?" Maybe it was unreasonable to expect, well, magic, but I was irritated that all she'd shown me was the glamour. *To be fair,* I reminded myself, *she hasn't been my patron for very long,* but before I could apologize, Aphrodite loomed in front of me, doing her larger-than-life trick again.

Her cheeks were tinted red with anger. "How dare you call my patronage nothing?"

I should have been frightened, but I thought about what Kali had said and stood my ground. "You saved me from that trucker. And you taught me the art of glamour. But what else have you done?" I felt frustration bubbling up inside my chest, and I started speaking faster, not waiting for a response. "Did you protect my parents when Hecate brainwashed them? Have you shown me any useful magic? It's no wonder Helen screwed up, with a patron as helpful as you."

She slapped me with an open palm, and I stepped back, stunned. With a gesture, she used air to seal my jaw and I stared at her, helpless.

"You will not speak to me in such a way again. It would be within my rights to call down a brutal punishment on you. Did you not vow to me that you would follow me with devotion and obedience?" The goddess smoothed her robes, her hands lingering over her hips. "However"—she smiled sweetly—"I am in the mood to be magnanimous. Consider this your last chance. You will not cross me again."

She turned away from me. I tried to open my mouth, but found I was still bound by her spell. I stood, mute, waiting for her to decide what to do with me.

"You are so eager to learn to do things. Fine. We will begin the real work tomorrow."

She vanished, but my jaw was still locked. If it hadn't been, I probably would have eaten the pomegranate right then just to piss Aphrodite off. But I guess she knew that and wasn't taking any chances. I only hoped my parents wouldn't notice my silence.

***

Luckily, Mom was in such a rush that morning that she barely noticed how quiet I was. As she flew out the door, she called over her shoulder, "Have a great day at school, sweetie!"

I smiled and waved, but my stomach churned. How much longer could I keep my parents blissfully ignorant of the situation? Telling them once had been hard enough; I couldn't imagine telling them a second time.

I cleaned up the kitchen in silence, waiting for Aphrodite to reappear. When all the dishes were washed and she still hadn't put in an appearance, I went upstairs. Xerxes raced ahead of me, determined to trip me up on the stairs.

Distracted, I knelt down and scratched him behind the ears for a minute. When I opened the door to my bedroom, I wasn't surprised to see Aphrodite standing there.

I tried to speak, but to my chagrin I found that I was still bound by her spell. I narrowed my eyes at her, and dipped my head in a slight bow. She smiled humorlessly.

"I've said it before; subservience is not a trait I like to see in Reds." She waved her hand carelessly, and I felt a popping in my jaw. I tried to speak again.

"I'm ready for my lesson."

She glared at me. "Didn't you learn anything last night? It's not up to you to call the shots. You will wait until I decide to teach you." She stopped, eyeing me for an immeasurable stretch of time. "I have decided to teach you how to work love magic."

My doubt must have shown on my face, because she shook her head in exasperation. "It's time for a field trip, Darlena."

With those words, the room swirled around me and everything went dark. It took a minute for my eyes to adjust, but even before I could make out my surroundings, I could smell stale popcorn. I shifted my feet, annoyed at the squelching sound they made on the sticky floor. When my eyes adjusted enough that I could see the screen, I realized we must be at a movie theater.

"Why are we here?"

"Sit back, watch, and learn."

Advertisements were scrolling on the screen, but I didn't think Aphrodite wanted me to learn about the hottest new soft drink. I glanced around the theater at the other patrons. There was a spattering of women older than my mom, some in groups and some alone, and here and there I glimpsed some girls who were a little younger than me. They were probably skipping school, but I didn't think the giggling girls were who Aphrodite wanted me to watch. Then I spotted them.

The couple was obviously still in school, because the girl kept looking around nervously. I wondered if she'd ever cut school before. The boy wasn't that cute, but he seemed confident, sitting there next to his date. I stared at them intently.

"Good. You aren't as dumb as you act. They are who we will practice on." Aphrodite's voice was a soft whisper beside me.

"What do we do?" I tried to whisper back, but I felt loud and conspicuous sitting at the back of the movie theater with a goddess.

"First, feel the situation. What do you know about them?"

"Are you crazy? We just sat down; how am I supposed to know anything about them?" Even as I argued with her, I realized she was right. I did know things about the young couple. I took a deep breath and struggled to put my strange knowledge into words.

"They're skipping class to be here this morning." She nodded encouragingly, so I went on. "She's never been on a date before, and she's never done anything that would get her in trouble, so she's doubly nervous." I paused, staring intently at the young couple. "He's not as confident as he looks, because even though he cuts class all the time, there's something about this girl that he really likes. He wants to impress her, but he doesn't know how. Skipping was his idea."

I glanced at Aphrodite and she smiled. "Very good. For your first time, you're very in tune with the energy and vibrations in the air." She rubbed her hands together like some kind of super villain. "Now, Darlena, what would you do with your magic?"

I sat very still, thinking. I knew I could make the boy fall head over heels in love with his date, if I wanted. I could also make him try to cop a feel, which would make the girl dump her popcorn over his head. I shifted uncomfortably. I didn't really like either option: they both felt so intrusive, so unfair. What right did I have to manipulate people in that manner?

I finally spoke. "I could do a lot of things. But what would I do? I think I would just use magic to bless this date, making sure they each have a great time. I don't want to do any more than that."

Aphrodite looked disappointed. "I had hoped you would have

higher ambitions, child. I had hoped you would do something interesting. But," she continued, "as this is your first lesson, you have my permission to practice in any way you want."

I concentrated very hard on the young couple, thinking about fluttering hearts, hands brushing in the popcorn, and an awkward goodbye where two people longed to kiss but no one took the first step. I thought about the tingling anticipation of sitting beside someone really cute in the dark, and I sent my thoughts forward. I could see red sparks flowing down the aisle of the theater and enveloping the first daters. The sparks lingered in the air for a moment before falling like snowflakes onto the girl and the boy in front of me. The air shimmered and the sparks cleared and Aphrodite clapped softly.

"Well done. You might not have a flair for the dramatic, but you certainly know how to wield power."

"Where do we go now?" I started to rise but she pulled me back down.

"Now"—she smiled—"we stay here. There will be two shows to watch: the one on the screen, and the one you created. See which one teaches you more."

Just then, the previews began to roll, and I sat back in my seat. Aphrodite had picked a corny romantic comedy for my training, a kind of movie I rarely watched on my own. At first, I was annoyed, but soon I found myself caught up in the missteps of the characters and the lead actress's convincing tears when she thought that she'd lost her chance at love. I'm embarrassed to admit this, but I teared up when the couple on the screen finally got together. I couldn't help thinking about Justin. Maybe, if we gave it another shot, we could find our own happy ending. My thoughts spiraled off into a fantasy, and the credits were over before Aphrodite elbowed me in the ribs and pointed.

Wiping my face, I noticed that the girl was leaning on the boy's shoulder, nestled happily at his side. I smiled; maybe Red magic wasn't just about destruction.

I grinned up at my patron, and she nodded once before vanishing.

22

"It was actually a lot of fun!" I lounged across Rochelle's bed that afternoon, watching her paint her fingernails. She was experimenting with designs, but I couldn't tell if she was trying to paint splotches or spiders. I didn't say anything, though.

"Sounds like hell to me." With a deft flick, she finished her nails and held her hands out, eyeing the results.

"I know." I laughed. "It should have been awful. But the movie was sort of sweet, and it felt really nice to know that I made those kids have a good first date."

Rochelle screwed the cap back onto the polish. "Oh, goody. You're all warm and fuzzy. Darlena, get a clue. Aphrodite didn't teach you anything today. She just had you play Cupid."

I tossed a pillow at her, which she dodged. "But I didn't know I could do anything like that. Even if it's nothing major, at least I'm still learning magic."

She snorted. "I don't think getting two horny teenagers to snuggle during a movie counts as anything magical."

I frowned, feeling the doubt of the previous night creep back into my mind. "What would you have done in my place?"

"First," she snapped, "I would never have sworn to such a pathetic goddess!"

"Pretend you did." My voice was tight with anger, but if Rochelle noticed, she gave no sign.

"Well, then, pretending I was as dumb as you, if I were stuck with Aphrodite and love magic, I'd at least do something interesting."

"Like what?"

She thought for a moment. "I don't know. Ruin the date somehow and make the girl cause a scene?"

I looked at her, feeling a little guilty. For just a moment, I'd had the same thought in the theater. "Why would anyone want to do that?"

She looked at me with pity. "Anger is more powerful than love. What good is it to make two people have a fairy-tale first date? That's such a waste of magical energy. You raised all that power, and then you let it fizzle out."

"But this is the first time I've used Red magic and not done harm." I tried to keep my voice level, but I was upset. "Can't you at least acknowledge that it's good to know I can stick to the Rede?"

She turned away from me and began putting on eyeliner. "If I were a Red Witch, I'd never waste my power on stupid little love affairs."

***

I was in a sour mood when I left Rochelle's house, and she didn't try to get me to stay for dinner. It was still light out, and I dawdled as I walked, taking my time and looking around at the brilliant colors of the trees. Fall had really decided to show herself, and the branches looked like they were dipped in gold and lit on fire. I drew a deep breath and struggled to push thoughts of Rochelle from my mind. I slowed down, lingering so I could enjoy the crisp air. Even if I did prefer Samhain, I found myself looking forward to Mabon more than usual. Although it might be awkward if Red sparks started shooting off my hands—my parents wouldn't know what to think—I was ready to celebrate the true arrival of fall.

Fall is sneaky in North Carolina, because summer likes to linger. But I can always tell when fall has really arrived. I'm not quite sure how to explain it, but I guess there's a certain smell in the air that I recognize. I took another deep breath through my nose and frowned.

The crisp scent of fall was still there, but underneath was a smell like burned food. I noticed a thick, gray cloud to my right. Acting on impulse, I turned the corner and cut across a side street. The closer I walked to the smoke, the stronger the smell became, and my heart hammered in my throat as I realized what it was. I prayed I was wrong, but the sight that met my eyes proved that my prayer came a little too late.

The coffee shop on the corner by Trinity was a charred mass of wood and melted glass. Flames still licked around the structure, but they seemed to be teasing the spectators: all the damage was already done. I spotted Cindy clutching her barista apron and sobbing. Firefighters were on the scene, but their hoses seemed worthless. It was eerily like the destruction I'd dreamt about before meeting Kali, and I shuddered, pushing that thought from my mind. Whatever had happened had nothing to do with Red magic. Steam hissed up into the air to join the inky smoke, and I crossed the street to see what had happened.

"Darlena!" I looked up, startled. Justin pushed through the crowd.

"What are you doing here?" I demanded as he got closer.

Instead of answering, he pulled me into a tight hug, crushing my ribs. "I thought you were inside!"

I looked at him, stunned. "Why would you think that?"

"Your text."

Suddenly, I realized why he was worried. I had texted him after leaving the movie theater to let him know I was going to hang out with Rochelle. He had texted back that he'd meet up with me later. He must have assumed we'd gone to our usual spot. I looked up at what was left of the building and suppressed a shiver.

"We were at her house. I was just walking home when I smelled the smoke."

He hugged me again. "I'm glad you're okay." He shifted his concerned gaze to the scene in front of us. "I wonder what happened?"

"That girl over there, that's Cindy. She worked here. Maybe she knows something."

Justin steered me through the crowd and I hesitantly tapped Cindy on the shoulder. Her eyes were puffy from crying, but I thought I saw a flicker of fear when she recognized me. Then she started crying again, and I wasn't sure.

"Cindy, what happened?"

"What happened?" She screeched loud enough that people around us turned to look. "What happened? Why don't you tell me, you crazy freak?"

I looked at Justin nervously. "I don't know. I just saw the smoke and walked over."

She shook her head. "I don't believe you. I saw you flip that car over, and you knew I saw you. You cursed me!"

Stunned, I took a step back. "Why would I do that?"

"'Cause you're some kind of satanic freak! You hexed me, and I'm lucky to have made it out alive!" She started sobbing again, and I felt a wave of fear. Cindy had seen me use magic on that car, but I would never have done anything like that on purpose. People were watching us, and I wondered when Cindy's voice would be enough to draw the attention of a police officer. I swallowed nervously.

Justin tried to come to my defense. "But what caused the fire? Darlena was nowhere near here when it happened."

Cindy shot him a dirty look. "Yes she was. I made her order ten minutes before the whole place went up in flames."

***

I looked at Justin. He was sitting beside me on my front porch, tapping the ground with his shoe. "Please say something."

"Darlena." He sighed, but then stopped as if he didn't know how to go on. After a minute, he finally said, "I trust you."

I exhaled, unaware until that moment that I had been holding my breath. "Thanks. I—"

"But," he held up his hand to stop me, "something happened today that I can't explain." He looked down at his scuffed tennis shoes. "I know you've hexed people before. You've never hid that from me."

I stared at him, dumbfounded. "So you think I hexed Cindy? Why would I want to do that?"

"Were you angry that she saw you cause the car accident?"

I recoiled as if he'd hit me. Was Justin blaming me for that, now? He had no idea what it had felt like when I'd realized I'd caused that horrific accident. I glared at him, and he repeated his question quietly.

"I don't know. I was confused." I tried to think back, to remember everything I'd felt that day. "I think I was too scared to be angry."

Justin nodded, still not meeting my eyes. "So why does she think you put a hex on her? And why does she remember seeing you right before the fire?"

I shook my head. "I don't know! But, Justin, you have to believe me. I was at the movies with Aphrodite all day." I ignored his raised eyebrow to continue. "And then I went straight to Rochelle's house. I left her house and then I saw you. How could I have been at the coffee shop before the fire?" He had to believe me. I'd done some nasty things, true, but I would never have burned down the coffee shop.

He shrugged. "The point is, someone who looked like you was there. Cindy believes it was you. How often do you go to that shop?"

"Every morning, practically, before I got kicked out of Trinity. I haven't been back since the accident, but Rochelle and I used to eat breakfast there."

Justin looked sad. "So Cindy knows what you look like. She wouldn't have mistaken a stranger for you, not if you were one of her regulars." He stood up to leave, his jaw clenched.

"Justin! Listen to me. I don't know what's going on, but something isn't right here. I promise you I'm telling the truth." Tears threatened to overwhelm me, but I tried to keep my voice steady. I needed his support; if I lost Justin now, after Mom and Dad had been brainwashed, I worried that I might go insane.

He shook his head and turned away from my house. "I don't know, Darlena. I need some time to think, and you make that hard. When I'm with you—" He drew a deep breath and stopped. When he spoke again, his words were soft. "Don't call me tonight, Darlena. I need some space from all this … chaos."

23

Even though I tried to sneak into the house soundlessly, Mom heard me come in.

"We're doing pizza tonight, sweetie, so get in here and help me decide what to order," she called from the kitchen. When I didn't answer, she came into the living room. "What happened?"

I shook my head wordlessly.

Mom crushed me in an embrace. "It was Justin, wasn't it? Oh, Lena, I'm sorry."

I couldn't help myself; I started sobbing earnestly into her shoulder.

"Shh, baby, it's okay. I'm so sorry." Mom brushed my hair away from my eyes. She smiled at me sadly and I tried to smile back.

Her eyes brightened. "I know! Why don't we play hooky tomorrow, just the two of us?" I stared at my mother skeptically. I couldn't remember a time in my life when she had allowed me to miss school without being really sick. She laughed at my expression. "Sometimes it's okay to take a break." She squeezed my shoulder and I started to smile. "Besides," she went on, "I know you don't want to be around Justin tomorrow."

I felt a stab of pain when I heard his name, but I swallowed it down and tried to smile at her. "But what about work? Can you miss a day?"

She waved her hand dismissively. "Nothing is more important than my daughter. I know just where we'll go." She glanced at her watch and frowned. "Are you willing to wake up at four?"

Surprised, I nodded. There were lots of places we could get to with just a few hours of driving. The mountains, the coast, South Carolina, Virginia—the possibilities were limitless, but Mom really loved the mountains and the ocean, so I figured it was one of those two. "Where are we going?"

Mom smiled. "Don't worry about that. You just get to bed early so you'll be awake in time. And dress warmly!"

Hmm. Definitely not South Carolina, then. "I'll try. And, Mom?" I turned at the foot of the stairs. "Thank you. I love you."

She smiled but her voice shook. "I love you, too. Want me to bring dinner up to your room?"

I paused for a minute, but then I nodded. "Dad won't mind, will he?"

She shook her head. "I'll tell him it was my idea. He and I haven't had a date since that concert, so maybe we'll watch a movie or something."

"I'll be in my room, then. Let me know when the pizza gets here so I can get out of your way." I was relieved that I wouldn't have to deal with Dad. I loved him and all that, but I didn't really want to listen to his comforting advice. I was glad that Mom hadn't asked any questions about what had happened with Justin, but I doubted Dad would be that in tune.

Mom smiled, but her eyes looked sad. "Alright, Lena. Just remember to get to bed early!"

***

I thought I'd be up all night worrying, but my body had other things in mind. I fell asleep almost instantly, and I plunged straight into a series of vivid dreams.

In one, I was looking in a mirror, but my reflection wasn't doing any of the things that I was. I lifted my left hand, she scratched her right knee. I smiled, she growled. I started getting upset in the dream, and I tried to smash the mirror with my fists. My hands began bleeding, but the me in the mirror was still there, laughing at me.

Then the dream changed. I was on a stretch of black rock, like wavy asphalt. It was hot out, the sticky, humid heat I'm used to in July. Strange birds flew close to me, and when I ducked to avoid them, I looked down and realized that my feet were embedded in the rock. I started to sink, slowly yet perceptibly, but it didn't occur to me to scream. I just watched the ripples of rock move up my legs to my torso. I closed my eyes when I was buried waist-deep.

When I opened my eyes, I was lying on a pink cloud. A mirror was next to me on the cloud, and when I gazed at my reflection, I looked the way I had under the glamour. The air smelled like roses, and I smiled at the mirror, happy to be away from everything as I floated on my cloud in the sky.

I rolled over and suddenly I was falling; the cloud had dissolved under me, and I was plunging fast toward ... nothing. I couldn't see the ground, I couldn't see anything. I just kept falling.

I woke with a start. I remembered my dreams vividly, and I had to count to one hundred while I lay there in bed before I really believed that I was safe in my room. The red numbers on the clock beside my bed were flashing twelve, and I blinked a few times before I understood. The power had gone out sometime in the night.

I dug my cell phone out from the bottom of my purse to check the time. It was almost four. I pulled on a pair of sweats and threw my hair into a messy ponytail just as Mom knocked at the door.

"Are you ready, sweetie?" She whispered through the door, and I opened it for her.

"Yeah. Do I need to wear anything special?" I hoped she'd say I was fine; I had no desire to fuss with anything right now. In fact, I was starting to question the wisdom of running off with Mom. All I wanted to do was curl up with a pint of ice cream and cry, just like the girl in the movie I'd watched with Aphrodite. But Mom looked chipper, and I didn't want to disappoint her. Besides, she never took time off work; I didn't want to spoil her day.

She shook her head. "Today isn't about how you look. It's about making you feel better."

In the kitchen, Mom grabbed the old blue cooler off the table. She must have packed it the night before. Either that, or she'd been up way earlier than me. When we got in the car, I peeked inside the cooler. There was water, juice, fruit, and granola, enough snacks to get us through the morning. I was relieved, since I hadn't grabbed anything for breakfast, and my stomach was starting to churn furiously.

"Do you want to stop for coffee before we head out?"

"No!" I blurted the words and Mom glanced at me, curious.

"I've never known you to turn down coffee."

I groped around for a reasonable excuse. "I'm still tired. I thought I might doze in the car." I hoped she couldn't hear the panic in my voice; the thought of explaining the decimated coffee shop to her was too much.

She accepted my answer, and I breathed a short sigh. I settled back into my seat, but even though I closed my eyes, I didn't sleep.

***

The drive to the Atlantic coast usually takes us anywhere from three to four hours, depending on the beach we're headed to. Mom likes to go fast, and she had the road mostly to herself, so it was just after six-thirty when I saw the sign for Wrightsville Beach.

There weren't any cars in the public lot that early, and as I got out of the car and stretched, I breathed a deep breath, letting the stillness wash over me. Mom grabbed the cooler, locked the car, and strode purposefully toward the deserted beach.

The sun was just breaking over the waves as Mom and I cleared the sand dunes. Just as I had done a million times before, I stopped to unlace my shoes. Beside me, Mom slipped her sandals off. Dad was the only one who ever wore his shoes at the beach. Shoes in hand, we headed for the water, only stopping to set the cooler down near the edge.

Even at dawn, the ocean was active. The waves rolled to the shore with the sound of sandpaper, and seagulls cried overhead. It was breathtaking, and the closer we got to the water, the more I felt myself growing calm. I dipped my toes in the icy surf, and let my feet melt into the sand.

Boldly, Mom waded out past me, and I began to follow her. Despite the chilly morning and the fact that we were fully clothed, Mom didn't stop until the waves lapped around her hips. I followed, and was instantly soaked. I stood next to her trying to keep my teeth from chattering. She raised her arms in the air, and recognizing the gesture from my ritual magic class, I did the same.

"Ocean, we beg you to wash clean our sad hearts." When Mom began to chant, I was startled. What did she have to be sad about? But I kept my arms raised, and I listened intently as she continued. "Mother and daughter, we have come to you this morning for the chance of a fresh start."

Wistfully, I thought of Persephone and the pomegranate seeds, safely tucked in the bottom of my sock drawer at home. I sighed, wondering if it was time for me to take my chances with the seeds. Mom started to lower her arms, and I followed suit, but she shook her head slightly. I raised my arms again, confused, and watched as she scooped up water in her cupped hands.

"May my daughter know no more sadness." She leaned forward, spilling the water over my forehead. I shivered compulsively as the droplets cascaded down my neck, but I felt a rush at the same time, a sense of energy just out of reach. Mom raised her eyebrow at me and I nodded, lowering my hands and reaching into the freezing water.

I scooped the water up and raised my hands over my mother. "May my mother know no more sadness." I repeated her words and doused her in salt water. She smiled at me, water dripping down her face like tears. My skin tingled in the crisp morning air, but I tried not to feel the cold. I wanted to savor this morning. I didn't usually do magic with anyone, especially Mom, and it felt special to share this with her.

It was a simple ritual, but it was beautiful. As we waded back to the beach, I knew that my problems weren't over, and I didn't think my mother would be always happy now, either, but the words and intent of our trip to the coast lingered in the air. For just that moment, I stopped being sad. With a burst of Red energy, I lit a piece of driftwood on fire, stepping close to it to dry off. Mom watched me for a moment, standing a few feet away from the fire.

"Come closer and get dry," I suggested, feeling the warmth coursing through me like magic.

She shook her head sadly. "Lena, that wasn't the point."

I felt like I'd missed something, but I didn't know what. Embarrassed, I kicked sand over the fire until smoke curled lazily into the air. "Um, I'm sorry?"

Mom shrugged. "It's okay. Let's walk."

24

We lingered at the coast for the morning, wandering around the beach barefoot and stopping to scoop up pretty shells every few feet. But by noon, we headed to the car and said goodbye to the ocean.

"That was really nice. Thank you." I felt shy being confined in the car with Mom after the morning's ritual. I hoped she wouldn't mention the fire; I still felt like I had screwed up her ritual somehow, but I couldn't explain Red magic without shattering the illusion that everything was fine. Mom and I didn't usually work magic together, and there was a sense of intimacy hanging over us that I couldn't reconcile with the fact that I had to lie to her about who and what I was. Still, I wanted her to know that our trip had helped me.

"Of course! Thanks for being willing to take an adventure with me." She smiled and turned the car back onto the interstate. We drove in companionable silence for almost fifty miles, but then Mom spoke. "Darlena, I know there's more going on right now. Justin isn't the only thing upsetting you, is he?"

Stunned, I shook my head.

She smiled. "I thought so. I know you think you love him, but I didn't raise you to cry that much over a boy. Can you talk about the rest of it, whatever it is?"

My heart swelled up with relief. She wanted me to tell her! I could reveal everything, and then I wouldn't be carrying my burden alone. She would help me. I opened my mouth, and the image of my mother kneeling to Hecate came into my mind. Even if she knew everything, how much help would she be allowed to offer me? Hell, what if it wasn't a question of offering me help; what if she would actively work against me to please Hecate? I closed my mouth and shook my head.

Her face fell. "I'm sorry you don't feel that you can trust me. Please remember, if you ever do want to talk, I would do anything in my power to help you."

My throat swelled, and I almost started to cry. Not trusting my voice, I nodded.

"Just remember, sweetie, whatever it is, you can't change everything. Don't bog yourself down worrying about things outside your control. Fix what you can, and leave the rest alone."

I nodded again and closed my eyes. Her words had triggered a thought: there wasn't much that I had any power to change. Even though Red magic was supposed to be strong and chaotic, I had felt utterly useless since stopping the hurricane. Aphrodite didn't want me meddling with anything except love.

My eyes popped open. If I couldn't fix everything, maybe I could at least heal the crack in my relationship with Justin. I needed him to trust me again. Love usually grows from trust, but maybe with a little magic, I could make trust grow from love.

***

That night, alone once more in my room, I grabbed a photo of Justin, my red candle, a box of matches, and the mirror Aphrodite had given me, then crept into my closet. My parents and the instructors at Trinity had tried to teach me not to use magic on another person, Witch or Non, but years of experience had taught me the value of sympathetic magic. I tried not to cast hexes that were too powerful, because I firmly believed what I had been taught about magic rebounding on the person who cast the spell. I didn't want to hex an enemy and end up in the hospital. But, I reasoned as I lit the candle, a love spell wasn't a hex. I wouldn't worry about any negative echoes from this spell.

Setting the picture in front of the candle on the floor, I held the mirror up and gazed into it for a long time. When I saw my image begin to shift to my glamoured self, I turned the mirror facedown over Justin's picture. I stayed there in the closet until the candle burned itself out, leaving a red puddle of wax on the floor, the mirror, and the photo. Leaving everything where it was, I whispered a prayer to Aphrodite before crawling out of the closet.

I couldn't fall asleep right away; I was too anxious about my spell. My body pulsed like I'd grabbed a live wire, and every time I closed my eyes, steamy scenes of flesh and lust filled my mind. My subconscious should have been embarrassing, but I reveled in the images my mind supplied, thinking about Justin's warm embrace. A part of me hoped the spell would work instantly, but when the clock said it was past two and the phone was still silent, I gave up and tried to sleep. Hopefully, I thought as I hovered on the edge of sleep, I would know if my spell had worked in the morning. At that moment, there was nothing I wanted more than Justin's love. I had screwed up once, but I wouldn't lose him again.

25

Wednesday morning dawned bright and clear, and I smiled as I looked out the window at the street. After the trip to the beach and my spell work the day before, I felt confident that today would bring better things than the rest of the week. I resisted the urge to text Justin, trusting that the magic I had begun would bring him to me. Instead, I took a long shower. I drew hearts in the fog on the bathroom mirror, then laughed at my foolishness and wiped them away with my hand. I had never been so silly, even the year before, when things with Justin had been intense. Brushing my teeth, I wondered if my mushy mood was a by-product of dedicating myself to a goddess of love. Or maybe, I wondered fleetingly, it was the rebound from the love spell.

"Good morning, sunshine!" Dad greeted me with a smile when

I strolled into the kitchen. "You look like you're in a fabulous mood!"

"I am." I grabbed a bagel and some peanut butter and sat down at the table with him. The paper was next to him, folded messily, and I glanced at the front page. "Anything interesting in the world?"

Dad sighed. "Interesting, yes. Good? Not really. There was an earthquake in Asia last week, and a lot of people are still without basic needs."

I hummed as I spread the chunky peanut butter on my bagel, not really listening.

"And I'm in the middle of a major project at work, so there's a lot on my mind. Did you have fun with your mother yesterday?"

I nodded. "Yeah, it was just what I needed."

Dad looked thoughtful. "I don't know if it was what your mom needed."

I looked around, realizing for the first time that we were the only ones in the kitchen. "Where is she, anyway?"

"She's got a headache, so she decided to lie down. I think she'll be staying home again today."

My mother had only ever missed three days of work that I could remember: yesterday, the time I broke my arm in third grade, and the previous winter when Dad had walking pneumonia. She never stayed home when she was sick, trusting instead in magic and herbs to heal her quickly. What if the ritual we'd done yesterday had sapped her strength? Fleetingly, I wondered if there might be a way I could use Red magic to recharge her. I'd never done anything like that before, though, and I didn't really want to experiment on Mom. Still, I should try to do something. "Maybe I should stay home with her."

"No." Dad shook his head. "You can't afford to miss any more school."

I shrugged, not making eye contact as I bit into my breakfast. "I guess. Well, I'll at least come right home at the end of the day. I'll tell Rochelle we can hang out later."

Dad beamed at me. "That's my girl. It wouldn't break my heart if you stopped hanging out with Rochelle altogether."

Usually, when my dad said something like that, I got angry. Today, nothing seemed to faze me. I shrugged again. "She's my best friend. I'm not going to ditch her."

Dad folded the paper and tossed back the rest of his coffee. "Just think about it, sweetie. You don't want to spend your time with someone so ... negative, do you?" He didn't wait for my answer as he picked up his briefcase and glanced at the clock. "I'll try to be home around six. Look in on your mother before you leave, okay?"

I nodded as the door swung shut. Finishing the second half of my bagel in one bite, I raced up the stairs two at a time. I tapped gently on the door, and when I didn't hear any response, I opened it slowly. My parents' bedroom was dark and I could barely see Mom's lumpy shape passed out on the bed. Quietly, I shut the door. She probably just needed to sleep, I reasoned as I grabbed my bag and cell phone off my desk. Once I was out the door, my worries about Mom were quickly replaced with heady anticipation. I had a feeling that my spell would yield results today, and I knew just the place to wait for that to happen.

***

It hadn't changed: the same ivy crept up the brick walls, and the same creepy gargoyle grinned down at me as I passed beneath the gate. I don't know why it would have changed. I hadn't been out of school for that long, but everything in my world was different. I guess I had expected that things would be different here, too.

School had already started, so the courtyard was deserted. I snuck past Snout's office and headed straight for the library. I could hide out there all day and no one would ever find me unless I wanted them to.

The library at Trinity was the one thing I had missed since my declaration to Red magic. The school had reappropriated the old gym when the book collection surpassed our athletic skills, and a new space hadn't been built yet to house the books. Shelves were arranged like prison bars across the court, and no matter where I stood, I could see at least two basketball hoops. It was weird, but kind of cool at the same time.

I slipped between the *biography* and *miscellaneous* shelves and began browsing. Some of the books were shiny and new, while others were bound in dusty leather with gold lettering. Still others were so old that they had no writing on the spines. It was insane how much knowledge was stored at Trinity, and for a moment, I wondered about Rochelle's suspicion. How much magical information was the school keeping from us?

I paused, my fingers hovering over a book entitled *Love, Lust, and other Longings*. It wasn't the kind of thing I usually went in for, but I was feeling all mushy that morning, so I pulled it off the shelf and curled up on the floor, leaning up against the bleachers. Before long, I was immersed in the book, fantasizing about trying some of the spells on Justin. There was one in particular involving feathers and cinnamon that I thought would be interesting, and I made a mental note of the page. I was totally focused on memorizing the spell when someone coughed.

"Oh, good, you're studying." I jerked my head up to find Aphrodite sitting next to me.

I exhaled in surprise. "I really wish you would stop sneaking up on me! You're going to give me a heart attack."

"You're a Red Witch, Darlena. Toughen up!"

I closed the book with a snap. "Are you here to lecture me?"

She looked genuinely surprised. "No, I'm here to see if your spell has worked yet."

"How did you know about that?"

"Darlena, when will you learn that there is little about you that I do not know?" Her words grated on me, but I tried to keep my temper.

"Well, if you know so much, you should know if it's worked or not."

Aphrodite eyed the dusty book on my lap and glanced around the room. "I'd say not, unless you've hidden your boy somewhere in the bookshelves." She stood up and crossed to the nearest shelf. "Come out, come out, wherever you are!" She searched around for a moment, then looked at me and smirked. "Nope. I was right. You aren't hiding a boy in here."

I glared at her, fighting the urge to blush. "It will work. I'm just waiting to be around when it does."

"Child," Aphrodite chided, "you are sworn to a goddess of love. You of all people don't have to mope around wondering if a boy will call. He will call."

I turned an even brighter shade of red. "Fine. While I'm waiting, maybe you can teach me something. We haven't had many lessons yet."

"You're right."

I was surprised that she agreed so quickly, so I stuttered, "Can you teach me how to bind the spell so it lasts?"

She looked at me for a moment, her face expressionless. "Are you so sure that you want it to last? It is not in the nature of love to be unchangeable."

I paused, trying to put my thoughts into words. "It's just that, in the past few days, I've felt like I'm totally alone. My parents don't remember anything about me being a Red, and now Justin stopped talking to me because—" I broke off, not sure I wanted to say anything to the goddess about my suspicions, but of course she could read my mind.

Her eyes grew wide and her face flushed in anger. "Someone has been using your image to work magic?"

I protested quickly, even though she'd just voiced my own deep fear. "Maybe not. Maybe Cindy just saw someone who looked like me, and in the chaos after the fire, she wasn't thinking clearly." I felt a sinking sensation in the pit of my stomach as I realized my theory wasn't plausible. Someone had posed as me. I just had no idea why.

"I am beginning to understand." Aphrodite's comment took me by surprise. She went on. "You said you feel isolated, and now because this boy thinks you are lying, you have lost his support, too. Someone is trying to make you vulnerable, Darlena. It is easier to attack one who stands alone than to target a person surrounded by love."

"But I don't understand. Who would want to attack me?"

Aphrodite narrowed her eyes. "Don't lie. You know exactly who is behind this."

I saw Hecate's flashing yellow eyes in my mind, and I swallowed. "Yes."

"What I don't understand," she continued, "is how she is going about it."

"What do you mean? She's the Queen of Witches!"

Aphrodite shook her head in irritation. "The gods are bound by different laws than mortals. You may remember our part in the Trojan War."

I thought hard, and grasped a scrap of memory. "You pushed the mortals to act, but when it came to the actual fighting, all you could do was watch from above and hope that they would carry out your conflicting wishes. Does that mean that you—any of you—can't actually do anything in the real world?"

She looked down and nodded. "I have always hated the fact that I am, essentially, powerless when it comes to the lives of men. I may manipulate, I may plan, I may cajole, but in the end, I may not act for myself." She clenched her robe in her fists. "For all that I am, a goddess, possessed of powerful magic, I am sometimes helpless without the assistance of my sworn mortals."

I thought about what she had said. If the gods couldn't act on their own, the attention of the various Red goddesses suddenly made a lot more sense to me. Filing that piece of information away to think about later, I asked, "So you're saying that Hecate isn't behind all this?"

She shook her head. "Not at all. I see her hand clearly. But she is not able to carry out these actions without mortal assistance. Someone"—she spoke softly—"has betrayed you."

***

Aphrodite spent the morning teaching me to shield my thoughts. "I hate to see you learn to close yourself from me," she said regretfully, "but it now seems imperative that I offer you whatever protection I can."

I agreed. Secretly, I wasn't as thrilled as I had expected to learn how to block my mind from invasion. It was irritating when the goddess read my mind, but her ability also meant I didn't have to waste time explaining things every time I saw her.

"Like any spell, this isn't permanent, but until you discover who means you harm, it would be best for you to shield your thoughts at all times."

"Even when I'm at home?" I argued.

"Especially then. Hecate would have no scruples about turning your own family against you; in fact, it would suit her purposes to not only weaken you through her magic, but also leave you betrayed by those you love most."

"But what does she want?"

"I believe that her hope is, once you are weakened, she will be able to influence you again."

I shuddered, remembering the satisfaction I had seen in Hecate's eyes the day of the car accident.

Aphrodite continued, making my stomach turn over. "If she can, she will wield you as a weapon of chaos. It would be best," she added wryly, "if you do not allow this to happen."

I felt a stab of guilt at her words. Even though I had not allowed Hecate to use me, I felt as though I had given her the advantage when I stopped actively trying to avert chaos. Since the hurricane, I had only focused my efforts on learning love magic. If I had continued to work with the more powerful Red forces, would Hecate have been able to gain a foothold in my life so quickly?

I didn't know the answer. I only knew that I had to prepare myself to stand against the goddess I feared most. Even my horror of Kali paled in comparison to the calculating appetite for death I had seen in Hecate's eyes. I worked hard at the spell Aphrodite showed me, and I had just sealed it with a careful knot when I heard the library door open behind us.

I spun around, hurriedly thinking of an excuse to justify my presence if the intruder was Snout, but I needn't have worried. Justin was crossing the court, peering at the bookshelves for a moment before he spotted me. I glanced back at Aphrodite, but she had vanished.

He walked up to the bleachers where I sat and bounded up them two at a time. All at once, he was there beside me. I grinned at him and tried to resist the urge to fling my arms around him. First, I needed to see if my spell had worked.

"Darlena." He whispered my name as if it were a prayer, and I felt a ripple of goose bumps cascade down my arms. Then his lips were pressed to mine, and I melted into his warmth. I forgot everything, savoring the sensation of his kiss.

26

Justin and I spent the afternoon walking hand in hand through the neighborhoods surrounding Trinity. The fall sunshine cast a golden light on everything, and I felt like I had when I'd snuck champagne at my cousin's wedding the previous spring. It was wonderful.

"I have an idea." Justin's eyes sparkled, and I smiled up at him.

"What?"

He shook his head. "It's a secret. You'll find out soon enough."

Turning, he led me through a labyrinth of streets lined with charming World War II–era homes. After a few twists and turns, I was hopelessly lost, but then we came around the bend and I spotted a brontosaurus through the trees.

"Seriously?" I laughed and squeezed his hand.

"Why not?"

"Because I haven't been here since my tenth birthday." We had stopped walking, but I was smiling.

"So? It's high time you went back."

I laughed and let him lead me through the entrance to the science museum. It had been one of my favorite places as a child, but I'd outgrown it a long time ago.

"We're the only people here without kids!" I whispered self-consciously, glancing around.

He slipped his arm over my shoulders. "Aren't we lucky? We can do whatever we want."

I relaxed and started to enjoy myself. We wandered past rocks and fossils, space mission equipment and X-ray machines. I was heading for the animals; the museum kept bears, wolves, and lemurs in outdoor habitats on the land surrounding the building, and even though I hadn't been there in years, I still remembered where my favorite exhibits were. Laughing, Justin grabbed my hand and ran with me to the first habitat.

"I love the bears." I was breathless from rushing toward the cage.

"They are pretty cute."

We pressed against the railing at the viewing area, wedging our way in between children and their parents. Shoulder to shoulder, we stood in silence while we watched the three brown bears sleep, eat, and splash in the water. I sighed in contentment. I would have been perfectly willing to stay right there for the rest of the day, but Justin wanted to see the wolves, so I reluctantly pulled myself away to follow him.

The keepers were just finishing laying out food when we

reached the second large fence. I watched, fascinated, as two red wolves slunk along the top of their enclosure, stalking the tray of raw meat. Justin turned away after a second.

"I don't really want to watch them eat."

But I was mesmerized. The first wolf had reached the meal and was sniffing it cautiously. Then, with a low growl, it began to tear at the flesh. The kids beside me let out a collective "Eeeew!" before their parents pulled them away. My ears started to ring, but my eyes were fixed on the feeding wolves. It was like I was entering a trance. My hands started to tingle, and I knew that at any second, I'd start shooting Red sparks into the air. Just then, Justin leaned down and kissed me quickly.

I looked at him, my reverie broken. He smiled at me, and my heart flipped.

"Let's keep walking."

I nodded, and let him lead me back to the path. I glanced over my shoulder toward the wolves once, but after that I kept my attention on Justin. It was amazing to be with him, and I whispered a silent thank you to Aphrodite for teaching me the importance of love magic.

***

When Justin left me at the door of my house, the sky was already turning the purple of twilight. He kissed my cheek gently, and I reached up to draw him close for a real kiss. After a long moment, he pulled away.

"I should get home." He didn't move.

I nodded and kissed him again.

When I finally broke away, I glanced at the house. The lights were on, but the front curtains were drawn. I giggled nervously. "I wonder if my parents are watching us." For a second, I thought I saw the curtain move, but it must have been my imagination. Still, I pictured my dad standing there with his eye pressed to the sliver of light, trying to see what we were doing. Just to be silly, I waved.

Justin glanced up at the window and smiled. "If they are, they must know how much I love you."

My throat tightened. "What did you say?"

"That I love you, Darlena." He said it like it was the most obvious thing in the world. There was a pause while I smiled up at him like an idiot, but then he playfully flicked my hair and said, "Well?"

I blinked, confused. "Well?"

His eyes looked troubled, but he didn't say anything.

"Oh!" I exclaimed. "Oh, of course. I love you, too." I'd thought the words often enough, but I'd never imagined I'd get the chance to say them.

He kissed me again, and a traitorous thought flickered through my mind: did he really love me, or was it just the spell talking?

"I'll call you tonight." He lifted my hand up to his lips, and gently brushed my fingertips against them. I shivered in delight.

"I know you will." I blew him a kiss as he turned and walked down the street. When he had rounded the corner, I looked up at the rapidly darkening sky. I put my arms out and started to spin giddily.

"That was even better than I expected!" I whispered when I staggered to a stop. I started to laugh, realizing that I was standing there, in the dark, talking to the clouds like a crazy person. It was a good thing Justin had already left! Even as I thought it, I knew it wouldn't matter. He loved me, and that wouldn't change because I was acting a little crazy. But would it change if he knew about the spell? I tried to ignore that niggling thought as I went inside.

***

That night, my dreams were filled with the heavy perfume of roses and summer, despite the autumn wind that blew outside my window. I didn't hear the pelting rain, nor did I notice the wind. I dreamt of fields of flowers and sunshine and had no idea that, as I slept, a late-season hurricane was inching closer to the Atlantic coast.

27

"Darlena, honey, I'm sorry to wake you." My mind was still groggy with sleep, but Mom kept pounding on my door.

I crossed the room and opened the door. "What's wrong?"

"There's a hurricane headed our way. We have a few hours 'til it reaches the Outer Banks."

I rubbed my eyes, confused. "So? We're far enough inland not to worry."

She shook her head. "Not this time. This one is strong, the worst of the season, they're saying. The radio even compared it to Fran. Your dad wants to be safe rather than sorry. I need your help sealing up the house and moving things upstairs in case it floods."

Groggily, I got out of bed. As I pulled on my sweats, I noticed my old atlas lying on the desk. I flipped it open to North America, feeling the tingles of magic still on the pages of the book. I looked long and hard at the map, considering.

I had averted a hurricane before, hadn't I? Maybe I could do it again. I drew a deep breath and tried to center myself, but my scattered thoughts kept latching onto the memory of Justin's lips pressed against mine. It was intoxicating, and I found it impossible to think clearly about anything else.

I shook my head and closed the atlas. I was clearly skilled at love magic; why did I feel the need to meddle in matters of chaos? Pushing away the memory of the last hurricane I'd altered, I headed downstairs and began stacking the kitchen chairs on top of the table. Mom worked with me, and it didn't take long to move most of the furniture either upstairs or as high as we could put it on the downstairs level. Then we went out to the shed to find the dusty old storm shutters.

"Will we need to postpone our Mabon celebration?"

She looked up at the sky and frowned. "Maybe. It wouldn't be a good idea to have the fire tonight, that's for sure."

"It'll blow over us. They always do, right?"

Mom nodded, but her forehead was still creased. "I hope so. Something about this storm feels funny."

I looked up at the sky, but it just looked stormy. Soon I had forgotten what Mom said as I struggled with the storm shutters. I had never helped hang them before, and it was tricky, heavy work. When we were done, I headed around the corner of the house, keeping my eyes on the ground. Mom usually put away her gardening tools, but I spotted her yellow trowel lying at the edge of the flower bed. Picking that up, I detached the water hose from the side of the house and dragged it over to the shed.

"What are you doing?" Rochelle had slipped up behind me, and I jumped, startled. I hadn't heard her come up, but the wind had started blowing harder, so that wasn't surprising.

"Getting things cleaned up. Mom says there's a hurricane coming." I handed the hose to her, but she made no move to take it.

"So?"

I looked at her, annoyed. "So I have to help get things put away. Shouldn't you go home and help out, too?"

She shrugged, smiling a strange smile. "My folks will be fine."

Glancing at the purple clouds, I shook my head. "I don't know. It looks like it's going to be bad."

"My storm will not harm them."

For a minute, I didn't understand her words, but then I turned, surprised. "What do you mean, 'your storm'?"

She smiled smugly. "Darlena , did you really think you were the only one who could fool around with weather?"

I felt a chill creeping across my neck. "What did you do?"

"Why, I did what you did! I used a map as a focus, but unlike you, I didn't try to fight the forces of nature. I helped them along."

Was this all a big joke? I stared at her, confused. "Rochelle, why would you do that? My mom says this storm is going to be dangerous."

Her laugh was harsh. "I told you, Darlena, you shouldn't waste your power. Other Witches would love to have control over chaos."

A terrible suspicion formed in my mind, but I tried to ignore it. "But Rochelle, you're a Black, not a Red."

"But I have friends, Darlena. Friends you ignored. And they seem to think that I would be a better Red Witch."

Her eyes were fiery, and I took a step back without realizing it. She snarled, and I realized then that I wasn't hallucinating; Rochelle had betrayed me.

"Too late to be afraid, Darlena. Once this storm hits, there will be nothing left of your house to hide behind. And there will be nothing left of you, either."

I said the only thing I could think of. "But we're best friends!"

"But we're best friends!" she mocked, her voice bitter. "What did you ever do for me? You took power, you could have mastered the world, and did you ever once think to teach me any of it?"

"Red magic is dangerous. There aren't supposed to be more than three Red Witches at a time. I couldn't have told you anything!" I kept backing away from her, frantically trying to think of a way to get out of this situation without harming Rochelle. No matter what, she was still my best friend.

"If you had cared enough, you would have. How do you think it feels"—her voice broke, but even her sob sounded frenzied—"to have a friend with so much power?"

I reached out to hug her, but she crossed her arms. I tried reasoning with her. "But Rochelle, you're a strong Witch, too."

"I'm just a Dreamer! My parents are Nons. I'm nothing! But you—you're a Blood Witch, and Hecate singled you out. It's not fair!" she shrieked, and I realized that while we had stood there talking, the wind had risen. I had to shout to be heard.

"I still don't understand. Why would you create a hurricane just to destroy me?"

She laughed. "You won't be the only corpse! And she promised me that if I made enough offerings, I could take up your vow instead."

My heart turned to ice. "Who promised you?" I thought I knew the answer, but I didn't want to believe it.

"Who do you think? Hecate!" Rochelle laughed wildly. "You should never have defied her, you know. But I'm glad you did. She didn't want me until you swore to Aphrodite." She shook her finger at me. "That wasn't very smart, you know. It's a bad idea to piss off a goddess like her."

I stared at her, openmouthed.

"But your bad luck was good for me. Because once you're gone, I'll be the next Red Witch!"

Lightning ripped across the sky, and Rochelle laughed, raising her arms. "The storm is almost here! And what a tragic accident. You got caught out in it. No one could have predicted that lightning would hit that tree, or that it would fall to the earth, crushing you beneath it."

My thoughts raced. Rochelle had betrayed me to Hecate. She wanted to kill me. My best friend wanted to kill me.

"You brainwashed my parents, didn't you?"

She laughed. "It wasn't hard to do. They wanted to believe that you were still their perfect little girl." She sighed. "For some reason, Justin didn't want to believe any fantasy. His mind clung firmly to the fact that you were a Red. I had to use other methods to convince him to desert you."

"It was you, wasn't it? You burned the coffee shop."

"I had to! You were getting stronger. If you lost Justin, I thought you'd lose your own power. You were pathetic when you guys broke up before; I figured you'd crumple again like the weak little girl you are."

I edged away from her, trying to scoot around the side of the house. Rochelle laughed.

"It's too late, Darlena. You're not going to live through this storm. And then I'll be the one with all the power."

I paused, tense and waiting for my chance. Rochelle turned to look up at the sky, and I moved quickly.

I threw the garden hose toward her and felt the tingle of Red magic course up and down my arms. The hose sailed through the air like a boomerang and wrapped around Rochelle. She stumbled back, stunned, but I could see her lips moving to form a curse. I still didn't want to hurt her if I didn't have to, so I turned and sprinted toward the front of the house, aware that she wasn't far behind.

I raced up the porch and tried the door, but to my surprise it was locked. "Come on, come on!" I jiggled the handle, pounding on the door. Why didn't Mom hear me?

"She's not there. Poor Darlena, nobody here to save you." Rochelle spoke from behind me and I tensed, flexing my palms and trying to ready myself for whatever she had planned.

Suddenly, my stomach clenched. "What did you do to her?" If

Rochelle had harmed my mom, I'd make her pay. Wild rage filled me, and I struggled to keep the Red magic from erupting uncontrollably. I didn't turn around, but I could see Rochelle's blurry reflection in the glass of the door. She grinned wickedly.

"Why do you think I would do anything to your mother?" Her voice dripped with venom, and she took a step closer to me. "Your sweet mother, who never liked me, who wished you would find a new friend. Now why in the world would I want to harm her?"

I took a deep breath. My palms were tingling, but I knew that when I turned I would have to act fast. Once Rochelle could see my eyes, she would know what I was planning. "My mom was worried that you'd be a bad influence on me. But she never did anything to you. You wouldn't harm her!" I tried to speak with more confidence than I felt, but my nerves pulsed, waiting for Rochelle to confirm or deny my fears.

"Wouldn't I?" Her voice was soft, and her reflection loomed closer.

"What about the threefold law, Rochelle? Are you really prepared to get three times as much pain as you've dished out?"

She laughed. "I haven't dished out any pain—yet. Your mother isn't here. That doesn't mean she's dead. She just had the sudden urge to run to the grocery store for some milk. Like just about everyone else on this street. What a shame," she laughed, "that the lines will be so long! What a shame she won't get home in time to help you."

Thank gods Mom was okay. I let my anger cool for an instant, and then I whirled to face Rochelle, raising my hands above my head as I spun. I had the satisfaction of seeing the shocked look on her face in the instant before she was blasted backward twenty feet. While she was on the ground, I quickly bound her with air, tying her hands first before sealing her mouth with the same spell Aphrodite had used on me. Part of me wanted to slice her throat and watch her bleed on the lawn, but I fought the impulse. I had sworn I wouldn't use Red magic to be destructive, and I certainly didn't want the guilt of my best friend's death on my hands. Still, I couldn't resist sending a little zap of energy at her, giving her a tiny magical shock.

"This isn't over, Rochelle. I'm still alive. You haven't finished your work." I tied off my spell, using a burst of magic that left me staggering and seeing double. Rochelle glared at me from the ground as I passed her.

I took off down the street at a run. The sky above me had turned inky black, and the wind was whipping through the neighborhood, bending trees in half. I hoped Mom stayed put at the grocery store. If she tried to drive in this wind, I didn't think she'd be able to keep the car on the road.

I was out of breath by the time I reached Justin's house. I pounded on his door, but no one answered. Where was he? Didn't he realize how much I needed him? Desperate, I turned back to the street.

"Aphrodite!" I screamed into the wind. "Goddess, hear me! Please! I need your help."

The only sound was the screeching wind, and the only response to my plea was the pelting rain that began to fall. I started back toward my house, moving in a daze. I barely noticed that Rochelle was nowhere to be seen as I raced up the driveway. The sliding door in the back was open, and I slipped inside. My mind was a mess, and thoughts kept slipping in and out of it like fish. There was something important I needed to remember, but I couldn't quite grasp it. It was maddening.

The sounds of the storm were only slightly muffled once I was inside the house, and I stood there, dripping on the kitchen floor for a minute, trying to get my bearings. Xerxes came around the corner but stopped when he saw me. His fur stood on end and his eyes looked wild.

"Xerxes, buddy, it's just me." I took a step toward him, and he took off like he'd been shot out of a gun. I could hear his claws scrabbling up the stairs. Cautiously, I started to follow him. I didn't want to give the cat a panic attack, but I needed to get to my room. I didn't know why, but I had the overwhelming sense that I would be safe there.

Upstairs, I didn't see any sign of the crazed cat, and I was grateful. Poor old guy had already been freaked out enough, and I didn't want to scare him anymore. The Red sparks had faded, but I could practically smell the magic pulsing off my hands; that was probably what had scared the cat. When I opened my door, I jumped back, startled by the electric shock that bit my fingertips as I touched the door handle.

My room was pitch black, and nothing happened when I flicked the light switch. The wind must have knocked the power lines loose. In the dark, I felt my way across the room to my desk. I groped around for a moment, and then felt a sharp pain as my hand closed around the unsheathed blade of my knife.

"Shit." I quickly sucked the blood off my finger. My tongue began to tingle and go numb, but I was distracted by the squishy shapes I felt under my left hand. The pomegranate seeds.

Time slowed down. I couldn't hear the wind outside anymore. I couldn't even hear the frantic beating of my heart. Everything was quiet and still, as if the world were waiting for me to decide.

Without thinking, I put the first seed in my mouth and felt the sharp sweetness explode on my tongue. I had never tasted anything so bitter and sweet; it was better than lemonade on a humid summer day. Quickly, I popped the second seed in my mouth, swallowing greedily. My hand slowed when I reached for the third seed, and the enormity of what I had done washed over me. Actually, I still didn't know what I'd done, but I knew that my actions had just changed everything irrevocably. Persephone had made that much clear when she gave me the seeds. I gulped and stared into the darkness, but nothing happened.

"In for a penny, in for a pound," I muttered, smiling slightly at the memory of my grandmother those words evoked. Deliberately, I picked up the last seed and plopped it on my tongue, savoring the flavors that were gone too quickly. When a bolt of lightning struck close to the house, I shivered.

Well, I thought, *what's done is done.* But the trouble was, I didn't know what I had done. Had I reversed the events since I declared to Red magic? Was I still bound to Aphrodite? Was Rochelle still waiting somewhere outside to attack me? The door to my bedroom creaked, and I turned in time to see it swing open.

The darkness in the hall made it impossible to discern any features on the shadowy figure that stood before me. I reached toward the desk and grabbed the athame, holding it point-up toward the door. I felt a twinge of guilt—ritual knives weren't weapons—but I pushed my guilt to one side. I didn't want to face whatever it was unarmed, and I didn't think I'd be able to use magic for a while; the fight with Rochelle had drained my strength.

"Darlena?" Justin's voice was laced with worry, and I sighed raggedly as soon as I recognized his voice.

"Justin! What are you doing here?" Hurriedly, I set the blade down.

"What do you mean? You called my house and left a crazy message on the machine." He took a step forward, glancing around nervously. I reached for a candle and matches on the top of my desk.

"I didn't call you. I can't find my phone." The smell of burning sulfur filled the room as I lit the stub of candle that I had grabbed. I held it cautiously in my hand, watching Justin's face sway in the candlelight.

"But what's going on?" Justin sniffed the air cautiously. "It smells like Black magic in here."

I took a whiff, but all I could smell was the lingering scent from the match. "I don't know."

He looked at me strangely. "I had a weird dream," he finally began, "about us."

"Oh?" I shifted my weight, not wanting to let my guard down, but suddenly desperate to sit down.

He took a step closer, shadows bouncing off his face. "I dreamed we got back together."

I exhaled loudly and looked away. "Was it a good dream?"

He shook his head, and his words were sharp. "You used magic. I felt helpless." The light from the candle made his head look like a grinning skull, and I swallowed.

"Would that be so bad?" I ventured, setting the candle down on the desk.

"Are you kidding?" He exploded. "Darlena, come on! Who wants to be forced into something against their will?" He clenched his fists. "It was just a dream, wasn't it?"

I looked down, passing my hand over the candle in a nervous motion.

"Darlena." I had never heard Justin sound so serious, and I looked up. I didn't say anything, but he held my eyes for a moment before he began to shout.

"Is that who you've become? Someone who would use magic to manipulate another person?" I couldn't answer, but he wasn't waiting for my response. "That's disgusting, Darlena! The fact that you would use me like that—" He spun toward the door.

My heart felt like it was imploding. "Justin!" I finally snapped out of my daze and took a couple of steps toward him. He stopped, but didn't turn around. I drew a deep breath. "What if I told you I only did it because I had nothing left? My parents couldn't help me, and you had stopped wanting to." My rushed words sounded pathetic, and I realized that he wasn't going to forgive me. My heart sank to the floor like a stone, and I reached for him, desperate.

He stepped away from my embrace. "I don't know about before. But I know I would never help you now."

As he went down the stairs, the lightning flashed again, and I thought I saw yellow eyes gazing up at me from the living room. I shut my door quickly and warded it, even though I desperately wanted to watch Justin to see if he would turn around. He'd have to deal with whatever was waiting in the living room by himself, I thought cruelly, although I was pretty sure it wasn't waiting for him.

I slid down the door, tears pouring down my cheeks. How had I made such a mess of things? The damn pomegranate seeds hadn't fixed anything! I sobbed brokenly, heaving great gasps of air. Maybe I should find Rochelle and let her kill me; it couldn't hurt more than what I was feeling at that moment. I think I came close to discovering whether it was possible to drown in tears, and I had all but given up when I heard a voice.

"Pain is good. Without it, you won't grow."

I looked up to find the cold face of Persephone in front of me. The goddess straightened up and cracked her neck.

"I've waited a long time for you, Darlena."

"What do you want?" I stayed crumpled against the door, craning my neck upwards to look at her.

"You."

Something inside of me reached the boiling point. "I am so damn sick of being a toy to you goddesses! I don't care who you are, or what you can do! I want to make my own choices."

A hint of a smile played about Persephone's lips. "You have. You chose to declare to Aphrodite, didn't you? And just now, you chose to eat the pomegranate seeds. Grow up, Darlena."

I gaped at her. She sighed, and her face softened, even if her words didn't.

"Do you really think it's the end of the world? There are worse things in life than making a bad choice."

"Do you regret your choice?" Instantly, I wished I'd never asked the question, because her face darkened dangerously.

"It's mine and I live with it. That's the bottom line, isn't it? Not the choices we make, but the way we handle those choices. Though"—her lips quirked in a bitter smile—"I can't say you've been handling your choices very well."

I wiped my face, feeling defeated. "I didn't choose to have my best friend try to kill me. Is she still? I mean, is Rochelle still trying to kill me?"

Persephone looked at me for a long minute. "That depends. Are you still a Red Witch?"

I flexed my fingers in my lap and looked away. "I don't know."

"Then I don't know if the girl is still hunting you."

"I thought you told me those seeds would give me a chance to undo something!"

She grimaced. "I never said that. I only told you to eat them if you ever regretted your choice. And you must have regretted something, because you ate all three of them."

I was silent, and the goddess slipped gracefully to the floor, sitting across from me. She reached out and took my hands.

"What do you regret, Darlena? What made you eat the seeds?"

I thought for a moment. "I regret the fact that I couldn't turn to anyone for help." I paused, trying to put my thoughts into words. "I regret forcing Justin to stay with me. And"—my voice hardened—"I regret not fighting harder when Rochelle betrayed me."

Persephone nodded. "Never once, child, did you tell me you regret choosing to follow the Red path."

"So the seeds only changed the things I was regretting when I ate them?"

She shook her head. "Magic is never that simple. You should know that by now. The seeds altered reality based on your thoughts, but what other effects they had still remain to be seen. However"—she smiled a genuine smile—"I believe that you are still a Red Witch."

"Why does that matter to you?"

She sighed, fiddling with the robes draped over her shoulder. "You have met some of the other patrons of Red magic. What did you think of my sisters?"

I hesitated, wary of a trap. The Red goddesses I'd met all seemed pretty nasty, but I didn't want to offend Persephone, since she'd just made it clear that she was a Red goddess, too.

She clucked her tongue at my frozen expression. "You may speak freely. Didn't you set a ward about this room yourself? I do not wish you harm, but I cannot reveal my meaning to you unless I know if your thoughts run in the direction that they seem to."

Surprised, I stared at her. "You mean you can't read my mind?"

She shook her head. "Your mind is swathed in shadow; you must be very powerful to keep even a goddess out of your thoughts."

I sat back, thinking. I hadn't really been practicing the tricks that Aphrodite had shown me in the gym, but evidently I was doing something right. The goddess waited patiently while I decided what to say.

"Kali frightens me. Pele was ... intense. And Aphrodite—" I licked my lips nervously, but continued. "She doesn't seem to care much about anything other than love spells. She wants me to use Red magic to meddle in people's lives."

Persephone nodded slowly, but she still looked wary. "And this is not to your liking?"

I hesitated, but something made me want to tell this goddess the truth. "Red magic is powerful, and, I don't know, it feels like a waste to mess around with romance when I could do something like stop a hurricane." I held my breath, waiting for her to say something.

A slow smile spread across the goddess's face. "Then it is as I had hoped. Darlena, you are right. Red magic is powerful. There are those who would harness that power for destruction, as Pele and Kali would wish. Then there are those who would struggle to find a balance between chaos and life."

I was surprised to hear the goddess voicing the thoughts I had held about Red magic almost since the beginning. "It doesn't have to be about destruction?"

She nodded. "A Red Witch who seeks balance is rare, yet she is also deeply powerful. You control one third of the world; if you used your magic to slow the inherent chaos, who knows what good things might arise?"

"But how do I do that? I've tried; Hecate keeps finding ways to slow me down. And now, if Rochelle kills me, she won't work for balance; she wants blood as much as some of the goddesses."

Persephone nodded thoughtfully. "That is a problem. It seems to me—"

She broke off and glanced around. Raising her hands in the air, she whispered a word I didn't understand, and I saw a shimmer of Red dust encase us in a tight bubble. I moved my hand wonderingly, and the Red dust stayed fixed to my skin.

"Not that I don't trust your wards, dear, but I wanted to add something of my own. No god can alter magic cast by another god. Remember that, Darlena."

I nodded and leaned forward eagerly. "What were you going to say?"

She paused and looked into my eyes. "You might not like it."

"Anything is better than this!"

She nodded. "I was going to suggest that we remove you from this sphere."

I sat back, confused. "What are you talking about?"

She sighed and gestured around the room. "This space, this existence. Rochelle may be a creature of Hecate, but there are limits to her power. She seeks you here, in the world you've always known. Wouldn't it be prudent to remove yourself to a place that

Hecate would never expect?"

I looked around my bedroom. Everything was the same as it had always been: my books arranged neatly on the shelf, the small bed covered with my grandmother's quilt, the thin blue lace that my mom had insisted on draping over the window blinds. I'd spent sixteen years in this room, in my parents' house, and I wasn't sure I was ready to leave. I swallowed, uncertain.

Persephone leaned forward. "They would not know you were gone, Darlena. Your parents would not miss you. Life for them would go on as before."

"How do you plan to make that work?" I was afraid I wouldn't like the answer.

"I will stay in your place."

"What?" I jumped up, the Red dust still clinging to me. "Are you crazy?"

"Is it not natural for one daughter to take the place of another?"

"But you're a goddess! And I'm ... not!"

Persephone laughed. "That much is obvious. But hear me out: If I am here, it will not only spare your parents' feelings. Hecate and Rochelle will also focus their energies on attacking me, while you are safely away, striving to undermine chaos."

A cold feeling had been sneaking up my spine ever since I stood up. "If you would stay here as me—"

"Is it not natural for one daughter to take the place of another?" Persephone repeated her words softly. I crumpled to the floor, my worst fears confirmed.

"You can't be serious! I can't go to the Underworld."

Persephone snorted. "If you paid any attention to the seasons, child, you would realize I have not yet made my annual descent. The weather is still fair, for another few weeks at least."

I gasped, "You want to send me to Demeter?"

Persephone nodded calmly. "Your mother is sworn to follow her. She will take care of you."

I studied her face. "Would she know who I am?"

The goddess paused, considering. Finally, she shook her head. "I'm sorry, Darlena. You would have to disguise yourself as me." When I opened my mouth to protest, she went on. "Hecate and my mother share a close friendship, and I cannot promise you that she would not betray you if she knew that you were the Red Witch Hecate seeks."

"How in the world am I supposed to convince Demeter that I'm you?"

"Easy." Persephone smiled. "You must fashion a glamour."

28

The plane lurched and the red seat belt sign began blinking. I leaned over and tried to look out the window, but the sky was black.

I was glad to have the window seat, but I wasn't thrilled to be sharing my armrest with a hulking businessman who smelled like he had brushed his teeth with cologne. He didn't seem concerned with personal space, and I'd tucked myself as close to the freezing window as I could get. Thankfully, he had been asleep for most of the flight, so I hadn't been forced to make small talk.

When I had asked Persephone why I had to take a plane, her response had been curt. "Some of us do not have enough magic to transport mortals such great distances." I didn't ask again, and she made all the arrangements. It was interesting to think that Aphrodite had more power than Persephone; maybe I'd been wrong to doubt her. But she never showed up, so I didn't get a chance to ask her if she was still my patron. I threw myself into planning for my trip, and the days passed in a blur.

I chewed my lip, worrying that perhaps we hadn't been careful enough. True, there had been no sign of Rochelle or Hecate in the days after the hurricane, but I wasn't confident that I had escaped so easily. Besides, how would I convince a goddess that I was her daughter?

"You've learned the art of glamour from Aphrodite," Persephone had said to me. "I will show you how to tie off a spell, so that it will remain without your constant attention."

I hadn't tried that yet; I was waiting until we landed in Athens before donning the face of a goddess. I hoped I had paid enough attention when she explained how to make the spell last. I didn't even want to think about what would happen if it really became permanent; I couldn't worry about that now. Until I went home, I just had to think like a goddess.

After eleven hours, the plane finally began its descent. The sky outside had grown lighter, and it was late afternoon when we landed in Athens. The wind whipped across the runway, throwing my hair into my mouth, and I rushed to get inside the terminal, not even stopping to look around. This wasn't a sightseeing trip, I reminded myself, and I moved with determination toward the sprawling airport building.

Once I had my passport stamped, I headed for the ladies' room. With my backpack, the only luggage I had brought, I locked myself into the large stall at the end. First, I used magic to change the backpack until it resembled a small leather drawstring bag, the type my grandfather used to keep marbles in. I checked the bag: everything, including the athame and mirror, had survived the transformation just fine. I'd glamoured my tools to get them through security; I wasn't sure what I would do with them, but I wanted all the help I could get. Drawing a deep breath, I turned my efforts to my own appearance. It was easier than ever before, and once again, I marveled at how badly I had botched the glamour I'd tried for Justin. Thinking about him was like touching a raw wound, so I pushed the memory of his face away. He hadn't been around since the storm, and I had to accept that I'd lost him for good.

I looked in the mirror, but all traces of my face were gone; Persephone's sad eyes stared back at me. Once the spell was cast, I imagined I could see two shimmering ends of rope in my hands. Swiftly, I knotted the rope and it pulsed and shimmered, changing from silver to gold. I looked down at my torso, now covered in a loose green linen tunic and brown pants. The goddess had suggested that simple work clothes would be best, and I trusted her. There was a gold-and-red braided cord at my waist, and I tied my bag to it firmly. Squaring my shoulders, I whispered a third spell, for invisibility, and headed out of the airport.

***

Persephone had given me very detailed directions to find her mother, so I started off with some confidence. It wasn't long before I reached the vineyard, just as Persephone had said, set into the base of a looming hillside. I glanced up at the mountain's peak and shivered. I would be in the shadow of the Greek gods, trying to pass myself off as one of them. It hadn't hit me until then just how dangerous this undertaking would be. My glamour had better hold!

I loosened my invisibility as I came into the vineyard, just as a figure came walking over the hill. I tensed for a moment, waiting to be discovered and punished. As she came closer, I realized that the woman approaching me reminded me of my mother. I figured out who she was in the instant before she spoke.

"There you are! We've been waiting for you." Demeter reached out her hands and clasped mine.

I squeezed her hands, surprised at their warmth. "I'm sorry. I don't know what's got into me today; my mind was wandering." I had to struggle to keep my voice from quavering.

The goddess laughed, shaking her head with a smile. My eyes were drawn to the wreath of wheat and bright red poppies she wore on her head. My mother's patron wasn't stunning like Aphrodite, but she was a stately woman. She looked like an earthy, tribal queen. Demeter squeezed my hand again. "That's my little one. Always thinking. What were you thinking about?"

She looped her arm through mine and we began to walk through the vineyard. I said the first thing that popped into my mind. "I was thinking how quickly the harvest has gone."

Her face clouded for a moment, but then she smiled again. "But it is not over yet! I will have you with me until the end of the harvest. Hades will not break his promise." Her tone was light, but there was something bitter about her words.

I felt a chill at the name of the god of the Underworld. "Has he ever broken his promise?" I didn't plan on meeting him, but if he decided to reclaim his bride by force, I might not have a choice.

She eyed me askance, and I realized that I had somehow said the wrong thing. "Just because he has been honest does not mean I have to like the arrangement!"

I relaxed slightly. Demeter seemed bitter about her daughter's marriage, but she hadn't said anything about Hades regularly storming to earth to take her before the appointed time. I hoped my question hadn't planted any suspicion in her mind, since it was clearly not something Persephone would have said. I decided then that I would need to listen before I spoke to Demeter; I didn't want to say anything that might give me away. I couldn't run the risk of her telling Hecate if she found out who I was. I had no desire to test Demeter's loyalty to her daughter. What if, when push came to shove, Hecate trumped all?

We walked on in companionable silence for a time. Demeter seemed more relaxed the farther we went into the vineyard, which made sense, since it was her home turf. When Demeter finally stopped, I was startled to see that we weren't alone anymore. We had stopped at the edge of a clearing, and it was surrounded by a rough circle of two dozen men and women. They looked perfectly ordinary to me, but it was clear that they could see the goddess— goddesses—that stood before them. Persephone had mentioned the gathering to me, and coached me on my role, but I was nervous.

Demeter raised her arms and spoke. "Friends, loyal devotees. Thank you for your work during this harvest. May your bounty be rich, may your hearts be full, and may your homes never hunger." She lowered her arms and nodded to me in expectation.

"May your joy never fade," I stammered out the words Persephone had taught me, "may your love only deepen, and may your winter be brief." Demeter frowned, and I tried to straighten my shoulders and steady my voice. "We will bless your harvest."

One by one, the people filed across the clearing, each bringing something. The first woman who knelt in front of me carried two jugs. "I ask your blessing on this wine." Her voice was strong, and I felt a sharp pang of guilt. These people wouldn't be blessed by their goddess this fall, but at least I could use my magic to ensure that they got something. Summoning up Red energy, I held my hands over the wine.

Keeping an image of a joyful party in my mind, I channeled the energy into the vessels, Red sparks shooting out of my hands. The woman looked at me in awe before she smiled and turned away. Beside me, Demeter was blessing the objects that people brought before her, but she looked up briefly to smile at me. I grinned back and turned to face the next person.

Persephone had told me that the farmers and vintners who sought blessing from her mother each year would bring a sample of their harvest, rather than go to the work of hauling all of it to the vineyard and back to their farms. She had explained that the blessing was symbolic and extended to the entire harvest. In ancient times, she said, the farmers would leave half of their sample at the temple of Eleusis, a place sacred to Persephone and her mother. Now, though, Demeter encouraged the farmers to leave their offering to some charitable organization, often the church in town or the orphanage on the hill. I had been surprised to learn that any Nons still remembered the old gods, but Persephone had just laughed.

"Witches are not the only ones who believe in magic, Darlena."

With her words echoing in my mind, I watched the farmers around us, and wondered what it would be like to stand in front of a goddess every season and ask for her assistance. The very idea fascinated me, and I gradually forgot to be nervous as I stood beside Demeter.

Watching her bless the people and their goods, I felt a pang in my heart. I missed my own mother. Here I was, with her patron, and yet there was no way I could tell her. She would have been so happy to help Demeter dole out blessings and donations. Like her patron, my mom always takes care of everyone around her, strangers and family alike.

I blinked back tears and turned to bless the farmer in front of me. He was a short man whose dark skin looked like a ripe grape in the sun. I smiled at him and held out my hands to take his token. He looked at me for a long moment, then shook his head and turned away. A few people in line behind him gasped, and I felt Demeter's sharp eyes on my back.

Had he seen through my disguise? Trying to ignore the way my stomach had started to churn, I focused on blessing the rest of the offerings, but it was impossible not to notice the cautious stares from the people in the field. And every time I looked up, Demeter was watching me, her expression unreadable.

29

Long after the sun had set, Demeter and I picked our way over the fields to a small farmhouse. Persephone had told me that her mother lived simply, but I hadn't been expecting the straw on the roof or the single lightbulb suspended from the ceiling in the large room. I guess I should have been thankful that she had electricity! Demeter flicked the switch, and the light buzzed to life. I crossed the room to the sink and began to pump water to wash my hands.

"That was a good harvest festival, I thought." I glanced over my shoulder when she spoke, but Demeter wasn't looking at me. She had crossed to the far wall of the cottage and was stirring the coals on the hearth.

I turned back to the sink, choosing my words carefully. "There were some lovely offerings. The children at the orphanage should eat well until spring."

She didn't answer, but the flames roared to life. I stopped working the pump, and the water slowed to a thin stream. The crackle of the flames and the trickle of the water filled the uncomfortable silence.

Finally, she asked, "Are you tired?" Demeter's voice was soft and motherly, and I again felt a yearning to be at home with my own mother.

I swallowed, and then nodded, trying to get a grip on the homesickness that threatened to overwhelm me. "It's been a long day." I crossed to the thin mattress under the window. Persephone had told me she liked to sleep where she could watch the stars in the night sky, so at least I knew which bed was mine. I yawned and knelt down on the bed.

"Sleep well, daughter. But wake early; we do not have many more days left, and I want to get a head start on the work of the day."

I nodded. She turned off the single light and moved quietly to her bed, next to the hearth. I thought I would fall asleep immediately, but between jet lag and my experience at the harvest festival, I was twitchy and wide-awake. I flopped around on the mattress, trying to get comfortable, but when I heard light snoring from the hearth, I rose and walked out of the cottage.

I wrapped the blanket from my bed around me and sat, shivering, on a large boulder not far from the cottage. I looked up, amazed by the dazzling display of stars. I had always lived in town, and even though we went camping every year, I'd never seen a night sky like this. There were three times as many stars as I was used to, and the sky looked like rich blue velvet. I drew a deep breath but started to cough when the cold air rushed into my lungs.

Not wanting to draw Demeter's attention by coughing near the open window, I began to wander aimlessly. I was too wound up to sleep, and there was something peaceful about being alone in the dark. I wasn't worried about being attacked; after all, I was staying with a goddess. She and Persephone must have protected their home with spells, so I walked around without any of the concerns I would have felt at home. Durham was a pretty cool city, but like any city, it had its issues. I would never have wandered around in a neighborhood I didn't know after dark, but it was different here.

There was a path leading away from the house and farther down the hillside, and I followed it carefully, watching my feet to make sure I didn't trip over any rocks or step into a thornbush. The path wound gently down the hill, past a slow stream before stopping at the mouth of a cave.

The pure darkness of the cave opening was a shock, even after being out in the dark night. The stars didn't seem to reach the cave, and it loomed up before me like monster. Everything around me was still; even the crickets had stopped their song. As I leaned forward, I thought I could hear something from deep within the cave, but I couldn't identify the sound. Suddenly, a hand closed on my shoulder and I squealed in surprise.

"Come back to the house." Demeter's voice was sharp, but her face was shadowed by her cloak and I couldn't see her eyes. Nervously, I followed her back up the winding path. I glanced back at the cave once and paused, but Demeter kept striding ahead of me, and I rushed to keep up. What would she say about me wandering around? Had I blown my cover? I cursed my insomnia as I hurried back to the cottage in her wake.

Once we were back inside, the stillness of the night dissolved.

"How dare you taunt me like that?" Demeter flung her cloak in a heap on the floor and started to pace.

"What do you mean?" Stunned, I couldn't stop myself from speaking. The angry goddess spun on her heel and slapped me hard across the mouth. Tears welled up in my eyes, and I glared at her in shock. My parents had never hit me, and I was surprised at how much her hand stung.

"It's bad enough that you abandon me for half of every year. Did you ever think, just once, to pretend to want to stay here with me?"

Still reeling from her slap, I stayed silent.

"But no! Sneaking out at night to look at the cave, making me feel like a burden that you can't wait to be rid of."

It was slowly dawning on me what that cave was. I couldn't ask, since Persephone would have already known, but I felt sure it must be the entrance to the Underworld. Demeter's next words confirmed that.

"You think I don't know that in just thirteen days you'll walk into that cave and I won't see you again until March? Why do you have to rush it?" Her anger gave way to tears, and she sank to her bed near the hearth, weeping. I crossed over to her and knelt by her side, even though I was still mad that she'd slapped me. Persephone wouldn't fight with her mother, I was sure of that, and

I had to keep reminding myself to act like her, not like me.

"I don't want to rush it. I'm sorry. You aren't a burden." I spoke softly, trying to heal a wound that was as old as the earth. I knew that Demeter had mourned the loss of her daughter when Hades first took her to the Underworld, but I hadn't realized that she still felt the pain, year after year, when Persephone descended to be with her husband. I tried to imagine how my mom would feel if she had to lose me again and again, and I shuddered. Pushing my anger aside, I reached out my hands and the goddess enfolded me in a tight embrace.

"I don't have to leave yet," I whispered, fervently praying that it would not be me who would make that journey this year.

30

When Demeter finally let me go back to bed, I fell asleep as soon as my head hit the pillow. My dreams were filled with whispers and cave openings, but even in my sleep, I never stepped inside. I had no desire to find out what waited for Persephone in the Underworld.

Sunlight was streaming through the window when I woke, and I realized that Demeter had allowed me to sleep in. The house was empty, but the fire on the hearth crackled brightly and there were fresh yellow flowers in a mug on the table.

I sniffed the flowers, smiling at the warm scent, and took a slice of the thick rye bread that had been left out. I figured Demeter hadn't stayed angry for long, or she wouldn't have left me breakfast. Munching thoughtfully, I looked around the simple room.

The two mattresses were against opposite walls, leaving the space free in front of the large stone fireplace. The floor of the cottage was unstained wood, swept clean by the broom that leaned against the doorframe. A round hunk of cheese sat next to the loaf of bread on the table, and I broke off a piece. It was salty and sharp, and better than anything I had ever tasted at home.

There was a shelf of old books near Demeter's bed, and I crossed the room to take a closer look. Leather-bound volumes of Homer, Ovid, and Apuleius took up most of the top shelf. I picked up a copy of the *Iliad* and flipped through it, but the text was strange; I wondered if it was printed in Greek.

The second shelf held rolls of parchment, and gingerly I unrolled one. The parchment was brittle and old, but the scroll didn't crumble in my hands, and in a moment I was looking at an old map. It looked hand-painted, and it was probably at least four hundred years old, because there was only a vague lump on the left side of the map to represent North and South America. I pulled it closer to see if I could make out any of the tiny writing that covered the continents.

"I'm glad you are awake." I spun around, terrified that Demeter had caught me hunting through her things, but instead of a goddess, a young boy with dark, curly hair stood in the doorway, smiling at me. His grin was infectious, and I smiled back at him as I replaced the scroll.

"What would you like to do today, m'lady?" His words surprised me; clearly this boy knew Persephone, but she hadn't mentioned any kids to me. For a moment, I was at a loss.

Before I could speak, however, the boy had crossed the room and taken me by the hand. As he pulled me out of the cottage, he rattled off suggestions for the day. "We could watch the men thresh the grain, or we could walk to the orphanage and bless their gardens. Or maybe we could go into the city, and pretend to be rich mortals with bags of money, and then laugh when the shopkeepers try to charge us!" He giggled impishly, but then looked quickly up at me. "Of course," he intoned solemnly, "I would never do anything dishonest. I serve the ladies of the harvest, and they want me to be good and kind." The words sounded like he'd repeated them many times, but his broad grin hindered the seriousness of his words, and I laughed.

"Isn't there some way we can go into town and still do good?" I asked him, liking the idea of seeing more of Greece than the airport and the fields around Demeter's house.

He thought for a moment. "I suppose we could go to the farmers' market, and bless the wares there."

"Weren't all the farmers here last night to receive a blessing?"

He looked at me strangely, and I felt foolish and exposed. "You know they weren't. Every year, fewer and fewer folk bring their harvest to you and your mother. You told me so yourself, just last week."

I thought quickly. "So I did. I just wanted to see if you remembered what I had said."

He nodded eagerly. "You said that the old ways are not

remembered because people think they can survive without magic."

I looked at him sternly. "And do you think we can survive without magic?"

The boy shook his head vigorously. "Never! Without magic, how could I do this?" He conjured up a toy, a small wooden frog. It sat on his palm and he tapped it solemnly with his index finger three times. The frog blinked its eyes, and croaked.

I laughed and clapped, impressed. The boy hadn't brought the toy to life, but he'd used a trick I hadn't seen before to animate the wooden figure. I leaned forward, curious, and the frog froze.

"You're very good at that."

"I've been practicing since you showed me last fall. I finally got it right!" He beamed up at me proudly, and I felt a twinge of guilt for taking this moment away from Persephone. My guilt was quickly replaced with joy that I was here, in Greece, watching a child do magic when I could have been in North Carolina, fighting Rochelle for my life. I drew a deep breath and sighed happily.

"We don't have to go to town," the boy said. "If you are tired, mistress, we could just walk in the field."

We headed away from the house, leaving it and the cave behind. "No, I'm not tired. Why don't you tell me a story?" An idea had formed in my mind, and I hoped I would be able to figure out who the boy was without asking.

He skipped eagerly beside me. "What kind of story? One about the gods?"

I laughed. "No, tell me a story about you. Tell it to me like it is about somebody else, like a great storyteller." Maybe he would tell me his name, at the very least.

"Well," he began thoughtfully, "once there was a boy named Dennis. He was a naughty little boy; his mother was always telling him so." I laughed, and Dennis frowned at me sternly. "Please don't interrupt, m'lady."

"I'm sorry. Go on, Dennis. Tell your story."

At least I knew his name. We were passing through the vineyard, and the morning sun was already baking the earth. I felt warm and content as I listened to Dennis talk.

Dennis continued, "His mother was a Witch-woman, and she learned her magic from Dionysus. She named her son after her patron."

I glanced down at the boy beside me. If his mother was a Witch, that might explain his magical abilities. But what was a devotee of Dionysus doing running around the fields with Demeter and Persephone?

Dennis looked up at me and winked. "But the boy grew up with a liking for other types of magic, and it wasn't long before a great lady found him outside her window."

"Which great lady found the boy, Dennis?"

He looked up at me and smiled. "It was your mother. I was listening to her cry after you had journeyed back to the Underworld—" He broke off and frowned. "You made me mess up the story!"

My heart contracted with grief for Demeter, but I ruffled his hair playfully. "But you know the best storytellers make their audience wait to hear the end of the tale. I will wait, and when you are ready, you can finish the story."

He smiled up at me, and for the first time I realized what it might have been like to grow up with a younger brother. I grinned at him.

"I'll race you to the hill." The words had barely left my mouth before he was off like a shot, running up the hill. I started to run after him, calling, "Dennis! That's not fair! Don't cheat!"

He laughed and slowed down, letting me reach the hill at the same moment.

"It's a tie!" I called jubilantly.

He shook his head. "No, m'lady. There cannot be ties between gods and men. You win, again."

31

Dennis and I spent the morning in the farmers' market, where I tried to summon up the same magic I had used in the field the night before. I managed to bless a couple of the farmers, but the Red sparks weren't very bright, and after a few minutes, I felt the energy drain out of me. Maybe I had been using too much magic lately, between the glamour and the spell in the field. I tried not to let it bother me, and I focused on enjoying the market and Dennis's company. At noon, we shared a meal of bread, olives, and goat cheese, sitting on the fountain in the middle of the market.

I sent Dennis home after lunch and returned to the cottage. I hoped Demeter wouldn't be back yet; there were some things I wanted to try out, but I needed to be alone. Luckily, the cottage was empty when I walked in. I shut the door firmly behind me and considered setting up a ward. Instead, I cast a spell around the cottage that would let me know if anyone was approaching. It wouldn't protect me the way a ward would, but it also wouldn't make Demeter suspicious if she came back to the house early.

Persephone had sent me to Greece to escape from Rochelle and Hecate, but she'd also wanted me to learn more about my power. "It's hard to learn when you are afraid," she'd pointed out. "In Greece, you will have nothing to fear."

I wasn't sure I agreed with her—I was terrified that someone would figure out that I was a fraud and alert Hecate—but I had to admit that for the moment, I wasn't in as much danger as I would have been at home. Ever since I'd declared to Red magic, I'd been too busy running and trying to defend myself to really figure anything out. I intended to change that, starting now. It was time I understood more about Red magic, and I wanted to start by determining the boundaries of my own power.

I fiddled with a small, pointed stone I had picked up on my walk back to the house. It was almost prism-shaped, and it felt evenly balanced. It would do nicely for the work I had in mind. I removed my bag from my waist and pulled out a thin piece of red string. I tied the string around the rock and let it dangle between my first two fingers. The rock spun until the thread hung straight, and then it stopped moving. Perfect. I should be able to use it as a pendulum.

I crossed the room to the bookshelf and removed the old map. Sitting down at the edge of the hearth, I spread the map out on the floor in front of me. Justin and I had tried to figure out which region I controlled, and because I'd successfully averted the hurricane, I thought the Caribbean must be part of my territory. I wasn't sure where else, though, and before I could start working to balance chaos, I had to know where to concentrate my energies. I just hoped that my idea would work; I couldn't afford to waste an afternoon playing around.

Lifting the stone, I leaned forward and held my arm stiff. Once the stone hung still on the thread, I shifted my weight and gently began to move the pendulum over the spot that should have been the Caribbean islands. The stone started swinging in small, clockwise circles. I paused for a moment, and the circles became more precise. *Good.* It was working.

Trying to be patient, I moved south on the map, pausing every few inches. The stone kept swinging. As I circled the continent of South America, the stone slowed. I moved my hand back and cut across the land instead of going over the water, and the stone began swaying again. Meticulously, I traced the map. I was surprised that the stone didn't respond when I hugged the western border of South America. I moved my hand slowly out over the water, but the stone didn't start swaying again until I came close to the eastern border of Australia.

When I was done, I had a rough idea of the territory that was under my control, and I shuddered. It appeared that I had power over most of South and North America, part of Malaysia, and the eastern edge of Asia, including the island of Japan.

That was a lot more than Justin or I had thought. I felt a pang when I realized I couldn't tell him what I'd learned. I doubted if he'd ever talk to me again. Shaking my head, I steered my thoughts in another direction. I couldn't get bogged down worrying about Justin or anything back at home. Persephone had sent me here to figure out how to use my power, and I needed to focus on that.

Just then, I felt a tingle on my neck. It spread down my back, and I realized it was the spell I had cast around the house. Someone was coming. Quickly, I rolled the map up and returned it to the shelf. I released the spell and dropped the pendulum into my bag as the cottage door opened.

I smiled at Demeter as she came inside. "You're home early." I had no idea if this was true, but the sun was still up, and I remembered that Persephone had told me her mother was usually working for the entire day during the harvest.

She smiled at me. "I wanted to spend some more time with you."

My palms started to sweat and I worried that Demeter had discovered my subterfuge, but then I remembered that Persephone was due to return to the Underworld soon. I relaxed slightly.

"Will you walk with me, daughter?"

I nodded and crossed the room. She clasped my hand tightly, and there was a flicker of confusion on her face for a moment. I pulled my hand away, and her face returned to normal. She shook her head as if trying to get rid of a mosquito, and we turned and walked around the side of the house. She'd had no problem touching me last night; what if the glamour was starting to wear off? I tried not to panic as I followed her outside.

Demeter led me to the meadow behind the house. In

the late afternoon light, it looked like a field of gold and precious jewels.

"I'd like to check on the hives, if you don't mind." Demeter spoke softly, not looking at me.

"That's fine." I glanced down at my thin tunic and trousers, worried. I hoped my glamour could fool bees.

A faint hum filled the air, like a helicopter in the distance, as seven boxy hives came into sight at the edge of the clearing.

Demeter crossed confidently and removed the lid of one of the boxes. The hum got louder and more distinct, and I realized I was hearing thousands of bees. The air seemed to vibrate, and my nose tingled. Demeter bent lovingly over the hive and pulled out a comb, examining it closely.

"We should have one more harvest of honey before they begin to sleep for the winter." I leaned forward, interested despite my fear of being stung. The bees were massed on the comb, working quickly and efficiently. There was one tremendous bee in the upper-left corner; it was easily as long as the first two joints of my finger.

"That's the queen, isn't it?" I felt foolish for my question. Persephone had obviously helped her mother many times, and wouldn't need to be told which bee was the queen of the hive. But I couldn't help myself; there was so much I wanted to ask Demeter. I was carefully storing away everything she said so I could tell Mom once I returned home. She'd want to hear all about it, I was sure.

Demeter didn't seem surprised by my question. "All the other bees in the hive live to serve her. None of them would dream of challenging their queen." Her deep green eyes looked into mine and I felt a chill. "Have you felt any tremors in your magic, lately, daughter?"

I looked down at the hive, trying to keep my face neutral. "What kind of tremors?"

"I have been told that you offered help to a new Red. Is that true?"

I laughed nervously. "We all did. Kali, Pele, even I were vying for her attention. It is difficult to be a patron of Red magic, Mother. We only ever have the chance for three devotees. There are never enough Red Witches to go around." I hoped that Persephone would have said something like that, and I tried to keep my voice casual. My heart was pounding so loudly that I was sure Demeter could hear it.

Demeter nodded slowly. "I understand the girl did not pick you."

I swallowed, wondering how much Demeter already knew. "No. She vowed to our cousin, Aphrodite. A waste of Red magic, if you ask me."

Demeter replaced the comb and moved on to the next hive. "Still, you had dealings with the girl. Hecate would like to question you."

"Why?" My arms grew cold and I struggled to keep my voice steady. Demeter shrugged, looking down at the bees.

"Evidently, this girl is strong. Hecate wants to learn more about her."

I was strong? That was good to know. "Why would this concern Hecate? Isn't she above all forms of magic?" I took a stab, hoping that my encounters with Hecate hadn't reached Demeter's ears.

She looked at me. "Hecate is above all magics, but *of* them. She is the Queen of Witches, after all. Of course she is taking an interest in this new child."

Silently, I walked to another hive. Demeter closed the one she was checking and followed me. "You know that I owe Hecate a great debt. She was the only one who was brave enough to tell me your fate. I won't have you treating her rudely just because you weren't able to win this mortal's devotion."

I shook my head, looking down. "Of course I will treat Hecate with all respect."

Demeter nodded. "Good. She should be here soon."

My head jerked up and I fought to keep the panic from my voice. "Soon? How soon?" Had Demeter figured out who I really was?

Demeter sighed. "She'll be here before you begin your descent, to escort you as she always does."

This was news to me. Why hadn't Persephone warned me about this? Maybe she'd figured we would swap places again before the dark goddess arrived. How would I hope to fool Hecate? Forcing myself to remain calm, I nodded at Demeter.

The goddess took a few steps away from me, keeping her face

averted, but her words were full of pain. "Must you really leave me?"

Gods, Persephone had to put up with this whining every year? How awful. I mean, I felt bad for Demeter, but she needed to get over it already. Still, I tried to keep my response kind. "There must be balance. It can't always be springtime." I held out my arms and hugged the goddess. "But I will be back. I always am."

Demeter nodded, stroking my hair. "I still do not understand the choice you made, daughter, and I have had centuries to think it through. I do not know what love you bear for my brother in his cold realm, but you have borne your choice like a woman." She sighed. "I simply cannot stop thinking of you as the child you once were."

"But I have to live with my choices. And so do you." My voice shook, and Demeter touched my cheek gently.

"Yes, little one. I live with your choice every day."

32

The next week was tense. Every day, I worried that Hecate would appear in the cottage, denouncing me and demanding that Demeter turn me over to her. I had no doubt that Demeter would obey Hecate. Persephone had been wise not to trust her mother with my secret.

But Hecate didn't appear, and Demeter and I spent the time walking the fields and speaking with the farmers who were her devotees. Dennis followed me everywhere, and although I teased him and chased him off each day, I secretly enjoyed his company. I would miss him when I returned to my own world.

Each afternoon, I arrived back at the cottage before Demeter and tried to practice Red magic. I could now sense its force if I was still, and I was beginning to feel the differences between Red magic and anything else. Red magic felt like a jolt of electricity, and it was the strongest force, but that didn't mean I couldn't feel the gentle tug of Green magic, or the warmth of White magic. One day, I even felt a sickening pull in my stomach that I assumed must be Black magic, but I shied away from that quickly, thinking of Rochelle. I didn't want to end up like her, and while I knew rationally that Black magic had nothing to do with her being power hungry, she had proved my parents' prejudices when she tried to kill me. Black or Red, whatever she was, she'd gone from being my best friend to my enemy, and I didn't want to be anything like her.

Before, I had only used Red magic when I was frightened, when I was desperate, or when I was angry. Now, in the small house in Greece, I tried to call upon Red magic when I was calm and quiet. It was hard. The more I tried, the more I wondered if it would be impossible to separate Red magic from chaotic emotion. I didn't want to do anything too dramatic, but I tried to light the hearth fire each evening and failed.

After I had been in Demeter's house for a week, I got particularly frustrated.

"What good does any of this do, if I don't know how to use it?" I slammed my hand down on the table in frustration. The fire leaped when my fist hit the wood, and I stared into the now-dancing flames. I took a step closer to the fire, excited. As a test, I tried to breathe slowly and evenly. As my mind slowed, the flames fell.

Was I going about this all wrong? Maybe I shouldn't try to distance strong emotion from Red magic; maybe the two were irrevocably bound. I didn't want to use Red magic irrationally, though. Instead of focusing on frustration, I stared at the fire and tried to call to mind the fear I felt of Hecate. The fire surged again.

Not all emotions were destructive, I reasoned. Staring at the flames, I pictured Justin's face, and for the first time I allowed myself to fully feel the emotions he stirred in me. Frustration and embarrassment swelled through me as I remembered his rejection. My cheeks burned, but the fire leaped high on the hearth, so I let myself keep retracing the emotions of our relationship. The relief I felt when Justin accepted my declaration of Red magic without question or judgment, the anger I felt when he refused to believe that I'd had nothing to do with the accident at the coffee shop. Images flooded my mind, and my heart raced. I focused on the feeling of his lips on mine after I cast the love spell, ignoring the fact that I wasn't likely to feel that again.

A loud boom brought me back to reality. The fire had grown so hot and the flames had gone so high that the kettle over the hearth had imploded. I fought for a calm state of mind, and the flames gradually dropped down.

Taking a rag from beside the hearth, I reached in and tried to rescue the remains of the kettle. The lump of smoldering iron looked like a misshapen skull, and I carried it out of the cottage gingerly. I flung it into the field and dusted my hands, feeling satisfied; I had made some progress, even if I had destroyed the kettle. It would be easy enough to walk into town and purchase a new one.

Smiling, I turned back to the house, but a sound in the grass stopped me. I turned slowly and spotted Dennis, who was running frantically toward the vineyard. I called to him, but he only ran faster. I didn't know how much he had seen, but I knew I wouldn't be able to keep up my disguise much longer. Dennis had clearly seen enough to know that I wasn't Persephone, and now he'd run off to tell everyone.

Frantic, I thought of the goddess I'd traded places with. We hadn't devised any way for me to contact her if things went wrong; she had said she'd check in on me, and I had trusted her. But so far, I hadn't seen or heard anything from the goddess. I started pacing, trying to figure out what to do now that my cover had been blown.

I didn't want to run the risk of Hecate catching me, not now when I was just beginning to understand how to use my power. And if Dennis went to Demeter, it wouldn't be long before she summoned Hecate. As if in answer to my thoughts, I heard the low rumble of voices over the hill. Someone was already headed my way from the vineyard; it sounded like a large group of people. I squinted in the distance, and saw Demeter crest the hill with a withered figure in black beside her. Hecate was here! How had everything fallen apart so quickly? I forgot that Demeter had said Hecate would be arriving soon to escort me to the Underworld; all I could think was that the Queen of Witches would soon have me in her clutches.

I panicked. Turning in the opposite direction of the crowd, I ran blindly down the path. I skidded to a halt outside the cave.

I stopped, weighing my options. If Hecate had heard what Dennis had seen, I didn't stand a chance. I might be starting to learn how to control my power, but I had no doubt that she could destroy me in an instant. The last time I'd pissed her off, I'd had Aphrodite's protection, but now I was totally vulnerable. I decided to take my chances with Hades, and I plunged into the dark mouth of the cave.

It was like being buried alive. Once I was in the cave, it turned sharply downward, and all light from the entrance was gone before I had taken ten steps. I paused, panting in the dark, fighting back fear. The cave was still, but I could hear the faint whispering that had drawn me to it that first night. Hecate was somewhere behind me, out in the light. With a deep breath, I continued into the darkness.

33

I emerged into a large, dimly lit chamber after what felt like hours in the dark. The trickle of water echoed off the cavern walls, and I realized with a start that I stood on the banks of the River Styx. In Greek mythology, souls passed over the River Styx to reach the Underworld. It had never occurred to me until now that Persephone had to follow the same path as the dead to reach her husband. I shuddered, wondering how she handled such a depressing journey year after year.

Why hadn't Persephone done something to help me? I'd been in Greece for over a week; shouldn't she have checked in to make sure I was still alive? My heart constricted painfully. I should have known better than to trust any of the gods. Hadn't they all tried to use me ever since I declared to follow Red magic? Hecate clearly thought my life was worthless; she had set my best friend on me, hoping that I'd end up dead. Why had I thought Persephone would be any better?

I shivered again. What if Persephone had known this would happen from the beginning? What if her mother wasn't the only one with a strong allegiance to Hecate? Angry, I stood there on the edge of the river. My fists clenched and released, and without even realizing what I was doing, I began to weave a spell. Red sparks shot up and down my arms, singeing my skin, but I was oblivious.

The boat was almost fully formed before I noticed it. Low to the water, it was red with a lantern hung off the prow. It looked sturdy, but I hesitated. Wasn't there something weird about the water in the Underworld? I couldn't quite remember, and pieces of myth teased at the back of my mind. *Oh, well.* Hecate was worse than whatever waited for me down the river. Glancing back over my shoulder one last time, I stepped into the boat.

There was nowhere to sit, but the boat began to move with the current as soon as I was aboard. I braced myself, trying not to fall overboard, and considered my options. Clearly, I would have to deal with Hades soon, and I had better come up with a plan before I met him. Making a decision, I closed my eyes and unbound my glamour.

I had never tried wearing a glamour for so long, and my skin tingled like a day-old sunburn as the spell faded. I glanced down at my arms; they looked familiar. Taking the mirror out of the pouch at my waist, I held it up to my face. My own eyes looked back at me, my own unremarkable and mortal features. I felt strangely relieved. At least whatever happened would happen to me, not to the girl who had been pretending to be a goddess.

The river cut through cavern after cavern, and the light of the lantern allowed me to make out the features of stalactites and stalagmites around me. Everything was still, except for the gently flowing water, and I didn't see any signs of life. The air around me grew colder, and I thought wistfully of the warmth of the ratty old sweatshirt that was probably still lying in a heap beside my bed, half a world away. I shivered and wrapped my arms around my body, wishing the boat would hurry up.

In the darkness, I worked to summon Red magic. I had nothing else to do, and a faint voice in my mind whispered that I was running out of time to master my powers. I allowed myself to dwell on my fear of Hecate, banishing all thoughts of betrayal or anger. The fear filled me, and I started to shake, but when I felt like I couldn't handle it any more, I extended my arms, palms down, and tried to open myself to Red magic. The boat surged, and I staggered to keep my balance. I peered into the water, startled.

The boat, which had been drifting quietly with the current, had sped up as if I'd attached a motor to it. The inky water was choppy around me, and I could see waves peaking in my wake. I raised my arms slightly, and the boat accelerated even more. I grinned broadly.

Lowering and raising my arms like a bird learning to fly, I played with the force I had summoned. The boat went alternately slow and quick under my command. It was a heady feeling. Sparks danced on my skin, and energy surged through me. I was having so much fun that I almost didn't notice where I was.

The lamp on the boat sputtered and went out, and I found myself plunged once more into eerie darkness. Looking up, I saw the silver illumination of a tremendous gate over my head, and I dropped my arms in awe. The boat slowed to a crawl, and I didn't even try to summon up any more magic. I knew I had just crossed into the Underworld, and my skin prickled.

The boat drifted to a ratty pier and bumped against it. Taking a deep breath, I grabbed the edge of the pier and stepped off the boat. The earth felt like it was rocking under my feet, and I waited a moment for everything to right itself. I looked around, nervous.

I had come ashore near a worn footpath, lit with randomly placed torches along the cavern wall. There was no one around, but I felt sure that someone was watching my every move. Turning my head slowly, I scanned the shore, but nothing happened. Still, I felt the hairs on the back of my neck stand up, and my fingertips tingled. Someone was watching me, waiting to see what I would do.

I sucked in my breath and squared my shoulders. Without looking back at the boat, I began to walk up the path. Whatever was watching me followed: I heard a faint rustling behind me, but I didn't allow myself to look back. In a few minutes, I would meet Hades, and I needed to come up with a story fast.

The path grew brighter, and I realized that the torches along the walls had been replaced with glowing candelabra and mirrored panels. One of the mirrors looked red, and leaning in for a closer look, I saw it wasn't a mirror, but a perfectly polished gemstone. The corridor was dripping with diamonds and rubies, emeralds and sapphires, and I felt a chill in the pit of my stomach. What would a god of such wealth need from a Witch like myself?

With that thought, I entered a room that was more like a cathedral than an underground cave. The ceiling soared hundreds of feet in the air and veins of precious metal sparkled up the walls, climbing as far as I could see. Spellbound, I turned in a circle, trying to get a sense of the size of the place. A voice spoke coldly behind me.

"It is not often that the living wander into my throne room."

I froze, still staring at the ceiling. Whispering a prayer to all the gods I'd ever heard about, I turned slowly to face Hades.

My first thought was that the Lord of the Dead looked sad. His robes blended into the cavern behind him, and at first I couldn't tell whether he was sitting or standing. But his face! His eyes looked like he hadn't slept in weeks, and the hard lines around his mouth spoke of a lifetime of sorrows. He rustled, and I realized he had been sitting. Now he towered over me. Gods, he was tall!

I knelt before him, lowering my head. I knew that, with the exception of Hecate, I was standing before a god more powerful than any I had encountered so far, and I didn't want to do anything to ignite his temper. Looking at the ground, I spoke. I had decided to keep it simple.

"Persephone sent me to you. My name is Darlena, and I am a Red Witch."

My words echoed off the cavern walls, taunting me. Hades said nothing.

I risked a glance up at his hard, impassive face. His eyes were the only part of him that seemed alive: they glittered as he looked down at me. Afraid that I had made a horrible mistake, I quickly looked down. The silence stretched, and I began counting my breaths, trying to calm the fears that were growing inside me.

"You are younger than I expected." Hades' voice was rough and deep, and his words resonated in the empty cave. I kept my head down, but I nodded slightly. "I knew there was much fuss being made over you, but I did not expect such an untried child."

I clenched my fist at his words, but said nothing. Hades could call me whatever he wanted, as long as he didn't blow me to smithereens or hand me over to Hecate.

"What do you understand about Red magic?"

Surprised at his question, I looked up. Hades sat back down and leaned forward slightly, his eyes fixed on my face. It seemed like every god I'd met had asked me that question, and they all expected a different answer. I eyed him, trying to gauge my best response, but his face gave nothing away.

"I know that it's the magic of chaos," I answered cautiously. He waited, his stare unwavering, so I continued. "It can be used to cause death, but it can also be used to manipulate love and other less deadly emotions."

"You think that love is not a deadly force?" His voice grated against my ears, and I paused, feeling trapped. "You will answer me, Witch."

I swallowed. "I used to think love wasn't very powerful." I paused, remembering Justin's face when he realized I had cast a love spell on him. "Now, I'm not so sure."

Hades seemed satisfied with this answer: his face didn't change, but he sat back in his throne slightly, as if he was relaxing. "What have you done since you became a Red Witch?"

I closed my eyes, thinking back to all the events of the previous few weeks. "I have caused harm, and I have protected myself." I didn't want to go into any detail, but I felt sure I didn't have to. Hades had known about me somehow, and I assumed he knew the answers to his questions before he even asked them. This felt like a test of some kind, but I couldn't tell if I was passing or failing.

Then he asked, "Why have you come here to me?"

Would it be better for me to lie? I didn't want to tell him that I had started to worry that his wife had betrayed me, but I couldn't leave her out of my explanation completely. Choosing my words carefully, I said, "Persephone sent me here. She and I had discussed finding a way to use Red magic to create balance, not chaos."

Hades nodded, and I blinked, startled. I had begun to get used to talking to a man as stiff as a statue. He gestured curtly with his hand, and I felt my legs move without my will, pushing me up off the floor into a standing position.

"Death is the ultimate balance, Witch. Would you seek to cheat me of my kingdom?"

I shook my head frantically. "Never. Persephone and I ... I want to find a balance for the living. I would never presume to control the dead."

"And yet, by your own admission, the magic you work causes death."

"But it doesn't have to!" Too frightened to check my words, I plowed ahead. "The first time I used Red magic, Hecate told me I had altered a fated pattern of death. I stopped death once, and I know I could do it again."

A faint smirk played about his lips. "Are you standing here, in my realm, telling me that you want to prevent death? Doesn't that worry you at all, Witch?"

He was right; I should have been terrified. I took a chance. "Everyone dies eventually. Does it matter to you if you get their souls now, or in a few years?"

There was silence in the cavern, and I was afraid I had gone too far. Then, all of a sudden, Hades threw back his head and laughed. His eyes crinkled up and his laughter echoed in the throne room. Suddenly, Hades seemed like a badly dressed version of Santa Claus. I stared at him, stunned.

When he finished laughing, he rose. "Little Witch, you are not as foolish as I thought. You are right; it matters not to me when the dead enter my realm. And"—his voice softened—"I know that my wife has often expressed a desire for mortals to live their lives in some degree of peace." He strode purposefully toward me. "You may stay here as long as you need. But know this: the living do not easily come and go among the dead. I do not know how long I will be able to offer you shelter without some lasting harm befalling you."

Hades held out his hand to me and I took it, uncertainly. His flesh was thin and cold, and I tried not to flinch. We shook hands once, solemnly, but I couldn't help wondering whether his final statement had been a warning or a threat.

34

Hades led me from the throne room along a narrow passageway. "I cannot offer you accommodations such as you may be used to, but until Persephone makes her journey to me, you may use her rooms as your own."

"Thank you." I hesitated, not wanting to ask a foolish question. "What will I do while I am here?"

He glanced at me, almost smiling. "I seem to recall that you are highly desirable to certain gods, including that old crone Hecate." I nodded nervously. "Rest assured that none can harm you here. Persephone sent you to me to seek sanctuary, and I gladly offer it. While you are here, you will practice your magic."

"Thank you. If I had time to practice—" I broke off, not wanting to think about Rochelle and Hecate hunting me and waiting for me back in the world. Things wouldn't be pretty once I went home, but I was determined to do better the next time I had to face Rochelle. Hades nodded, hearing my thoughts.

"When you leave my realm, you will again have adversaries to face. But for now, little Witch, you have time to rest, to strengthen, and to learn." We had reached a carved wooden door fitted snugly into the cave wall. "I'll leave you here to get your bearings. Feel free to use anything in these rooms."

I hesitated for a moment. "What will I do for food?" I didn't want to offend him, but I needed to ask; what if he decided he wanted to keep me there in the Underworld? I wouldn't fall for the same trick that had bound Persephone.

Hades chuckled. "Don't worry, I have no desire to trap a second wife. I will have some brought from aboveground." I must have looked skeptical, because he sighed in exasperation. "Witch, I am not one for breaking faith. I have offered you sanctuary because of my wife, and I will not renege on that promise. As long as you are in my realm, you will be safe from all harm."

"Thank you. I didn't mean to offend you." I tried to smile.

Hades looked sad. "Mortals rarely trust me. I should not have expected otherwise."

Without another word he turned and stalked back toward the throne room. I felt bad for him, and I resolved that I would try to trust him. He'd been kind to me so far, and just because I had started to be suspicious of everyone didn't mean that they were all out to get me. Hades had no reason to be my enemy, and from the way he had talked about Hecate, I wondered if he might even be my ally. It must be hard to be a god who no one trusts. I doubted that any Witches ever took Hades as a patron. Was it lonely? He seemed lonely, but maybe that was just because Persephone wasn't here. Either way, I liked him. When he was out of sight, I opened the door to Persephone's rooms.

The smell of dust rushed to greet me, and I coughed. Cautiously, I entered the room. Dried flowers were everywhere, arranged in vases, hanging from the ceiling, strewn across the floor. It looked like a postponed funeral, and I felt a twinge of sympathy for Persephone. Obviously, she missed her life aboveground: she'd tried to recreate springtime here in her cave, but the flowers were brown and battered. Petals and leaves crunched under my feet as I explored the vast chambers.

The ceiling of the first room was so high I almost couldn't see it. It must have reached all the way to the top surface of the earth, because a jagged skylight cut into the ceiling allowed a patch of natural light into the room. There were candle stubs on the furniture, and an unlit torch waited by the door that led into the next room.

That room was darker; evidently, Hades' architect had only felt like installing one skylight. Squinting, I waited while my eyes adjusted to the dim light, but the room didn't look very interesting. There wasn't much in it, just a full-length mirror in an ornate wooden frame, and a simple square table. The surface of the table was empty, but something on the floor caught my eye. It was blurry, but I could just make out the smudged outline of a white circle in the center of the floor. I didn't walk near the circle; I recognized a magical workspace when I saw one, and I didn't know what kind of protections Persephone might have left in place. Crossing the room carefully, I passed through another doorway.

The third room had an odd, bluish light. It took me a minute to realize that instead of a skylight, this room boasted a wall of glass looking out over a river. I assumed it must be the Styx, but the part that flowed beneath Persephone's chamber looked nothing like the inky water that had brought me to Hades. Here, the river was crystal clear, and the banks were awash with color. At first, I thought the colors were flowers, blossoming impossibly underground, but then a sparkle caught my eye. The banks of the river were lined with piles of gemstones, like the ones in the walls of Hades' throne room.

As I stared at the gems in amazement, a figure caught my eye. I couldn't tell whether it was a man or a woman, but whoever it was looked too frail to be pushing such a large wheelbarrow. The figure stopped at the bank, overturned the wheelbarrow, and moved off. As it moved, it flickered like a dying lightbulb, and I wondered if I had just spotted one of the dead. I made a mental note to ask Hades about the worker with the wheelbarrow, then turned to continue my explorations.

There was a low, arched doorway leading out of the room, and I had to duck to avoid hitting my head. The cavern I now found myself in was almost perfectly circular, and the walls sparkled with veins of gold. I stood in the center of the room and turned in a slow circle, marveling at the wealth that surrounded me. The room didn't have any furniture, but rich red pillows covered the floor invitingly. Feeling my shoulders relax for the first time in weeks, I sank to the floor and curled up like a cat on the cushions. I was asleep almost instantly.

I don't know how long I slept, but when I finally woke up, I had a disorienting moment of fear. I couldn't remember anything for an instant: not where I was, not even who I was. The sensation passed almost instantly, and I wondered if I'd imagined it. Maybe the Underworld was playing tricks with my memory. I shook myself and stood up. The room was dark, but every so often the gold in the walls would reflect a shimmer of light from the adjoining room. Remembering the view of the river, I went back to the window in that room.

The gems that had been piled haphazardly when I first arrived were now arranged into beautiful patterns. Hypnotic swirls of rubies skirted around geometric patches of sapphires, and I stared, transfixed. It was like a sand painting or a mosaic made from precious stones. I'd never seen anything like it.

"Do you think she will like it?" Hades spoke from behind me, and I jumped, startled. He hesitated in the doorway between the magic room and this one, and I looked at him curiously.

"Who?" I asked dumbly.

He sighed, still lingering at the entrance to the room. "Persephone."

I looked out the window again. "It's amazing."

"But will it please her?" he asked anxiously.

I didn't know what to say. "I don't know her that well. I mean, I just met her when I declared—" I broke off.

His face fell, and I felt like I had just told a child that he would never get a puppy. I took a few steps toward him, trying to think of something to say.

When I moved, his eyes refocused and the vulnerability I thought I had seen was gone instantly, replaced by his imposing, immovable mask. "How do you find your accommodations?"

I crossed my arms. "Fine. But I still don't know what I should do here."

"Use the golden room for sleep, as I see you already have." I self-consciously ran my hand through my hair, trying to imagine what I must look like. "For magic, work in this space." He gestured to the room behind him.

"Um," I interjected, "not to be rude, but isn't that her workspace? Witches don't usually share their magic with anyone."

"She is not here to decide, but since she sent you to me, I will decide for her. You will practice your Red craft there. Maybe," he added, "your own work will be aided because it is her workspace."

I nodded. Persephone was a goddess of Red magic, and that room was sure to retain some residual energy from whatever spells she had cast. Still, I was nervous about invading her space; it already felt weird enough to be hanging out in her home with her husband. Hopefully, she wouldn't mind. "What magic should I do?"

He looked at me hard. "You want to find balance. Start practicing."

"But I don't even have an idea of where to start!"

"Little Witch, you told me yourself that Red magic brings chaos and destruction. Have you any idea of the realm your powers will affect?"

Thinking back to the map in Demeter's cottage, I nodded slowly.

Hades bared his teeth in a grin. "Good. Focus your efforts on effecting change in that region."

"But it's huge! What do I focus on?"

Hades sighed. "I cannot tell you how to do this, but I can tell you that I am expecting many new souls very soon. As we speak, the ground is quaking in a small yet mighty island. The tremors even rattle the red sun." He opened his eyes wide, as if he was trying to communicate something to me without speaking, but I just stared at him in confusion. Was he talking about an earthquake? Would I be able to stop it like I'd stopped the hurricane? But where was it?

Hades saw my confusion and sighed. Without another word, he turned and left the cavern. I heard the outer door close behind him and I let out a groan of frustration.

"I don't know how I'm supposed to do anything if no one will really help me!" My words filled the empty room, and I felt foolish for having spoken. Nervously, I crossed into the workspace. For a minute, I lingered at the edge of the circle, but I didn't feel any warning zaps of magic, so I crossed the line. Nothing happened, and I exhaled in relief. Maybe Persephone hadn't bothered to ward her space, since no one but her would ever wander into the Underworld. But I was there now, and I couldn't let the opportunity to work without distraction go to waste.

I sat down on the floor in the center of the white circle and tried to focus. There wasn't much in the room to distract me, but I couldn't keep my eyes off the mirror. Seated on the floor as I was, I could see my full reflection just two feet away from me. I looked awful.

While I was studying the dark circles under my eyes, I started to feel dizzy. My image in the mirror grew fuzzy and doubled. I leaned closer, and, with a shock, I realized that there were two figures reflected in the mirror. I turned quickly to look over my shoulder, but the room was empty. When I looked back, my own image was completely gone, replaced by a woman in a long, white kimono. She glowed as if lit from within, and I realized that she must be a goddess. I had thought I would be safe here; had Hades set me up?

"Who are you?" I whispered, frantically trying to draw on enough energy to protect myself if needed.

The beautiful woman shook her head sadly. "I should have known you would not know me. You are too fond of the Greek gods, Darlena, and you have ignored the rest of us."

She spread her arms out, palms up, and nodded her head deeply. Her formal bow tugged at my memory, and I nodded back, wary; although her actions seemed to indicate she would do me no harm, I had learned the hard way not to trust the gods.

"I am Amaterasu, keeper of the noonday sun, and throne mother to the nation of Japan."

"Japan!" I blurted. "That must be what Hades meant."

Amaterasu nodded, her face weary and lined with trouble. "He knows that my people are suffering. But they are also your people, Darlena."

I stared at her in confusion. How could the people of Japan have anything to do with me? Then I remembered the map in Demeter's house where I had traced the boundaries of my power. Japan lay within my control. They were my people; I was their Red Witch. I squared my shoulders. "What can I do?"

"You cannot stop the quake, for the first rumbles have already subsided. But you must stop the Black magic at work in my land!"

"But I don't understand!"

"Earthquakes are a part of life to my people. They do not expect to live without seeing a dozen. They have learned, though, to build homes that are strong. They have many systems in place to ensure the safety of as many people as possible, no matter what the rolling earth may do to them. But," she wailed, her eyes brimming with tears, "some Black force has been at work in my land. The houses that should withstand a century of abuse are falling like children's toys at the first tremor."

Could this possibly be the work of Rochelle? I shuddered, thinking about the damage a normal earthquake could cause. How much worse would it be if magic played a role?

"You are the only one who can abate the chaos. The quake will happen, for it has already begun, but what magnitude it will be rests in your hands. Without you, I fear this disaster will topple my nation into the sea once and for all."

Shaking, I drew a deep breath. "I don't know if I can do anything. But I'll try."

A sad smile filled Amaterasu's face before she faded from the mirror. It was empty for a moment, and then I was once again staring at my own reflection.

"So," I said to myself, "Rochelle thinks she can control chaos. She's not a Red Witch yet, and she won't be. Not if I can help it." Closing my eyes, I opened myself to the anger I felt at Rochelle's betrayal. How dare she meddle with the lands under my control? Even though I'd never thought about Japan before, I was filled with a fierce protectiveness at the thought of Rochelle harming anyone within my third of the world. I felt my hands tingling with power, and Red sparks filled the air.

I lifted my hands in front of me and began to shape the power into a sphere between my hands. Swirling Red sparks became visible as I moved my hands faster and faster. When I could clearly see the red ball, I stilled for a moment, just holding it and feeling it pulse with energy. The energy was angry, vengeful, and dangerous, and I suddenly knew that this would only make the quake worse. What was I thinking?

I looked around the room, searching for a place to dispose of the energy ball I had created, but I realized I was stuck with it. Exhaling in frustration, I held the ball, trying to shift my focus from Rochelle. I thought of my parents, and Justin, and slowly the ball began to grow warm. It wasn't sparking anymore, but it was glowing with a steady light. Now it looked more like a pink flower. Had I calmed it down? It certainly looked less dangerous, and I hoped it was strong enough to do what I wanted.

I didn't have time to try and figure out if I was doing this right.

Cupping the sphere gently in my hands, I lowered it to the earth floor of the cave. I hesitated for a moment, trying to fill my mind with the image of the Japanese goddess, hoping that focusing on her would help me direct the energy to her island. Taking a deep breath, I pushed the glowing ball into the ground until it disappeared completely. I held my hands there, pressed to the ground, counting slowly. I didn't know how long the spell might take, so I stayed there until my count reached three hundred.

Hesitantly, I lifted my hands. The room was absolutely still. I glanced once more at the mirror, but all I saw was my own tired face. Whatever I had done, I hoped it wouldn't bring more harm. I was trying so hard to use Red magic for good, but I felt lost. There was no one to guide me, and I knew that guessing in magic could sometimes be as dangerous as malicious intent.

"Please, let it be enough," I whispered to my ragged reflection.

35

I didn't know how long I'd have to wait to see if my spell had any effect, but I didn't want to wait locked in Persephone's rooms. Nervously, I headed into the corridor and turned in the direction opposite the throne room. The passage soon widened and I found myself once again walking along the River Styx, but this time I was far from alone.

Across the water, I could make out the forms of hundreds of people—but just barely. I squinted, but they looked wispy. They reminded me of the figure I'd seen with the wheelbarrow, and, up close, my thoughts were confirmed: I was looking at the dead. I stood for a moment, staring at them in shock. *Is this what happens after death? We just become wispy spirits, like smoke?* I shuddered at the thought.

While I stood there, some of the dead noticed me and began to move closer to the bank of the river. Not all of them came forward, but two dozen or so did. Entranced, I moved closer, too, ending with my feet just inches away from the river. We studied each other. I saw old faces and young faces, and as I peered at the dead, my heart dropped out of my chest.

Directly across the river from me was a young boy. His features were blurry, but I was absolutely certain that it was Dennis.

"Dennis!" I called, waving frantically. The boy glanced at me and drifted away. I started to follow him, but a rough hand on my arm pulled me back. I spun around, angry.

"Don't step in the water, little Witch." Hades spoke softly, but his words were firm. "The living do not cross that river twice."

"But I think I know that boy!" I pointed across the river, where Dennis had vanished.

Hades looked at me in pity. "All of the living know someone among the dead. That doesn't mean that they come here, trying to converse with the ones on the other side." He pulled on my arm, forcing me to come a few feet away from the river, but I dug in my heels.

"But that boy was alive before I came here!" What had happened to him after he saw me destroy the kettle?

"Death comes suddenly, sometimes. Have you not seen this with your Red magic?"

I paused, swallowing a lump in my throat as I remembered the car accident. "Yes. But that boy helped me."

Hades looked moderately interested. "And you say you saw him just before coming here?"

I nodded. "His name is Dennis, and he helped Persephone and her mother with the harvest." Had he died because of me?

Hades brooded for a moment. "I do not usually inquire about the fate of the souls in my keeping, but I will make an exception in his case, if you like." His eyes searched my face. "Are you worried that his death is in some way connected to you?"

His words echoed my own fears, and I nodded.

Hades tilted my chin up with his hand and looked at me. "You are a magic worker, and a Red Witch. There will be many souls in my realm as a result of your actions." I tried to jerk my face away, not wanting to listen to him, but he held me firmly. "These things you will have to bear. Magic never comes without a price."

Finally he released me and I rubbed my arms, suddenly cold.

"Come," he said, "there has been food delivered from above, and I am sure you are hungry."

I looked back once at the river, searching the bank for Dennis. I hoped it wasn't him, but the more I thought about it, the more sure I became. My stomach felt hollow when Hades put his hand on my elbow and led me away.

"I will inquire about the boy. Now come with me."

The food Hades presented me with could have fed an army. I didn't think I could eat, but as soon as I smelled the food, I felt my stomach grumble in response. I realized that the last meal I remembered was breakfast in Demeter's cottage. It had been at least a day, if not more. I'd lost track of time since I got to the Underworld.

Hungrily, I tore into a loaf of bread and offered a chunk to Hades. He recoiled as if I'd offered him poison.

"I cannot partake of mortal fare. Eat your fill."

"But there's so much! I can't possibly eat all this." I spoke with my mouth full of bread, and Hades cocked an eyebrow.

"And I cannot possibly eat any of it. Eat, Witch. Then I would suggest that you return to my wife's chambers; it would not do well for you to fall into the river when I have offered you safety."

"Will you tell me as soon as you know anything about Dennis?"

He nodded. "I will."

I grabbed an apple, chewing thoughtfully. "I guess I'll go back and practice some more."

Hades hesitated. "Have you already been working with magic?"

I nodded. "I think I figured out what you meant earlier, about the land of the red sun. I tried to do what I could to slow the disaster."

He held up his hand and I fell silent. "I do not need to know too much about you, Witch. It is enough that I know your name and your magic."

I understood. Even my own mother hadn't wanted to know the details of Red magic. "How will I know if I've done any good? Do you get news reports from the outside world?"

Hades laughed harshly. "If you have done anything lasting, I am sure we will hear of it."

***

When I returned to Persephone's chambers, I slept again in the gold room. I woke feeling refreshed, and the outer cavern was dimly lit, as before, so I decided to assume it was another day.

My stomach agreed with me, growling loudly as soon as I sat up. Smoothing my hair and rumpled clothes, I headed toward the throne room to ask Hades for some breakfast. I also hoped he'd found out something about Dennis. As I drew near, however, a screeching voice echoing around the cavern made me freeze in the tunnel.

"I know you have her, you old fool. Hand her over now or suffer my wrath."

Hecate's words sent chills up my spine, and I crept along the corridor, hoping to catch a glimpse of the angry goddess. Hades, however, didn't sound at all fazed by her threat.

"Hecate, you know that your words have no force here. I allow you to enter my realm at will, but once here, you are as powerless as those dead souls across the river." Hades chuckled. "And you must think I'm a complete idiot if you believe I'd ever face you aboveground. No, Witch, you can do me no harm."

"She's mine! Red magic is of no interest to you. Give her to me!"

I peeked around the wall. Hecate stood before Hades, her robes seething around her like mist. Hades was seated casually on his throne, his face the expressionless mask he had worn when I first met him. I gulped, hoping Hecate wouldn't turn around. Despite the danger, I kept listening. I had to know what they said to each other.

"Magic is of no interest to me, be it Red, Black, or White." Hades steepled his fingers under his chin and leaned forward. "However, as you well know, my wife is a patron of Red magic. So for her sake, I think I will take an interest in this girl."

Hecate laughed harshly. "Then you and your wife are both fools. This girl has already chosen her patron, and she didn't choose Persephone."

Hades stared at her impassively. "Perhaps. And perhaps you have been misinformed."

The goddess fumed. "She's weak, and foolish, and thinks she has more power than she really does. You would be doing the gods a great favor if you just surrendered her now."

"She must not be that weak; it's obvious that the girl frightens you, Hecate. Why would you be afraid of a weak little Witch?"

Speechless, Hecate glared at him for a moment. Then she turned and stalked toward the corridor where I was spying. I jerked back quickly, trying not to breathe. Even though Hades had said he would protect me, would he really do anything to stop Hecate if I were stupid enough to let her catch me?

"I know she's here. If you won't help me, I'll find her myself."

Quickly, I backed away from the throne room. As I moved up the corridor, I heard Hades' voice ring out in command.

"You have entered here as a guest, but you are now abusing my hospitality. You will leave now, or I will fetch Cerberus."

I paused, barely daring to breathe, listening for Hecate's response.

"Fine, Hades. Let it be that way. I'll leave. But it would be wise to tell your little pet," she spat, "that the longer she hides here, the more harm she will cause. And," she said, raising her voice to carry to where I stood, "if she attempts to meddle in the chaos of the world again, those she loves will very shortly be joining the ranks of your subjects across the river. Like the little boy your wife took such a liking to."

Her words hung in the air unanswered, and I recognized the foul smell of sulfur burning, the scent I had learned to associate with the Queen of Witches. Was she gone? I hesitated a moment, then stepped into the throne room, my fists clenched. The goddess was nowhere in sight.

Hades looked at me, unsurprised. "You have your answer about the boy."

I nodded. "That's what I was afraid of." I was sad to know that he had died, but I wasn't really surprised. I only hoped she hadn't done anything to my family yet.

Hades rose from the throne and crossed to me. "And you heard most of that conversation?"

I nodded again.

"What are you planning to do, little Witch?"

It was an easy choice. I looked him in the eye, unflinching. "I have to go back. I have to protect my family."

He frowned slightly. "That might not be possible."

Squaring my shoulders, I said, "I know." I had a good idea of what I was up against with Hecate, but I wouldn't hide in the Underworld, letting her do whatever she wanted on earth. I had to try to balance chaos, and I needed to keep my family safe. They would always be in danger now because of me, but at least if I were home, I could do something to protect them. Here, I was powerless.

Hades put his hand on my shoulder. "I offered you sanctuary, and that offer still stands, for as long as you desire it."

"But you can't protect them from Hecate. And you can't work Red magic. I'm the only one who can do that."

Hades raised his hand warningly. "No. Never think so much of yourself that you believe that you alone possess any powers. Remember that there is balance, even within Red magic."

I sighed. "You're right. There are three of us. But right now, I'm the only one I know who can do anything to stop Hecate."

"It might be wise of you to seek the others like you and win their support."

I nodded. It wouldn't be a bad idea to find the other Reds, but there wasn't time for that right now. Hecate had threatened my parents. "First, I have to go home."

36

The house was still standing, but the flowers along the front walk were dead and the yard looked like it hadn't been mowed in weeks. I used my key and entered through the kitchen, bracing myself to face my parents. I had a lot of explaining to do.

"Mom? Dad?" I called. "I'm home. I need to talk to you."

The house answered me with stillness. I moved through the kitchen into the living room, turning on the lights as I went.

Heading up the stairs, I felt my stomach spinning around in circles. The house felt empty; was I too late? Had Hecate already made good on her threat?

"Mom? Are you in here?" I opened the door to my parents' bedroom. The bed was made and a basket of neatly folded laundry sat on it, but there was no sign of my parents. I entered the room and looked under the bed.

"Xerxes, buddy, where are you hiding?" No green eyes glowed up at me, and no sound greeted my voice. Everything was eerily still.

Truly frightened now, I opened the door to my bedroom. The desk lamp was already on, illuminating my large volume of Shakespeare open on the desk. I crossed to it, looking down. The book was opened to the last scene of *King Lear*, when Lear discovers that his daughter has been killed trying to save him. There was a red sticky note in the middle of the page.

Swallowing hard, I picked it up. "You or them," it read, "your choice. Meet me at Trin."

I recognized Rochelle's handwriting from the countless notes we'd passed in class. I should have expected her to do something like this, but I'd been so focused on Hecate that I'd almost forgotten about Rochelle's betrayal. But Hecate couldn't act alone, I reminded myself, and Rochelle was more than willing to be her pawn. I crumpled up the note and sat on the edge of my bed, trying to think.

Rochelle had my parents, and I knew now that she wouldn't hesitate to harm them. But what tricks did I still have up my sleeve? I pulled the athame and the mirror from the bag at my waist and laid them out beside me. Then I removed the polished crystal sphere that Hades had given me when I left the Underworld.

"Use this to see clearly," he had told me when he handed me the crystal. He had hesitated a moment, then leaned forward and kissed my forehead gently. When he pulled back, there were tears in his eyes.

"And if you see Persephone, please tell her that I dealt fairly with you. Ask her—ask her when she will be coming home."

Rolling the sphere over in my palm now, I felt a pang of regret. I had hoped that Persephone might still be here, and I had planned to tell her how much her husband had helped me. But I was alone. I couldn't talk to the goddess or rely on her for help, I realized. I had to deal with this myself.

I held the crystal ball cupped in my hands and I looked deep into it. For a moment, all I saw were the whorls in the stone itself, but eventually, an image began to appear. Justin's face became clearer, and I almost dropped the ball in shock. How could Justin help me now? Annoyed, I shook the crystal, and the image faded away to nothingness. I kept looking into the stone, but no other image appeared.

I thought for a moment. Even if he hated me, I decided, it would be nice to tell someone where I was going. I didn't know if I'd survive another confrontation with Rochelle, but I had to rescue my parents, even if it was the last thing I did. I turned on my cell phone and sent a quick text to Justin before I left the house: "SO sorry. Rochelle has Mom & Dad. Going to Trinity. <3."

***

The school was dark and deserted when I approached. Dusk was falling, and I knew that soon it would be even darker. Moving silently, I opened the large iron gate with a quick spell and slipped inside. It had always surprised me that a magical school wasn't better defended, but then again, I guess none of the teachers ever expected any trouble they couldn't handle. They only taught us enough magic to get by, never enough to be any kind of threat. I laughed silently to myself. They sure screwed up with me and Rochelle!

In the vestibule, I hesitated. The school was a labyrinth of classrooms, hallways, and staircases. It had always seemed corny to me, when I was a student there, to be studying Witchcraft in something that could have been a Gothic mansion. Now, I realized there were countless places that Rochelle could have hidden my parents. Drawing the crystal out of my pocket, I drew it close to my face.

It was hard to see, but after a moment, I recognized the gruesome image of a gargoyle. Trinity's roof was covered with the creepy things, adding to its odd appearance and to its façade as a religious school. I knew my way to the roof; it was a favorite spot for all the students when they wanted to practice big, flashy spells. I headed for the janitor's staircase at the back of the building, trying to come up with a plan. I knew Rochelle wanted me dead, and I hoped that if I offered to fight her, my parents could get away. That is, if she hadn't already done anything to them. I crept up the stairs, waiting for Rochelle to attack me from above.

I was surprised when I reached the roof unharmed. As I opened the door onto the roof, I was hit with a wave of freezing air. While I was in Greece, fall had deepened, and the crisp night air around me bit at my cheeks and made me think of winter. Drawing in a deep breath of cold air, I crept onto the roof, my eyes darting around, looking for recognizable shapes in the darkness.

A muffled sound drew my eyes to the western side of the roof. My parents were pressed up against the wall, bound and gagged with air and floating a foot off the ground. Mom's eyes looked panicked when she spotted me, and she shook her head frantically. Dad's head lolled to one side. I fought back the fear that he was already dead and headed across the roof, not caring if I made an easy target for Rochelle.

My hands started to spark. With a single word, I directed the energy out to my parents, slashing through their invisible bonds. The Red sparks flared for an instant when they hit Rochelle's spell, but then my parents dropped to the roof, released.

"Darlena, run!" Mom coughed.

I rushed to her and hugged her tight. "Are you okay?" I was so grateful to see her, but I knew we didn't have time for a long reunion. "What's wrong with Dad?"

She shook her head and didn't answer. "You have to get out of here, now. She's just waiting to kill you."

I flexed my fingers, feeling the power that still flowed through me. "Let her try."

"I thought you'd never ask." Rochelle stepped out from behind a vent and took a step toward me. Before I could even react, she raised her hands and sent a blast of Black energy surging across the roof. I jumped at the last minute, but the bolt passed close enough that I could hear the hiss it made when it hit the stone behind me. It took all my self-control not to fling myself at her.

Instead, I turned to my mom. "You have to get out of here,

now. Can you manage Dad?" My father was still unconscious, but Mom nodded and reached over to pull him up. She struggled for a minute under his weight, but finally she stood, Dad leaning against her body. He let out a soft groan, and relief surged through me. He wasn't dead!

"I can manage." Her voice shook, and tears welled up in her eyes. "But what about you?"

"I have to handle this." I crouched in front of her, shielding her from Rochelle's view, but no attack came.

"But I want to help you! Two Greens together—"

I interrupted her. "Mom, I'm a Red. I can't explain now, but I promise I'll tell you later."

She recoiled as if I'd slapped her. "A Red?" Fear and revulsion were plain on her face, and I sighed. If I survived, we'd have a lot to talk about, and I didn't think it would be any easier to tell her the truth for a second time. Silently, I cursed Rochelle; couldn't she have left my parents' memories alone?

"There's a lot we need to talk about. But first I need to deal with Rochelle. Take Dad. Call a cab and get home. Set wards on the house. I'll see you soon." I kissed her cheek and she flinched. She looked like she wanted to stay there and argue with me, but she lifted my father and moved quickly for the stairs.

"How touching." Rochelle sneered, stepping closer to me. "Darlena is trying to save her family." She raised her hand and pointed at my mother.

"Don't!" I snapped at her, raising my own hands. Energy crackled in the air, but I didn't want to strike her just yet. I was worried about using up all my strength early on in the fight; I'd never used Red magic for prolonged periods of time, and I didn't know if I'd be able to. "You won't hurt them, Rochelle. It's me you want."

Her lip curled in disgust. "Do you really think I'd have a problem hurting them?" Before I could react, she flicked her wrist and Black sparks struck my parents just as they reached the stairs. Mom fell backwards with a cry, taking Dad's prone form with her, and I heard the heavy thud as their bodies tumbled down.

"How dare you?" I raised my hands, shaping a sphere of power, but I made no move to attack yet. I needed to give Mom and Dad time to get away. I just hoped they weren't unconscious.

Rochelle laughed. "I'm not afraid to use my power, Darlena! Unlike you, skulking like a coward." She sent another pulse of energy toward me, but I used the Red sphere in my hands to deflect it. It was like deadly dodgeball. Black sparks shot into the sky.

"I wasn't hiding, Rochelle, I was learning." The sphere in my hands pulsed, but I held onto it.

"Oh, I see. Learning." She zapped me again, and I moved, slipping behind an air conditioner vent. "I don't know how much you were learning while I was out here working." Black sparks bounced off the vent in front of me again.

"What do you really know about Red magic, Rochelle?" I put the finishing touches on my sphere, but I still crouched behind the vent, holding the molten ball of energy.

"Know? What is there to know? You're an idiot. I should have been the Red Witch, not you! I'd never stand in the way of chaos like you want to."

I peeked around the side of the vent, but I didn't see her. "So you're willing to cause countless deaths?"

Her laughter was sharp. "Didn't you learn anything from Hades? Death brings power. I would grow and grow in my power with each disaster I caused, until one day the entire world would bow down to me."

How had she known where I was? Hecate must have told her. Did she realize that her pawn was talking about world domination? Somehow, I doubted Hecate would let Rochelle get that powerful. The Queen of Witches didn't strike me as someone who was willing to share power. "That'll never happen, Rochelle! There are laws! Don't forget the Rede."

"Laws!" she spat, moving into view and closer to my vent. "Those laws protect Nons. They'll be the first to go. I will reshape the earth into a magical world, and all the beings on it will revere my name."

"Rochelle, you're insane." I felt the Red sphere pulsing in my hands and I knew I had to act quickly before the magic overwhelmed me.

"Maybe, but I'm the one who's going to live through this."

"Don't bet on it." I spun out from behind the vent and flung the Red ball at her just as she released another bolt of Black magic. It hit me dead in the chest, and I fell backward, bruising my elbows. Rochelle sailed off the roof, the Red sphere of energy propelling her like a deadly comet.

Gasping, I tried to pull myself upright, but the Black energy had turned to tar when it struck me, and I was pinned to the roof. If Rochelle had survived her fall, I was trapped, a perfect target.

"Rochelle?" I yelled into the night sky. There was no answer. Struggling against the Black stuff oozing over me, I tried again. "Finish what you started!" I waited for her to reappear. Maybe it was stupid, but I sort of hoped she'd survived; I didn't want to be responsible for one more death, especially not hers. "I'm sorry!" My words were lost in the wind.

The door to the roof burst open and Justin rushed out. "Darlena!" His voice echoed off the rooftop as he hurried toward me.

I looked at him, dumbfounded. "What are you doing here?" I struggled to sit up, but the residue from Rochelle's spell still held me hostage.

He knelt beside me, White light radiating out of his hands. "I got your text."

The Black goo dissolved and I sat up, rubbing my raw elbows. I couldn't look at him; the last time I'd seen him, he'd said he would never help me. Why was he here now? "So?"

He laughed. "So? That's all you have to say to me?"

"I thought you were angry at me." My voice dropped, and I blinked back tears.

To my surprise, Justin hugged me tight. "I was. But I don't want to lose you."

His embrace felt too good to be true. I glared up at him, trying not to let him see how affected I was by his touch. "So you decided to rescue me." The bitterness in my voice made him drop his arms to his sides quickly.

"No. You look like you had that under control. But I wanted to tell you that I still love you, and I was worried that after tonight, I wouldn't have another chance."

His words sank in. "You love me?" The world spun.

He nodded, blushing. "I always have."

There was a pause, and then I flung my arms around his neck, squeezing him tight. Our lips met, and I melted. "But why did you think you wouldn't have another chance after tonight?"

Justin sighed. "I had a vision. I don't think now's the time to discuss it."

Suddenly, I remembered my parents. "Justin, when you came up the stairs, did you see—"

"Your parents?" He finished for me, and I nodded. "Yes. I healed them both, or at least I tried to. Your mother kept insisting that she could do it without my help."

I laughed, relieved. "So they're okay?" He nodded and I stood up. My legs were shaky, but I took a step away from him, my mind reeling. I was alive, my parents were safe, and Justin was there beside me. It was almost too much to take. Then I glanced over the side of the roof and took a step forward. I looked down to the dark street below.

Realization hit me like a truck, and I burst into tears. Justin looked surprised, but he drew me close and started stroking my head. "It's okay. Everything is okay. You did it."

At his words, I cried harder. What exactly had I done? I'd

become the person I swore I wouldn't be: I'd murdered my best friend. I sniffled. "Justin, I killed Rochelle."

He didn't look surprised, but I thought I saw him clench his jaw. "She was trying to kill you, Darlena. You acted in self-defense."

I shook my head, tears streaming down my face. "But I'll have to answer for that! You know the threefold law."

"But not right now, Darlena." He stroked my hair, whispering. "Right now, you're safe with me."

I let him hold me while I cried, exhausted and frightened. Even as he stroked my hair and whispered soothing things, I knew that Rochelle's death would come back to haunt me.

37

"I have to go talk to my parents." We had reached my house, and all the lights were on, illuminating the dark street.

Justin shoved his hands in his pockets. "But I'll see you tomorrow, right?"

I hesitated. "Justin—there are things I need to do."

"So I'll help you!"

I shook my head. "Look, I really appreciate everything you've done, but I don't want to put you in any more danger. Hecate has no problem using the people close to me, and I don't want her to get her hands on you." I hated myself then, but I didn't want to put anyone else in danger. Still, pushing Justin away felt like I was sticking a nail into my heart.

"I'd like to see her try." Justin clenched his fists and I grabbed his hands, shaking my head.

"No, you wouldn't. I don't care how strong a White Witch you are, Hecate will always be stronger. She's stronger than me, too, but I'm not trying to beat her."

A confused expression crossed his face. "Then what is all this about?"

I sighed. "I want to use Red magic to find some kind of balance. Hecate wants things to tip in favor of chaos, I don't know why. But I need to find the other Red Witches and see what we can do together." I had realized that Hades was right. I didn't have to do this alone. It wasn't about winning; it was about using Red magic for good. Maybe if I found the other Red Witches, I could learn something.

He frowned and looked at the ground. Gently, I touched his cheek.

"Justin, look at me." Reluctantly, his eyes met mine. "I love you. Nothing changes that."

His frown deepened for a moment, but then he nodded. I kissed him lightly.

"Thank you." I hoped he understood what I meant: I wasn't just thanking him for tonight.

"I still think I can help." He sounded petulant, and I smiled.

"You already have."

My parents were sitting in the living room when I opened the door. Xerxes crept out from under the couch, purring regally as if nothing had happened. He hopped up beside my dad, who began petting him absentmindedly.

I drew a deep breath. "I have a lot of things that I need to tell you both."

Mom shook her head. "No, you don't, honey."

"But—"

"Darlena," Dad interrupted, "we knew when you made your declaration that there would be certain things you couldn't tell us."

I stared, confused. Mom got off the couch and crossed to me. "You're a Red, sweetie. And we can't help you very much." She embraced me tightly.

"You know I'm a Red?"

Dad nodded and Mom patted my cheek. "We've known since the beginning. Don't you remember when Hecate visited us?"

I stared at them, confused. Had their memories just been miraculously restored? What if the spell Rochelle had cast had dissolved when I killed her? My stomach flipped at the thought, and I tried to ignore the memory of Rochelle sailing off the roof to her death. "But what about tonight?"

Mom sighed. Dad stared at the crackles of electricity flying off the cat's back as he stroked him.

"Tonight," Dad said firmly, "you saved us. I still don't know what was going on, but I know we're safe. And so are you."

"We've missed you, Lena."

"Missed me? What … " I trailed off as Persephone walked out of the kitchen. "Oh."

She stood in the doorway, her face expressionless.

I crossed to face the goddess. "Well?"

Her eyes flashed. "Well, what, child?"

"Shouldn't you be in the Underworld?"

Surprise showed on her face. "Aren't you concerned about the past weeks?"

I shook my head. Whatever had happened while I was gone, I trusted her. It was a nice feeling to finally have a goddess I could trust. I looked up at her. "Thank you."

She sighed. "In the end, my glamour wasn't enough to fool that Black Witch."

"I know. It wasn't your fault. I gave myself away, too."

Her eyes studied me for a long moment, but she didn't speak.

"Persephone," I hesitated. "I have a message from your husband, and there's something I should tell you."

"Go on."

"Dennis is dead."

Her temper flared. "Is that the message my lord would send to me?"

"No, no," I hurried on despite my fear, "that was my fault. He died when I ran to the Underworld." Tears filled my eyes, but I brushed them away. What was done was done, and I couldn't spend too much time thinking about the people who had died because of me. If I did, I might go crazy. "I'm sorry. He was really special."

She nodded, struggling to master her emotions. "And the message from my lord?"

"He loves you, and hopes you'll come back soon."

Persephone made a sound that could have been a sob and

287

began to dissolve in a cloud of Red light. "Perhaps, little Witch, you will bring balance after all." She kissed my forehead before she vanished, but her words hung in the air. "We will meet again, Darlena. I swear it by the River Styx."

She faded, and I was left alone with my parents. Squaring my shoulders, I turned around.

"I know you don't want to know a lot, and I don't want to tell you anything that could hurt you," I drew a deep breath, "but I can't stay here very long."

"We expected something like that. Persephone told us that you were in conflict with Hecate." Dad's voice was calm, despite his words.

I nodded, trying not to laugh at the way he phrased it. Dad made it sound like Hecate and I were just having a minor disagreement rather than a war. "It's not over yet. What happened with Rochelle was just the beginning. I need to find a way to balance Red magic. I can't let chaos happen unchecked."

"You can't start right now," Mom said softly, and I could tell she was trying not to cry. "It's too dark outside. Besides, even heroes should be able to sleep in their own beds once in a while."

I laughed and hugged her. "I'll stay tonight. I don't know when I'll need to leave, but when I do, it will be fast. Will that … will that be okay?"

Dad rose and embraced me. "Of course. We trust you to make the right choices, Darlena."

"You always have," Mom added, brushing strands of hair off my forehead and kissing me.

***

It felt strange to lie down in my own bed after everything that had happened. Xerxes curled up on my stomach, purring contentedly, while I stared at my ceiling, thinking. There was still so much I didn't understand. But the biggest question that was weighing on me had to do with Aphrodite. "I wonder if she's still my patron?" I asked the cat, scratching him behind the ears.

"She may be." Aphrodite stood near the window, her back turned to me. Xerxes lifted his head and sniffed before hoping off the bed and crossing the room to wind around her ankles. I sat up in bed and watched the goddess.

After a moment, Aphrodite turned around. "I love the moon." She sighed. "So peaceful, so beautiful."

I raised an eyebrow. "Is that what you came to talk to me about? I thought we already had that lesson."

She sighed again and crossed to the foot of my bed. Sitting gently, she plucked at the quilt with her fingers. "No. I wish it were that simple, though."

I hugged my knees into my chest. "Are you still my patron?"

Her eyes met mine. "I can't read your thoughts anymore."

I frowned. "Does that mean no?"

"Darlena, when you ate the pomegranate, what were you thinking about?"

I thought back to that night. It seemed like it had happened in another lifetime. "I was thinking about Justin," I began slowly, "and the spell I cast, and—" I broke off, realization dawning on me.

"And you were thinking about me." She spoke softly, and her voice sounded sad.

Swallowing, I nodded. Was the goddess about to kill me? I thought about the oath I'd sworn to her, and waited for the waters of the sea to attack me for breaking faith. I squeezed my eyes, not wanting to see what would happen. After a moment, I opened them again, confused. I was still sitting in bed, unharmed. The goddess was watching me.

"You could choose to swear yourself to me again," she began, "but I doubt that you will."

I shrugged, uncomfortable. "I learned a lot from you. And I'm really grateful."

"But you don't think I'm strong enough to help you now, is that it?"

I shook my head quickly. "Not at all! You are strong, and I'm lucky you were protecting me and helping me." I chewed on my lower lip, choosing my words carefully. "It's just that … I need to be able to focus on Red magic, not just love magic." Seeing the stormy expression on her face, I hurried on. "Not that I think love magic is weak! Believe me"—I laughed ruefully—"I learned my lesson. It's strong; it's just not the right kind of magic for me right now."

Aphrodite was silent. Anxious, I leaned forward, willing her to understand.

"I made my declaration to Red magic without any thought,

acting on impulse. And then when I swore myself to you, I was more afraid than anything else. I never thought I'd have the chance to reconsider some of the choices I've made."

"I'm surprised you didn't reconsider your choice of Red magic in general."

I shook my head. "I still don't understand it all, but something about this just feels right."

She nodded slightly. "You are going to be powerful, Darlena. You have already exceeded my expectations. But"—she glared at me—"don't assume your power will buy you another chance once I've left here tonight."

My voice trembled. "Are you threatening me?"

She smiled sweetly. "Oh, not at all, little Witch. But I want to make one thing clear: if you want me as your patron, you must decide now. I will not offer again."

I looked at the crescent moon shining through my bedroom window. I closed my eyes and drew a deep breath. "I'm not ready to vow myself to a patron. I want to make that choice when I am ready."

She stood. "Then you will never serve me. And"—her voice softened—"I must admit, I'm disappointed. You showed great promise in the art of love."

"Thank you. But I think there are other things I need to learn."

Aphrodite nodded, but her smile looked forced. "Then I'll take my leave." She turned to go.

"Wait, please." I hopped out of bed and crossed to my closet. I rummaged around for a minute before emerging with the mirror she had given me when I swore my Dedicancy. I held it out to her, hesitantly.

She looked at it for a moment, and then shook her head slightly. "You may have need of it in the future. And I am not in the habit of taking gifts back." Her tone was acidic, but it was clear that she meant it.

I nodded, hoping I hadn't offended her. "Thank you. For everything."

When I looked up, the only other creature in the room was Xerxes.

That night, I had a vivid dream. The chanting was familiar, like I'd dreamed it before, but this time, the images became clear. Three women were leaning over a massive cauldron, their faces hidden beneath hoods. They were chanting and pacing around the cauldron in a wide circle while I stood nearby, watching. The woods surrounding us were thick and ancient, and the sounds of battle echoed through the trees.

Suddenly, a man burst into the clearing. He had a haunted expression, and the kilt he wore was stained with blood. Instead of looking at the women, he pointed his sword at me as he stalked across the clearing.

"One Red Witch in my land is one too many! I'll not suffer you, too. Go back, if you value your skin!"

His sword flashed through the air, and the dream changed. A man with fire for hair crouched in the shadows before me. He held out his right hand, beckoning me forward. Confused, I dug in my heels and refused to move. The fire on top of his head flared, and a great snake of flame shot upwards, circling through the air and heading toward me. I turned and tried to run, but the king with his sword waited for me, slashing the blade in the air near my face. I woke up with a start.

I was covered in sweat and shaking from fear. I grabbed the notebook beside my bed and hurriedly jotted down the sensations and images I could remember from my nightmare. I crept out of bed into the bathroom, splashing water on my face and telling myself that it was just a dream. When I looked at my reflection in the bathroom mirror, however, I noticed an unmistakable well of blood across my cheek. Lifting my hand, I pressed the cut gently, and pain shot through my face. Dabbing peroxide on the strange wound, I thought back to the dream. It was like a scene straight out of a Shakespearean play. The women reminded me of the three Witches from *Macbeth*.

Macbeth.

Suddenly, everything made sense.

Rushing back to my room, my wound forgotten, I pulled my old atlas off my shelf and flipped through it. I reached down to trace my finger along the northern coast of the British Isles.

"If there were Red Witches in Scotland before," I said, "who's to say there isn't one still there?"

The images of my dream seemed to point to one thing: Scotland. The old king had warned me to stay out of his land. But I wasn't afraid of the ghost of a man long dead. If there was another Red Witch in Scotland, I would find her.

ACKNOWLEDGEMENTS

There are so many amazing people who have helped me along my path to publication. I would like to offer my deepest thanks to these wonderful folks.

First, to all of my Twitter friends: thank you for keeping me infinitely entertained, and for squeeing with me whenever good things happen. To my students: past, present, and future. Thank you for inspiring me!

To Marietta, for selflessly sharing your knowledge and encouragement with me. To Josh, for pushing me to intensify the title. To Danielle, for invaluable feedback. To the SCBWI community; thank you for helping me grow and giving me the chance to learn!

To Kat, for believing in this book when it was still a baby.

To Georgia McBride and the entire Month9Books team; I am grateful every day to be a part of this wonderful family.

To Deanna, for reading early drafts and listening to me ramble over countless cups of coffee. To Amanda, Austin, Victoria, and Wanda. You are magical! To Boyce, for continued support and friendship. To Laura and Deb for reading and falling in love with Darlena's quest. To Kara, for pushing me to submit that first poem all those years ago: thank you for always believing in me!

To the YA Valentines: Anne Blankman, Bethany Crandell, Lindsay Cummings, Bethany Hagen, Kristi Helvig, Sara B. Larson,

Kristen Lippert-Martin, Lynne Matson, Sara Raasch, A. Lynden Rolland, Philip Siegel, and Paula Stokes. Thank you for making me laugh and letting me be a part of such an awesome group. Valentine love!

A huge box of chocolates and eternal love to Jaye Robin Brown: YA Valentine, CP extraordinaire, and wonderful friend.

Huge thanks to my family on both coasts for the never-ending support. What would I do without y'all? An extra big hug for Mom; I'm a writer because of you.

To Matt, now and always: thank you.

And finally, deepest gratitude to you: thank you for reading!

Jen McConnel

Jen McConnel first began writing poetry as a child. Since then, her words have appeared in a variety of magazines and journals, including Sagewoman, PanGaia, and The Storyteller (where she won the people's choice 3rd place award for her poem, "Luna"). She is also a former reviewer for Voice of Youth Advocates (VOYA), and proud member of SCBWI, NCWN, and SCWW. A Michigander by birth, she now lives and writes in the beautiful state of North Carolina. When she isn't crafting worlds of fiction, she teaches college writing composition and yoga. Once upon a time, she was a middle school teacher, a librarian, and a bookseller, but those are stories for another time.

Website: http://www.jenmcconnel.com/
Twitter: @Jen_McConnel
Blog: http://jennifermcconnel.wordpress.com/
Goodreads: http://www.goodreads.com/author/show/6451403. Jen_McConnel
Facebook: http://www.facebook.com/jenmcconnelauthor
Pinterest: http://pinterest.com/jenmcconnel

Preview covers from forthcoming books.

Learn more by visiting www.month9books.com!

Find the diary, break the curse,
step through the looking glass

THE LOOKING GLASS

JESSICA ARNOLD

JACKIE MORSE KESSLER

TO BEAR AN
IRON KEY

27845650R00186

Made in the USA
Charleston, SC
24 March 2014